JADE
LADY
BURNING

MARTIN LIMÓN

Published by
Soho Press, Inc.
853 Broadway
New York, NY 10003

Library of Congress Cataloging-in-Publication Data

Limón, Martin,
Jade Lady Burning / Martin Limón.
p. cm.
ISBN 978-1-61695-090-3
eISBN 978-56947-801-1
I. Title.
PS3562.I465J3 1992
813'.54—dc20   92.27572
CIP

Design and composition by The Sarabande Press

Printed in the United States of America

10   9   8   7   6   5   4   3   2   1

For Aaron, Maria and Michelle.

Ship me somewhere's east of Suez, where the
best is like the worst,
Where there aren't no Ten Commandments,
an' a man can raise a thirst.

"Mandalay"
Rudyard Kipling

JADE
LADY
BURNING

1

Ernie and I finished the black-market case in Pusan, did a little celebrating, and caught the Blue Line night train back to Seoul. The dining car served only Western-style food and a few snacks to go with the ice-cold liters of OB beer that they offered at inflated prices. Ernie and I avoided it, preferring to carry our own sustenance aboard.

The U.S. government wouldn't buy seats in the first-class cabin for GIs, but the coach was quite comfortable, with large padded chairs and plenty of legroom. It was nice enough so that Korean men usually wore suits and the women dressed up. But that didn't stop them from bringing along small tins of pungent kimchi and rice, and maybe a little fish for their meals.

Bringing your own was the only way, the Koreans pointed out, to have any "real" food.

The man and his wife in the seat in front of us were sharing the fermented bounty from the same tin while their three children bounced playfully around them. Occasionally the parents would pop a morsel in their children's mouths and they would squeal and return to their frivolity.

It wasn't doing my hangover any good. I elbowed Ernie. His arms were crossed, his legs stretched out. One eye partially opened. He leaned forward, and from under the seat pulled out his brown leather traveling bag. He removed two cans of Falstaff.

"Breakfast," he said.

My reaction was Pavlovian. We popped them open and white froth rose in a mound around the top of my can. I sucked greedily, letting the lukewarm liquid slide down my throat until the juices got flowing in preparation for the full onslaught, and then I tilted the can way back and let the hops revitalize my brain and body.

My eyes were watery; we both leaned back in our chairs to luxuriate in the feeling.

"You're a genius, Ernie."

"Logistics, pal. Simple logistics."

Outside, the winter countryside was brown, white in places where snow clung: acres of frozen rice paddies. Farm folk hustled from chore to chore, bundled against the weather. Dark pillars of smoke rose lazily skyward; the clouds rolled and drooped low to the earth. Gradually the rice paddies gave way to storage yards, then warehouses, truck parking lots, factories.

"There it is," Ernie said, sounding impressed, his breath clouding the window glass. The OB brewery stood out against the overcast, a huge gray plant with a monstrous red and yellow sign mounted on its tallest smokestack: OB. Extending for acres in all directions were countless rows of brown beer bottles in wooden slat-crates piled twenty high. A majestic sight.

We sped through Yongdongpo Station, past crowds of huddled commuters, through a small wooded area and suddenly out over a vast expanse of blue—the Han River. And we could see, off to our right, the city of Seoul floating on a cloud of river fog. Yongsan Station flashed by; the engineer was balling it to the end of the line. The windows radiated cold.

"Lock and load," Ernie said, gathering up his bag.

We jumped off the train just as it stopped and tried to beat the crowds streaming off and up the stairways leading to the main hall. Seoul Station was old and large and Slavic—made of mortar and brick—a present to Korea from the czar, left over from the days when Russia still had designs on the Land of the Morning Calm.

At the top of the stairs, we hung a left and headed toward the Eighth Army Transportation Office in an adjoining old office building whose entrance opened into the hall. We used it as a shortcut out so we wouldn't have to wait in the long lines of passengers turning in their expended tickets. Out on the street, we dove into a milling throng. The large, open area in front of Seoul Station was full of responsible citizens hurrying in all directions: uniformed girls on their way to school, businessmen toting briefcases, old ladies with huge bundles on their heads.

Stands of vendors offered refreshments and quick food, like *kodung*, being warmed in large pans. *Kodung* were a favorite of Ernie's: insects in pill-sized shells from which you sucked the meat and conveniently discarded the shell. Signs advertised *nakji*, raw squid in hot sauce, and *yakulut*, liquefied yogurt sold in little plastic bottles. Despite our hunger and the cold, we resisted and hurried to get in line at the taxi stand. In fifteen minutes we reached the end of the queue and jumped into a small cab. In Korean I told the driver where to take us. He nodded, clicked his meter on, and jammed the gas pedal to the floor. He reached forty-five quickly, even in the heavy traffic. The driver weaved in and out, taking any opportunity to advance. The roadway ostensibly had four lanes, but at any one time the swerving cabs and trucks formed at least six.

Ernie stared serenely at the automobiles careening wildly around him. "I could use a little something."

We climbed up the ramp to the Samgakji Circle and, without taking his foot off the gas, the driver forced his way into the bumper-to-bumper flow. On the far side, he veered off the circle and, a few yards further, came to a screeching halt at a stoplight. The ROK Army Headquarters buildings, on the left, faced the Ministry of National Defense, on the right.

"*Hana, tul, seit, neit!*"

A high-pitched female voice was barking out a cadence. Two female soldiers ran to either side of the intersection. They each thrust out one hand to halt traffic, and came to a snappy parade rest. Marching proudly into the intersection was an entire platoon of the Republic of Korea Women's Army. The drivers of the backed-up trucks and taxis revved their engines impatiently, cursing and jeering. The sergeant shouted out her orders, continuing to march, impervious to the petty civilians.

The women wore brown skirts and matching uniform jackets, with bright red stripes slashed across their arms. The black oxfords gleamed. Squared at the nape of the neck, their hair was uniformly straight and cut in bangs. Brown, box-like caps balanced atop their bobbing heads. All seemed exactly the same height. We leaned forward in our seats, straining to catch glimpses.

The cab squealed off as soon as the last woman passed.

I fell back in my seat. "Damn. I feel a little woozy."

"Yeah," Ernie said solicitously. "You do look a little flushed."

Until you got to know Ernie you'd never guess. I mean, he looked normal. "I make a good first impression," he used to say, as if he were amazed by the fact. He was Caucasian and just a little above average height at about five foot eleven. His weight was probably right at what an insurance salesman's chart would say it should be. He wasn't handsome but he was highly presentable. Wasn't muscular or thin or fat, but uncompromisingly right in the center.

He wasn't ethnic, but also not so white that he would stand out in a crowd. His ancestors were from Europe, though exactly where you wouldn't be able to say. He lulled you to sleep. Officers tended to trust him; the girls in the ville expected him to be civilized. He did look a lot, his eyes slightly bulged out behind thick round lenses. His nose was pointed and his lips were set in a simple, noncommittal parallel.

You couldn't figure out what he was thinking. Not that anyone was trying. Ernie just fit into a crowd: he didn't make anyone nervous.

It was me who made people nervous. I was big and noticeable and people always wondered what I was doing there. And while they were wondering about me, I was wondering about Ernie.

Worried about what was going on behind that noncommittal gaze. That gaze that lingered on every woman's rear, head rotating behind his pointed nose like radar homed in on a target. The calculating mind behind the blue eyes was scheming. I spent a lot of time worrying about Ernie.

The taxi sped on. The city was everywhere. Building after building, sign after sign, an endless jumble of streets, alleys, and overhangs. People were crammed into buses full to bursting, jostling each other on the packed sidewalks, and riding bicycles piled six feet high with goods of all descriptions.

I looked at the girls: their dresses, their coats, their hairdos. My eyes jumped rapidly from one to another, each with straight black hair to her waist.

A GI bus drew alongside, bearing the spare, stenciled markings of the U.S. Army. It didn't stop for civilians. The Korean populace stood at their own bus stops, patiently waiting while the drab green bus sped by them, stopping only for GIs, or Korean women frantically waving their Military Dependent identity cards.

The Korean buses were packed. Heads and arms pushed up against the steam-smeared windows in a flesh-colored jigsaw puzzle. I spotted a pretty girl. She stared blankly ahead.

Large and green, Namsan loomed over everything, standing just south of the city's center. The "South Mountain" was about halfway between the King's Palace and the Han River. Radiating from it in all directions were millions of buildings and houses and the skyscrapers of the downtown business district.

"It wasn't anything like this my first tour," I said. "There weren't hardly any buildings over two stories tall. And there weren't hardly any girls asking more than ten dollars for an overnight."

"The two must be related," Ernie said.

Another two blocks and we came to an abrupt halt. Ernie fumbled with some coins and gave the driver the exact change indicated by the meter.

"Shit, pal," I said. "You're not going to embarrass me and not tip this guy?"

"Hell no, I'm not going to tip him." He picked up his bag. "These guys don't know what a tip is. Korean custom."

Across the street we entered Yongsan Compound, headquarters of the Eighth United States Army. A block past the gate, we passed through the Moyer Recreation Center and went straight to the snack stand. I ordered a hot dog and a medium Coke and Ernie had the same.

The buns were steamed, the dogs hot, and we piled them high with mustard, sweet pickle relish, and onions. They didn't last long. Then we looked at each other, hesitated . . . and got up to order two more. It had been a long ride from Pusan.

"How was the teenybopper?" I said.

Ernie shrugged. "She did what I told her to do."

My voice husked down a few decibels. "What did you tell her to do?"

"Routine." Ernie leaned back in the vinyl-covered seat and pushed his pelvis forward a little. "Had her work on my joint for a while. She wasn't very good but she tried real hard. I like watching them while they try to figure out what to do with it." He crossed his arms and stared straight ahead. His blue pupils threatened to melt the thickest part of his round wire-rimmed glasses. "That's what brought me back," he said.

"Brought you back? I thought that was the first time you'd ever seen her."

"I mean back in the Army. Back here." He twisted his head towards the window. "The American girls, they want you to talk. They want you to understand them. Even with all this stuff back in the States about free love, I never yet ran into one that didn't claim she was old-fashioned."

"Weren't getting enough nooky, huh?"

"I could have," he said. "I just didn't want to talk to them." He looked back out the window. "It's better here, where you just pay them." He leaned back, pushed his hands into his jacket pockets, and tilted his head against the hard metal siding of the snack stand. "The price in the States is too high."

He closed his eyes. I thought of the college courses I had taken courtesy of Uncle Sam. The ones I had signed up for were mostly on the Orient: Asian history, Asian languages, the anthropology of the Far East. The friends I had made were mainly veterans, and there weren't many of them. I had drunk a lot and tried to talk to some of the girls just out of high school but it hadn't worked. It never had. But now it wasn't working for a different reason.

"Come on," I said, checking my watch. "It's game time."

* * *

Bile percolated up my throat and pumped gas into the hollow of my chest. I popped the last of my antacids and swore.

"They found her at zero four hundred this morning," the first sergeant said. "The body was badly burned but the neighbors are certain that it's the young girl by the name of Pak Ok-suk who lived in that hooch."

The first sergeant sipped his milky brown coffee, grimaced, and placed the porcelain mug in the center of his immaculate desk. Down the long hallway an ancient radiator whistled and clanged while the snow outside swirled in a howling wind from Manchuria.

Ernie Bascom fidgeted in his chair and tucked his tie into his trim belt line.

"So far, the Korean National Police don't have much information on Miss Pak other than that she was a registered prostitute and her hometown was Yoju. The neighbors claim that she had an American boyfriend, actually a number of American boyfriends, but that for the last two or three months it had been the same guy. The KNPs didn't get much of a description of him: under six feet, light brown hair, average weight, early twenties. Could be a million GIs. He'd been living with her, bringing her stuff out of the PX to black-market. Routine. They never seemed to have any fights, except around payday, when she pushed him a little, and no one noticed whether or not he came to her hooch last night. Normally he arrived around six P.M., after work. There were no other bodies found in the hooch, just hers, and by the time the neighbors were awakened by the flames, it was too late to save her. No one else was hurt since they were able to get out in time."

The first sergeant rattled the paperwork in front of him and took another sip of his coffee. Ernie sat perfectly still, leaning back in his chair, his right ankle crossed over his left knee, a Caucasian Buddha in baggy coat and tie.

"All of this would be just routine—a fire starts in a business girl's hooch out in Itaewon, she's burned to death in her sleep, and life goes on—if it wasn't for the findings of the Itaewon fire marshal. The girl had been bound hand and foot, trussed up, actually, and some sort of bonfire had been built under her body. So it was clearly arson and apparently murder. She might have been dead before the fire started. The neighbors heard no struggle or fighting that evening and were unaware of anything unusual until they smelled the fumes coming from her hooch. Strange enough by itself, but things sort of get worse when we get to the final entry in the fire marshal's report. Upon examining what was left of the girl, they discovered that a large wooden stake had been shoved inside her body. This, taken with the unusual, trussed-up position they found her in and the bonfire that had been prepared, led them to believe that it had been some sort of ritualistic killing. It almost seems as if the girl had been skewered and prepared for roasting."

Ernie reached in his coat pocket and fumbled for a stick of gum. The bile in my stomach hit my head and threatened to burst it. Last night's booze or this morning's killing, I wasn't sure which.

The first sergeant cleared his throat and continued. "The young lady's close association with American servicemen, of course, casts immediate suspicion on Eighth Army personnel. The story didn't break in time for the Seoul morning papers but we expect the afternoon editions to be screaming about it. We'll have to wait and see if the Koreans broadcast the details of such a grisly murder on TV. What makes this case even worse than if a GI had just murdered a Korean woman is the way the assailant did it. The corpse was treated as if it were a beast. And I know you two guys have read your Eighth Army training manuals and know that Koreans are particularly sensitive about any implications that they should be treated in any way less than human. Being called an animal, something nonhuman, is the supreme insult to a Korean.

We can expect the TV and radio people to whip up a frenzy of anti-Americanism over this one.

"The provost marshal, Colonel Stoneheart, has already gotten the word from the commanding general. Pull out all the stops. Take all needed investigators off all other details, get to the bottom of this murder, and bring the culprit to justice. ASAP."

The first sergeant set the paperwork down, positioned it perfectly, and looked at us.

"I know I've been on you guys lately, what with keeping you on the black-market detail and keeping the pressure on to get as many arrests as possible, but that's what the colonel wanted. And you've got to remember some of the shit you've gotten into before, like overstepping your jurisdiction. You, Sueño." The first sergeant pointed his finger at me.

"We got that all cleared up, Top."

He shook his head at the memory. "But, anyway, it's over. The Army likes things to proceed in orderly fashion. You need to remember that. You, too, Bascom."

The first sergeant put his big hands flat on the desk. "Still, after all is said and done, I've got to admit that you two are the best ville rats I've got. Nobody can go out there, work with the Koreans, and come back with the goods like you guys."

A compliment, the first one in months. And it obviously hurt him to say it, judging from his rictus grin. He was setting us up for a big one.

"That's why I've called you into this one. I need you to get out there and find out all you can about this Miss Pak Ok-suk. Who she knew, what she was up to, and how she ended up the way she did. I'm taking you off the black-market detail effective immediately. You can consider yourselves on this case twenty-four hours a day. Just report back to the office every morning prior to zero eight hundred hours. You got that?"

"What about our expense account?" Ernie said.

"Sixty dollars a month."

"Make it a hundred."

The first sergeant gazed at Ernie for a moment and then at me.

"Okay. But I want results. And I want 'em fast. And if I find that you're out there screwing off on me, you'll be cleaning grease traps from here to Pusan."

We lifted ourselves out of our chairs and strode out into the hallway.

Ernie stopped in the Admin Section to shoot the breeze with Miss Kim, the fine-looking secretary. I found Riley, the CID Detachment's personnel sergeant, hair greased back, working away frantically on a pile of paperwork.

"So what's the deal, Riley?"

He looked up at me through thick square glasses. "It's hitting the fan, George. Find out who dorked that girl and you'll be a hero."

"And if I don't?"

Riley jerked his thumb over his shoulder. "Back to the DMZ."

"I've walked the line before."

"Yeah," he said, disinterested.

Ernie and I walked out into the cold wind of Seoul. Snow crunched beneath our feet, left over from the off-and-on fall we had had the night before. We jumped into the old motor-pool jeep and Ernie brought it coughing to life.

"Where to, pal?" he said.

"Where else?" I said. "Itaewon. The home of my fevered dreams."

They say that Seoul is not as cold as other parts of Korea. Particularly not as cold as up north in the hills near the Demilitarized Zone or down south in the flat, unprotected plains of Taegu. But it's cold enough. The Chosen peninsula has all four seasons; the summer almost tropical, the spring and autumn achingly beautiful. This was a big change for me. I was used to the flat, unrelenting sunshine of East Los Angeles, with the only variable being the thickness of the smog layer.

The streets I grew up on were mean but they never became part of me. Primarily because I kept moving. From one foster home to another. My mother died when I was two. Some people say she was killed. And then my father disappeared into Mexico, the ancient land whence he had come.

I don't know the truth of how my mother died or why my father disappeared. As a child I had no choice but to accept it, and just before I was scheduled to graduate from high school, I joined the Army. I've thought a few times since then of going back, talking to some of my cousins and my uncles and aunts scattered around the city. After all, I'm a trained investigator now, but I've been busy and I've been overseas and maybe you could say that I'm afraid to find out the truth.

The foster homes I lived in were grim, a child always knows when he's not wanted, but there was one bright spot. Mrs. Aaronson, one of my foster mothers and the one I lived with the longest, took a special interest in my schoolwork when she realized that the math and reading weren't sinking in. She showed me what they really are—puzzles. She made sure I brought my books home and made sure I did some homework, whether it was assigned or not, every night. And after a while she didn't have to check very close because the thrill of surprising the teachers and my fellow students with a perfect test score became my incentive to work on my own.

It didn't last long, though. After I left Mrs. Aaronson, I climbed into the rebellious shell of all adolescents, and soon I was looking for a way out of high school other than the car washes or factories that swallowed whole legions of Mexican-American kids.

I dropped out and joined the Army. My high test scores

landed me a clerical job and for a couple of years I kicked around in the States, my newly found buddies spinning off occasionally to Vietnam, spit out like tickets from a rotating drum in a lottery drawing. With a little more than a year left on my enlistment, I got orders to Korea. At first I couldn't believe my luck. No getting shot at. And then they bused me and about a hundred other guys over to an Air Force base, strapped us into a chartered jet, and we were on our way. Hours later I saw Mount Fuji through the clouded porthole. We refueled and another couple of hours later we landed at Kimpo Air Field.

Like rats we wound through a maze of partitions, getting shots, having papers stamped, exchanging our greenback dollars for Military Payment Certificates, and then they put us on a bus for the Army Support Command Replacement Depot. I saw my first stern-faced Korean soldiers manning sandbagged machine gun emplacements.

I loved Korea. It was a whole new world of different tastes and smells, and a different, more intense way of looking at life. People here didn't take eating and breathing for granted. They were fought for.

I got a job at Eighth Army Headquarters in Seoul and I did a lot of typing and filing and driving and standing for hours in the sun with an M-14 rifle that I never used, waiting to be inspected. I started taking classes in the Korean martial arts, tae kwon do, and the Korean language, and I got twisted into knots by Suki, one of the greedier girls out in the village of Itaewon.

When my year was up, I went back to the States reluctantly and figured I had to get out of the Army. Everybody else was. I started drawing on the GI Bill, attended Los Angeles City College for one semester, and then, just after I bought my books for my second term, I decided to hell with it all, and I went down to see the local recruiter and made his day by signing up as fast as he could fill out the reup forms.

I got assigned to the military police but I was a college boy now, so after a brief stint at Fort Belvoir, Virginia, I got sent to the Criminal Investigation School. My good study habits got me through, and I kept my mouth shut rather than ask the instructor why someone who steals some communications equipment, say, should be seen as a criminal while a colonel who leads his troops into combat from a helicopter three thousand feet in the air should be seen as a hero.

This was the Army, after all. You can question the Green Machine but don't expect answers. And then I got orders to go back to Korea. Actually, I had pestered my local personnel sergeant until he called up a buddy at the Department of the Army and got me the assignment. At first they sent me down to Taegu and that's where I met Ernie.

Ernie's my kind of guy. Completely devoid of emotion. Unless they lock him out of the NCO Club on a Sunday. Ernie's one of those who pulled a lottery ticket to Vietnam. He was in a transportation company there, driving a big deuce-and-a-half, rolling through thatched-hut villages in mile-long convoys at fifty miles per hour. Spikes in the road. Not stopping to change the tires until you got back to the base camp at Chu Lai. Nights in dugout bunkers, waiting for the random rockets to drop in. Pure heroin sold by children outside the wire for two bucks a pop.

After they sent him back to Fort Hood, he volunteered to return to Vietnam. One more year at the same base camp. And then he was out of the Army. He kicked around on the beaches of southern California for a while and then he came back in.

He hit Korea a couple of months before I did.

The night before, we had bounced from one Pusan bar to another like metal spheres in a Japanese pinball machine. And with about as much conscious thought. We had ended up in a club with two good-looking girls, business girls—registered prostitutes who kept their VD cards up to date by going to the public clinic every month and getting the little red chop in the appropriate box. You're supposed to check to protect yourself but I never did. Except sometimes the following morning, as a matter of curiosity. I always wanted a VD card as a souvenir.

The girl I had been with last night was slightly harelipped, I think, with a long, slender, unblemished body. She sneered at me through the whole thing. I think I hadn't paid her enough money. And then she wouldn't let me have any in the morning.

Just as well. I was so hung over I hadn't really wanted it anyway. The attempt was a matter of form.

Ernie pulled the jeep up onto the sidewalk in front of the Itaewon Police Station, which was under the command of the Korean National Police, KNP. There was no other place to park, but normally I wouldn't have let him do it because I was always careful to consider what Captain Kim, the commander of the police box, might find insulting. I figured he'd forgive us this time because it was sort of an emergency.

Sergeants Burrows and Slabem stood in front of the Korean desk sergeant's counter, trying to look like they were doing something.

Jake Burrows was tall and thin with a pockmarked face that had long since healed over into a rough approximation of the Mojave Desert. Felix Slabem was short, soft, and round and for some reason he still had pimples, like an adolescent. He spoke first.

"Take the streetcar?"

"Yeah," I said. "We figured you'd have the culprit by now."

Burrows piped up: "The first sergeant told us just to perform liaison. The case falls under Korean jurisdiction."

"Lucky for you."

Ernie and I had been at odds with Burrows and Slabem from the start. They were always careful to push an investigation only far enough so it fit neatly into one of the categories on the provost marshal's briefing chart. Our investigations were always a little more unconventional, involving people who maybe weren't under suspicion in the first place and causing the honchos at the headshed to come up with some fancy explanations. At least that's the way we saw it. As far as everyone else was concerned, we were just screwing off—making wild accusations in an attempt to justify the time we spent in the ville.

In the Army, going after the truth is usually seen as a criminal waste of time.

We nodded to the desk sergeant and walked down the short hallway to the little cubicle that was Captain Kim's office. His face was buried in a stack of paper. Brown pulp. The Korean government couldn't afford the reams of letter-quality bond that were routinely churned out of every Eighth Army office for no discernible reason. The Koreans didn't have the redwoods for it. Or any other types of trees except for the ones they had planted since the Korean War.

Captain Kim looked up, kept his face impassive, and nodded. Coming from him that was like a joyous embrace.

I said a couple of polite things to him in Korean. His English was okay, my Korean barely passable—mostly culled from long intimate conversations in barrooms with beautiful women—but somehow we managed to communicate.

He treated Burrows and Slabem like any other interlopers from an alien planet. Us, he treated with bored indifference, which was one hell of a step up.

His face was flat and leathery with heavy, horizontal eyebrows that extended almost the width of each eye. His uniform was neatly pressed, open at the collar, and a deep brown color, reminding me of Sheriff John standing next to his wiener-mobile in back of a big shopping center in Pacoima. The uniforms of all the other cops were faded and patched.

He already knew what we were there for, to see the murder

site, and he already knew that it was our job to come at the case from the GI angle. The Koreans were maintaining jurisdiction. When only GIs were involved in a crime, they often turned the prosecution over to the U.S. military authorities. But when a Korean was victimized, and the newspapers had gotten hold of it, there was no way they were going to let it go. He did realize, however, that he needed us to infiltrate the world of the U.S. soldiers and their Korean girlfriends.

He got up, put on his hat, and barked some instructions to his desk sergeant. We followed him out the door.

Next to the police station was a bank—smart move—and beyond that a few shops and then the nightclub district. The UN Club was first—big, blue, and boxy, with a little neon sign touting it as the gateway to Itaewon. Up the road, coiled neon hung off the sides of cement brick walls, looking dusty and sad in the gray morning air.

Alleys wound up the hill and formed a network like a giant spider impaled amidst the jumble of Korean homes.

Captain Kim leaned his head forward and trudged quickly up the incline, not turning left, as I expected, at Hooker Hill, but marching straight up past the King Club and then left, up a narrow alley, and right through an open metal gate imbedded in a ten-foot-high stone wall. The hooches formed a U shape. The one closest to the gate was gutted. It was charred and black and Captain Kim told us that the landlady had acted quickly to get the fire department there in time to save the rest of the rooms.

She had gray hair yanked straight back over her wrinkled face and knotted in the back with a polished wooden pin. I thought I saw worry in her eyes. Maybe it was just from living, maybe something else.

I talked to her briefly. She said she was an old woman and a light sleeper and she had a phone right next to her bed so she called as soon as she smelled smoke.

I decided not to be impolite and question her at length, since Captain Kim had told me in firm tones that he had already personally conducted an interrogation.

That was another thing I was sometimes accused of when somebody other than Ernie watched my investigative technique—being too soft, on Koreans usually. And taking too much instruction from the Korean police. The U.S. Army's not real big on subtle moves.

The hooch itself didn't reveal much. The body had been removed a couple of hours ago. There were the remnants of the usual business-girl apparatus: a big charred armoire for storing clothes, a melted-down stereo set, and the skeleton of a Western-style bed.

Ernie picked up a wooden stake that seemed to have been untouched by the fire. "Why wasn't this one burned?" he asked.

Captain Kim understood the question and answered in Korean. Before I could translate, Ernie turned his back on us and started poking around in the remains. He uncovered a pile of charcoal in front of the bed. The bonfire. Probably what was left of a perforated cylindrical briquette, the type that is fired up in outside heaters to spread warm air through flues that ran beneath the house. He kept flipping with the clean wooden stake until he turned up a blackened pair of long straight tongs. It looked as if they had been used to carry the flaming briquette into the hooch.

The old woman and the other neighbors knew nothing more about the GI boyfriend than that his name was Johnny. The description they gave was vague and where it was explicit it could have applied to half the guys in Itaewon.

Ernie dropped the stake, dusted off his hands, and turned to the old lady.

"Where did Miss Pak Ok-suk work?"

"The Lucky Seven Club," she said.

We asked the old woman for a list of her other tenants.

Captain Kim didn't like it much since he'd already interviewed them all and come up with nothing.

The only one who seemed worth interviewing was the one with the room that wasn't much larger than a closet. Kimiko. We knew her well. In Itaewon, everyone knew her well.

"Where is Kimiko now?"

The old woman waved her hand towards the village.

We thanked her and walked down the hill in silence. I could think of a few places where Kimiko might be. All of them raunchy.

Burrows and Slabem were still waiting at the police box.

"Like a couple of hounds guarding a store," Ernie said.

"Or waiting for us to make a mistake."

Captain Kim didn't say goodbye. Neither did we. Ernie cranked up the jeep and swiveled his head almost completely around to back off the curb.

"What'd Captain Kim say about that stake? The one that hadn't been burned?"

"He said it couldn't have been burned because it was protected."

Ernie popped the jeep into first and edged out into the rushing traffic.

"Protected?"

"Yeah."

The jeep lurched forward. Tires squealed and fourteen horns at least blared as Ernie bulled his way into the careening stampede.

2

Life in the Army isn't anything like what most people think. Especially when you're stationed on Yongsan Compound, the headquarters of the Eighth United States Army.

First of all, we don't stand any formations. In the CID you're not even issued rifles, only .45s, which we could check out of the arms room when we felt like it, which in my case was never. And we don't wear uniforms. Of course the CID, the Criminal Investigation Division, never did, no matter where you were stationed. You always wore a coat and tie. The civilian clothes were supposed to help you blend into the civilian population. That probably made some sense in the 1930s and '40s, when everybody who could afford it wore a suit. But nowadays the only people who wear suits are either getting married, on their way to a funeral, or they work for the U.S. Army Criminal Investigation Division.

Our rank was classified. So if young buck sergeants, like me and Ernie, had to investigate a full-bird colonel, we wouldn't be intimidated. That's another one of those things that doesn't really work in practice. After you've worked at Eighth Army Headquarters for a while, everybody knows you. And the colonels have this habit of protecting themselves and their fellow officers. In that order. Of course, the generals don't have to worry about anything. They're just one step below God.

People also have this idea of some sort of sad sack existence. I haven't touched a mop since I left the States. We have house-boys. Every night I throw my dirty clothes on the floor, in the same spot, and in the morning after I shower and shave I put on the clean clothes that were laid out for me the day before. About an hour before I leave for work, my houseboy shows up and brings my footgear to a high spitshine. When I get back to my room, usually at lunch or in the late afternoon, the place is clean, the bed is made, and my work clothes for the next day are hanging in front of my wall locker.

I never call Mr. Yi a houseboy to his face. He would consider that insulting, especially since he's about a quarter-century older than me. And I don't call him *Ajosi*—"Uncle"— which would be the normal form of address for a younger man to his elder. I call him Mr. Yi. The Western way. To Koreans it sounds neat and clean—businesslike—and doesn't get us involved in their complex hierarchical relationships.

Koreans use different forms of address, and different verb endings, depending on what your relative status is to the person you are talking to. Status that is defined not by money but by the writings of Confucius. Don't even try to get me to explain it to you. They say that, because of these status considerations, a for-eigner can study for years and still never learn how to speak

Korean properly. I've been trying—and I communicate—but I know they make a lot of allowances for me that wouldn't apply if I didn't have a Caucasian face.

In the mornings we hit the Yongsan Snack Bar, which I love. I love the shuffling feet, the tinkling porcelain cups and silverware, the incoherent mumblings, and the crinkling of newspapers being opened. Ernie and I never miss the morning edition of the *Pacific Stars & Stripes*. They fly it in from Tokyo. Unless there's a typhoon or something, they airlift it all over the Pacific: Vietnam, Thailand, the Philippines, Hong Kong, Okinawa, and of course to Korea. It's a real rag, with William F. Buckley, Jr., on the right and Art Buchwald on the left. So much for socialist leanings. But it's good for a laugh and without my copy of the *Stripes* and a nasal-cleansing cup of Snack Bar coffee, I just don't feel right in the mornings.

For lunch we go over to the Lower Four Club and order the special, which usually runs under a buck and a half but sometimes they go hog-wild and put a bunch of beef on the plate and try to charge a dollar ninety-five—ice tea, rolls, and salad included.

My favorite waitress over there is Miss Lee. Everybody tries to tell me she's a little sweet on me but she's sort of old—I've heard thirty—and so I've never tried to get her alone. We call her the Titless Wonder, but her can is really great and she's very pretty and tiny. Not petite. Tiny. Since I'm six foot four, two hundred and twenty pounds, I'm sure we would make a heck of a couple.

If you don't want the special, you can drink your lunch in the cocktail lounge and watch the go-go girls or the stripper or whatever the club manager might have arranged for the noontime entertainment.

A lot of guys don't get out much. Their Korean wives keep them at home after working hours and so lunchtime for them is their chance to kick out the jams and have a little fun. At Eighth

Army Headquarters, beery breath always reminds me of afternoons. At night we hit the ville.

More often than not I run the ville with Ernie. We've gotten used to each other.

Ernie keeps his body pretty well saturated with liquor. He says it's better than heroin. Besides, heroin is virtually impossible to get in Korea—not like Vietnam. And liquor is not only accepted but embraced by the U.S. Army.

Me, I've always been afraid to try any of the hard drugs. Marijuana, speed, a little acid once or twice, okay, but I doubt that I'd have the willpower to put down heroin like Ernie did.

I really admire him.

We call his girlfriend "the Nurse." She's a stout but shapely young Korean woman who dropped out of nursing school and now takes care of Ernie full time. When he shows up at their hooch, that is. They've had some pretty hellacious fights about him staying out all night. He always claims it's an investigation, but she knows better.

Ernie enjoys the fights. Even the time she dropped their big folding Styrofoam mattress into the public well near their hooch. Ernie just heaved it out and took it, dripping, in a cab back to the compound. Later, after getting a few stitches in his hand from the butcher knife she took to him, he moved back into her hooch. But he kept the mattress in his barracks. Prudent guy, that Ernie.

When they're not fighting they spend a lot of time talking about injections. It's Ernie's favorite word. The Nurse meticulously explains all the preparations necessary for giving an injection, even mimicking the hand movements, and then performs the act, keeping her face stonily serious, while Ernie watches the imaginary needle pop in his arm.

Every couple has to have a hobby.

Lately Ernie's been seeing a lot of Miss So. She's got long straight black hair and a serious expression—he's got a thing for serious expressions. But one thing she has all over the Nurse is that she wears glasses.

Ernie wears glasses. Round, wire-rimmed jobs with thick lenses, and girls who wear glasses just about drive him mad. Miss So seems to have injected herself into his soul.

She's one of those chicks who hang around Itaewon, wearing the latest stateside outfits, because she's fascinated by the American GIs. She's been watching American movies for so long and listening to the music and studying English in school that she's got some sort of idea that all the wise, punk-ass, jitterbugging GIs hanging around the ville are actually worth a damn.

Anyway, she's not a professional so she has to watch herself. Mainly she hangs out in the rock-and-roll clubs where fewer straight business girls work and a few more of the strays wander in from time to time. Her running partner is her sister, who's a year or two younger than she is, taller, doesn't wear glasses, and doesn't look anything like her.

Ernie tried to set me up with her once but it didn't work out. I think I'm too serious for her. She likes guys who are bubbling over with enthusiasm and can barely contain themselves over something indecipherable, like maybe just being alive. I get enthusiastic about books and things, or a particularly knotty investigation, or just getting laid.

Definitely not her type.

Not that I hold any grudges. There are plenty of other girls in Itaewon. Like Miss Oh, the cocktail waitress who works at the King Club.

She was a big help to me on my last investigation, after she got tired of bonging me on the head with her cocktail tray. She's tall, slender, with flowing black hair, and a figure than can make grown men cry. At least she's brought me to tears a couple of times.

I try not to push her too hard. I know she's got something

going with one or two of the guys who run the local Club Owners' Association here. Got to pay her dues. So I just see her occasionally, when we both have time. If I wander into the King Club, have a drink, and she's a little brusque with me, I get the message. If she lingers at my table and asks me to buy her a drink, then I know I'm in. But Miss Oh would have to wait until at least nightfall.

There would be nothing for us until then so Ernie and I decided to take advantage of the first sergeant's loose reins. Ernie went over to South Post to do some jogging, and I rolled up my *gi* and made it to the twelve o'clock tae kwon do class.

Mr. Chong, our instructor, had been holding classes at the main gym on Yongsan Compound for the last couple of years, ever since he'd won the Korean national title in the tae kwon do middleweight division.

It's the most competitive division, mainly because almost everyone in the country is a middleweight. He's a calm man, with a sculpted body, extremely precise in his movements, and as quick as a cobra when he wants to be.

I'd no more want to meet him in a dark alley than walk through an impact area during a Second Infantry Division field exercise.

"You're late again, George."

We were in the locker room, changing into our white outfits.

"Yes, I'm sorry. They had me working."

Mr. Chong finished tying his long black belt around his trim waist and walked over to me slowly, shuffling his plastic slippers.

"You could be a very good student, one of my best, if you'd only work harder."

"I will try," I said. "It's this job. . . ."

The worst part about every tae kwon do workout is the stretching exercises at the beginning. My skeleton had set into a brittle knot years before I ever thought about taking up this stuff, and to get my head to my knees or my ankles behind my neck was perfect torture.

We had a couple of American girls in the class, mainly there to ogle Mr. Chong, and they went through the stretching exercises like eels through a net.

Later, when we finally got back on our feet and into the endless repetitions of our kicking and punching routines, I felt a lot better; the sweat flowing, air coming hard. And then the solid feeling of knuckle and instep smacking against the swinging heavy bag.

It was during the free fighting that Mr. Chong always got me.

"You defend yourself too much, George. You must open up. You must attack."

That was difficult for me to do since I'd always thought that the best offense was a good defense. And I was about twice the size of most of the people in the class. How can you open up when you don't really intend to hurt anyone?

After the cool-down exercises, more stretching and bending, we bowed to Mr. Chong, in unison, and were dismissed. I walked over to the weight room and, still in my *gi*, pumped iron for a couple of hours.

In the sauna room I thought about Miss Pak and her short career.

A lot of GIs, especially those just in from the States, are always hung up on whether a girl is a professional or not. As if there's some sort of clear-cut, fluorescent line between a person who is evil and one who isn't. I've done enough things in my life to be ashamed of that I don't have much problem with a girl who lives alone in a drafty hovel, works for a salary of thirty dollars a month, sees a couple of boyfriends, and then asks me for a few bucks the morning after.

I'm a GI. I clear almost five hundred dollars—cash—a month.

And I've got a free place to live and free food to eat. Not to mention medical care if I get sick. I'm like a millionaire compared to Miss Oh.

To be honest, there are some totally straight girls around, ones who aren't as desperate as Miss Oh. It's sort of hard for a GI to meet them, though, especially if you're like me and Ernie and spend all of your free time in the village of Itaewon.

I did once.

Ernie and I were pulling security, along with about eight thousand other guys for some big mucketymuck from the U.S. government who was visiting the Israeli Embassy in Seoul. Ernie was driving a big unmarked sedan and I rode shotgun. We spotted her leaving the embassy, walking towards the bus stop, so we slowed down and offered her a ride. At first she didn't understand me but then I spoke Korean to her and everything was all right.

I took her to lunch at the Naija R&R Center downtown and then on a date where we walked through Duksoo Palace, and one afternoon I even went home and met her oldest sister. I don't know what came over me. Just going along out of curiosity, I guess. Anyway, I took her to the Frontier Club after that on Yongsan South Post, let her listen to the live band, and bought her a Brandy Alexander. We spent the night together in a little *yoguan* I know in Samgakji. It was the first night she ever spent with a man.

I saw her a couple of times after that but then I got tired of it and I stood her up once and then I wouldn't return her calls. Her brother-in-law, a Korean man of about forty, called me and in faltering English told me I couldn't do that to her. I was hung over, in a bad mood, and I told him to go screw himself.

I've never seen her again. I'd be afraid to now. It's things like that that have piled up in my life, that keep me aware that I'm no better than Miss Oh or any of the girls in Itaewon like her.

However, I'm not completely nonjudgmental and there is one thing I'm sure of—I'm better than that son of a bitch who murdered Miss Pak Ok-suk.

3

At the Lucky Seven Club we shoved some stools out of the way, leaned up against the bar, and ordered a couple of beers. We were the first customers in the joint. Most of the GIs had just gotten off work and hadn't yet had time to eat chow, shower, shave, and get on down to the ville.

A couple of business girls scurried in and out, playing grab-ass, and only three or four of the waitresses were yet on duty. Ernie hit up the barmaid first.

"Where's Kimiko?"

"Kimiko?"

"Yeah. Old woman. Long hair. Big *jeejes*." He cupped two hands in front of his chest.

"You mean Ok-suk *onni*." The barmaid thought about it for a minute and then shook her head and got back to washing glass-ware. "I no see her for a long time."

Ok-suk *onni* meant the older sister of Ok-suk. If that's what everyone called Kimiko, they must have been close.

The barmaid was a nice-looking gal, sturdy and squat, like maybe her ancestors had ridden in from the central plains of Asia, but she was shapely in all the right places. Her long black hair sat atop her round head, knotted by a single polished chopstick.

I waited until she finished her glasses and then I asked her name.

She looked up at me, surprised, the drying towel still in her hands.

"Mangnei," she said, which wasn't an answer because *mangnei* just means little sister. GIs wouldn't know the difference, though.

"What's *your* name?" she asked.

"Opa," I said, which wasn't an answer either because *opa* just means older brother.

Her eyes widened and she started to laugh. Soon we were speaking Korean together and I bought her a Coke. GIs walked in and she got busy but after the first flush of business there was a lull and she came back to us and I asked her about the woman named Pak Ok-suk.

I expected reticence, a closing of ranks against a foreigner. What I got was a girl who wouldn't shut up, a girl who seemed proud that Itaewon had finally hit the Korean equivalent of the tabloids.

Everyone had heard about the murder and the manner in which it was done and "Mangnei" was as fascinated by the grotes-querie as anyone. Other girls walked over and started to add their embellishments and before long I had more information than I really wanted.

Pak Ok-suk had drifted into Itaewon from the countryside, cast off by a family that could no longer afford to keep her. Not that they couldn't afford to feed her. They could manage that. What they couldn't manage were her eccentricities—her demands for new clothes, her willfulness in going out at night with her friends, and her refusal to take her father's word as law. The cramped quarters of the Korean rural home got tighter each day until the walls were about to explode and the family lashed out at her for being the source of their shame, for being a grown daughter yet unmarried.

The young men her age were in the Army, manning a fighting force almost as big as America's in a country one-sixth the size. The country was crammed with armaments and soldiers that pushed up against the Demilitarized Zone, threatening to burst across.

Her choices included the textile mills and the factories, filled with white-bandannaed female automatons churning out high-tech equipment for the world's consumers. Or collecting tokens, sweeping out buses, jamming the passengers in the door, straddling the exit to keep anyone from falling out, shielding them with her body.

Instead she chose Itaewon.

At first she was just a barmaid's helper, doing lowly work: the sweeping and the cleaning and the washing of the bar rags. She hid from the GIs but watched them with her big round eyes and, as time went by, she became more bold. She poured Cokes for them or popped open beers, saving the more complicated highballs for her wiser sisters. And she even went so far as to collect money from them and hand it over to the old crone who guarded the cashier's box, receiving change from gnarled hands.

And she loved the music and the dancing and the clothes and the hairdos and she longed to have nice things of her own.

She slept in the bar, on chairs pulled together after the Lucky Seven Club closed for the evening, before the midnight curfew. And at first she couldn't sleep because she was too wound up by all the things she had seen. And she listened to the young men who were the ushers by night and the janitors by day, as they crept from their rickety multilegged beds and crawled in with some of the older girls who rated soft vinyl-covered booths for their boudoirs. And she listened to their giggles and then their grunts, but none of the young men crawled in with her. There wasn't room.

And she dreamed of home and how warm it had once been and how it would never exist for her again. When she met Kimiko, everything changed.

Kimiko hadn't frequented the Lucky Seven Club much in the last few years. They hadn't let her in since the spitting and scratching contest she'd had with a girl she found with one of her GI boyfriends. When she got through with the girl, she punched out the GI and two of the young ushers. Soon whistles were blowing and the Korean National Police joined the fray. Snarling and clawing and kicking, she had fought them off until one of the cops whipped out his baton and ended the altercation with one clean swipe to her head.

But time has a way of draining rancor, and Kimiko was eventually allowed back into the club again. All the young help had changed, maybe two or three times, and no one was too anxious to tell her to leave anyway. The old crone, hunched over the cash box, remembered her and kept an eye on her but didn't say anything when she started a restrained and civil conversation with the young little Pak Ok-suk.

Kimiko was known to all the GIs of Itaewon and some of them called her Short Time, a reference to the way she financed her life.

She freelanced, strictly, rolling from bar to bar searching for GI prey, getting them to buy her drinks. Not those overpriced sweetheart drinks, with hardly any liquor in them, but beer and straight shots of bourbon. And she held her liquor well. But sometimes her heavy makeup would get smudged or her skintight dress would seem a little twisted, off center, and she would look like some demented doll that had been dressed by a clumsy child. Hemline riding high over spindly legs, neckline bursting with bosom.

Kimiko had been around long enough to know GIs. She knew about the problems they had getting an overnight pass, she knew that they'd get shafted if they were caught on the street after the midnight curfew, and she knew that some of them would do anything to get promoted and others didn't care. Some of them just wanted to do their time and get out and some of them had much more money at home than the U.S. Army could ever pay them. And she kept looking for that one starry-eyed young GI from a rich family who would flip for her. She was like an old sourdough in the desert, pulling her old burro along, searching for that last shining vein of boyish El Dorado.

When she came back into the Lucky Seven Club after such a long absence, she was prim and proper. She behaved herself. And she didn't get drunk. She sat at the bar, sipped on a Chilsung Cider, and left early. She didn't hang around for those last few GIs who were too drunk to walk—her normal clientele—but instead held a polite conversation with the one person behind the bar who seemed to have some sort of respect for her age and her experience: Pak Ok-suk.

None of the girls remembered exactly when they had started talking together. It was something that just happened. Kimiko would pontificate, waving an American-made cigarette in the air and punctuating her discourse with sips of beer, while Pak Ok-suk leaned across the bar, a devotee at the feet of a guru.

Some of the girls tried to warn her: Stay away from Kimiko. But they couldn't give concrete reasons. Kimiko had never messed with the other girls in the village unless she caught them with one of her boyfriends, one of her sources of livelihood. Mainly she was just aggressive about making her living.

The girls were unanimous in not blaming her for that. After all, who else would take care of her? But they knew that Kimiko was bad news for Miss Pak, yet Miss Pak didn't listen, and now all their dire warnings had come to pass.

"Did Kimiko kill Miss Pak?"

Mangnei pulled her head back, her eyes and mouth rounding. "Of course not."

"Then who did?"

She didn't know. But Kimiko had probably gotten Miss Pak involved with a man she couldn't handle. Who?

She didn't know that either. She only knew that Miss Pak had quit her job behind the bar and started wearing nice clothes and getting her hair done and learning how to dance, until she was the sexiest girl in Itaewon. Often she had left the club in the company of Kimiko. On important missions. And each day she seemed to have more money and more clothes and soon had her own hooch. After a while she stopped talking to any of the girls who worked in the Lucky Seven Club.

"What about her boyfriend, Johnny?"

"He was crazy about her and used to follow her all the time."

"Has he been in lately?"

"Every night. He sits over there, same table." She pointed. "Waiting for Miss Pak. But she didn't have time for him. She talk to him for few minutes and then goes with Kimiko."

"Was he here last night?"

"Yes. Early. But then left."

"What time?"

"Maybe ten o'clock."

"Where does he work?"

The girls buzzed amongst themselves on that one. They mentioned some other names—Freddy and Sammy—friends of his, and one of the girls seemed certain that they worked at the motor pool.

I turned to her. "How do you know?"

She blushed. The other girls laughed. She'd spent the night there.

We didn't bother to ask the girls where we could find Kimiko. She could be anywhere and then turn up where you least expected her. We'd find her ourselves. Or she'd find us.

As we walked out of the Lucky Seven Club, the amplified instruments on the bandstand clanged to life and the ballroom began to whirl with multicolored light. People jumped up from their tables and chairs and soon the dance floor was packed with gangly GIs and sweet young girls just in from the lush green valleys of Korea, all dancing to Motown.

GIs bounced up the main road of Itaewon, hands in their pockets, breath and laughter billowing from their mouths, ignoring the slippery ice as they headed for the neon.

The village was a huge web of brightness, shrouded in snow. Nightclubs lined the main road, and alleys branched off, up steep stone steps, to smaller, cozier clubs. Old women lurked in the darkness ready to lead any willing GI to a brothel if he didn't have the time or the temperament for the dancing and the booze and the laughter.

Ernie took a deep breath of the biting air and let it out slowly. "It's good to be back."

"After forty-eight hours away?"

"Entirely too long."

We popped into the King Club, elbowed our way through the crowd, and asked a few questions. No one had seen Kimiko. We got some strange looks. Normally people tried to avoid her.

At each club the answer was the same. No one had seen her.

"Sort of like the dog that didn't bark," Ernie said.

"What do you mean?"

"Well, normally when you come to Itaewon there's three things you can count on—cold beer, women, and Kimiko bugging the shit out of you. So if we come out here one night, get all the cold beer we want, have to push our way through bunches of sweet young girls, but still we can't find Kimiko no matter how hard we look, there's got to be something wrong."

"What's that got to do with a dog that didn't bark?"

"Like in Sherlock Holmes. If a burglar breaks into a place and the dog didn't bark, that's got to mean that maybe a burglar didn't break into the place."

"Not in East L.A. The mutts just snarl and attack."

We decided to hit up Ginger at the American Club. It would be good to get in out of the cold. Relax, have a beer, and maybe learn something.

When she saw us, she pounded down the planks behind the bar, squealing all the way.

"Georgie! Ernie! Long time no see! Short time how you been?"

Ginger made a point of making all her customers feel welcome.

She was a big girl. Round. Maybe not chubby but definitely husky. She was Korean through and through but her bobbed hair was light brown and her face was dotted with freckles across her cheeks and the bridge of her nose. All the old NCOs and retirees who hung out at her place kidded her about it: "A little *Miguk* in the woodpile, eh, Ginger?" Meaning, she was half Caucasian—a mixed blood.

She called herself Ginger because it was a spice used in a lot of Korean cooking. When she found out that Americans used it too *and* it was a woman's name, she couldn't resist.

She took pains to be the sauciest gal at any gathering and she was the smartest woman in Itaewon, as far as I was concerned. The only one to own a club outright, and not part of a family-run operation.

We ordered a couple of beers. The place was full, with quite a few nice-looking women, but most of them escorted. No heavy-handed hustle in Ginger's place. A row of beer bellies, belonging to middle-aged American men, lined the bar. Luckily, the country-western band was on break.

Ginger poured our beers, made change, and then propped her elbows on the bar.

"I got a problem, Ginger," I said. "We can't find Kimiko."

Her eyes widened and then set back into their normal position.

"Information?"

We laughed. "How'd you know?"

"You guys can't be looking for a woman that old for sex. Not unless you're getting kinky on me. And you're not looking for her for black market. Nobody does black market with Kimiko, except for a newbie. So you must be looking for her for some sort of information. Hot information. Like maybe something to do with that poor little girl who was murdered last night."

"Don't stop now, Ginger," Ernie said. "We'll just drink beer and listen."

"In Itaewon during the day, when the GIs are at work, the main thing everybody does is wait for beer deliveries and gossip. Today there was only one subject, Kimiko and Pak Ok-suk. Kimiko had been running that girl around, making money off of her, and she must have got her involved with some mean guys."

"Anybody know who they are?"

"Not that I've heard. Kimiko always took little Miss Pak out of the village, away from Itaewon. Nobody knows who they were seeing. Everybody expects Kimiko to disappear for a while. Eventually she'll come back and try to find a new girl."

"Has she done this before?"

"Yeah. The last one wasn't killed, at least not that I know of. She just disappeared."

"Do you know who she was?"

"No. But I can find out for you. Check back tomorrow."

Nothing like a little murder to convince people to support law enforcement.

We ordered a couple more beers just before the band started and if we hadn't I probably would have left before the first song was over. They were young, Korean, and enthusiastic but that didn't make up for their lack of skill. Of course, I'm not too crazy about country music even when it's played well. The old guys at the bar didn't seem to mind. Already anesthetized. And at least it wasn't rock and roll.

Ginger had jumped into an intimate conversation with a woman down the bar. She was elegantly dressed, tall, with a big shining rock on her finger. Ernie pointed his nose at a few of the girls on the dance floor and finally one of them walked over to him and stood leaning against his bar stool, his legs spread-eagled around her.

Ginger brought me another beer and leaned over to talk in my ear so I could hear her above the dulcet sounds of "The Orange Blossom Special."

"This is from her. She wants to talk to you."

I glanced down the bar for a second. The woman was older than I usually liked, closing in on thirty. Her eyes were cast demurely down.

"No sweat," Ginger said. "She's my friend, here from the States. On vacation."

I walked down the bar and she smiled when I took the seat next to her. Ernie got lost and, by the time the band was ready to start another break, so did we, scooting out the front without even saying goodbye to Ginger.

Her name, she told me, was Miss Lim and she claimed she owned one of those hostess bars in Honolulu that cater to Japanese tourists and mainlanders looking for something exotic.

What it meant, probably, was that she was married to a GI, worked in one of those bars, and made more in tips during one good weekend than he made for the entire month.

She told me about how she prepared the *puupuus*, the free snacks, for her customers every night. What she didn't tell me about were the handjobs under the table. When I asked, she just laughed.

She'd been here in Seoul, staying with her mother, for a few days and had to leave Korea in another week or so. I figured she could afford a nice hotel room but she didn't think much of the idea.

"You man," she said.

Since I was paying for it, we went to a rundown *yoguan*.

She didn't want to wash me like the business girls do and she balked when I asked her for a particularly intimate sexual favor.

"It's only our first date," she said.

They go to hell fast when they go to the States.

At dawn, gray light filtered through the tattered cloth curtain covering the small window. Miss Lim lay next to me, naked. Thanks to Miss Lim I was not too hung over and I lay still in the bed, trying to put myself in Kimiko's place and imagine where she might have gone.

Kimiko was old enough to have been born during the Japanese occupation of Korea. That's probably why she used a Japanese woman's name, Kimiko, as her working name. She had seen Korea transformed from an Oriental colony into a hideous battlefield for warring superpowers and now into what verged on a modern industrial state. During all that time she had remained firmly entrapped on the lowest rungs of society.

I couldn't begin to imagine what must be going through her mind. We were too different. My guess was, though, that she understood me and others like me—completely.

4

When the first sergeant heard about Johnny he tried to take over the operation.

Ernie said, "You don't want to do it that way, Top. Let me and George go in quietly and find out what's going on with this guy before you send in the cavalry and the sirens and every glory hound in Eighth Army."

The first sergeant stood up from behind his desk and leaned forward.

"All right. But I want this guy Johnny, whoever he is, arrested before close of business today. And don't screw it up. The CG is screaming for a suspect. He has to keep explaining to the Koreans why no GI has been arrested yet and they don't really want to hear it."

"International relations, eh?"

· "Don't get cute, Bascom. Just get us the suspect."

The first sergeant sat down and started to take a sip out of his coffee mug but realized it was empty. He got up, walked over to the metal coffee urn on the counter, tilted it, and cursed. It was empty, too.

Ernie and I looked at our full, steaming cups nervously. The first sergeant turned and looked at them, too.

"*And* you were late again. Both of you." He sat back down behind his desk. "And why didn't you give me the lead on this guy Johnny last night? We could have had him behind bars by now. The provost marshal is at the command conference room, as we speak, giving his briefing on our lack of progress on the case and getting his ass chewed. Don't you guys have any loyalty?"

"Loyalty?" Ernie said. He looked at me. "Sure, We got loyalty."

I sipped on my coffee. "Loads," I said.

The first sergeant glared at us. One of his management techniques. His day was going too smoothly, I decided.

"What if he didn't do it?"

"What?" He looked startled.

"What if Johnny didn't kill Miss Pak Ok-suk? I mean all we have established so far is that he knew her and spent some time with her. No particular reason to believe that he was the guy who offed her."

"He's the boyfriend, isn't he?" the first sergeant said. "It's always the boyfriend."

"Maybe he can prove where he was the night of the murder," Ernie said. "Maybe he didn't have an overnight pass. Or maybe he was Staff Duty Driver that night."

The first sergeant toyed with his coffee mug. He gazed at it sourly. "We'll worry about that shit once we get him behind bars."

Burrows and Slabem breezed into the office.

Ernie stood up. "We'll take care of the arrest, Top. Don't sweat it."

"What arrest?" Burrows said.

I tapped him on the chest. "Cardiac arrest. The one Top would have if you two guys ever actually dug out some information on your own."

"What information?" Slabem said.

When we got to the Admin Office we waved at Miss Kim and trotted down the steps to Ernie's jeep.

If we hesitated about going to the motor pool, the first sergeant might change his mind and send Burrows and Slabem. Not that they'd do a better job, they'd just do a more reliable one. Since Eighth Army needed a suspect, they'd arrest a suspect, and not pay any attention to frivolous bothersome facts.

Ernie popped the clutch, the wheels caught on the ice, and we jerked forward.

"Looks like Mr. Johnny stepped into a world of shit," he said.

"Either that or we have."

The jeep slid swiftly along the tree-lined avenues of Eighth Army Headquarters. My skin tightened at the rush of frigid air.

21 T Car was one of those great GI acronyms that actually stood for the Twenty-first Transportation Company, alias the motor pool: the place that provided the jeeps and the sedans and the buses and all the other requisite wheeled vehicles in support of the activities of the Eighth United States Army Headquarters. The huge open parking area was surrounded by a chain-link fence topped with trident-pronged barbed wire. At the entrance a green arch covered the guard shack, emblazoned with a martial welcome and the insignia of the U.S. Army Transportation Corps.

The Korean guards waved us through. They knew Ernie.

Most of the other CID agents had to use the handful of

sedans provided for their use at the detachment. Usually it was a half day's work trying to prioritize the various cases everyone was working on and playing politics to see who got which sedan. After ending up with the clunker most of the time, Ernie took matters into his own hands and romanced the dispatchers down at 21 T Car into assigning him a jeep that they had managed to slip off the ready-for-duty list.

Two quarts of liquor every payday kept the jeep reserved and all regular maintenance was thrown in. We had the added advantage of being a little harder to spot by the bad guys, who had the makes and models of the CID sedans memorized.

"Where to first?" I asked

"Chief Winkle."

Ernie jerked the wheel to the left and pulled up to a big ramshackle one-story wooden building that was the dispatchers' office. He parked, locked the chain, welded to his floorboard, to the steering wheel, and got out.

Inside the building, he waved at the Korean dispatchers, who flashed big block-toothed grins, and we walked down a long narrow hallway until we came to the last office with a small wooden sign over the door that said CHIEF, DISPATCH.

Chief Warrant Officer-3 Frank Winkle sat ramrod straight in neatly pressed fatigues behind his cluttered desk. Talking on the phone, he looked for all the world like a worried doctor taking a discouraging lab report. He peered up, calm but concerned, then smiled when he saw Ernie.

"Okay, you got it," he said. "Minus three on the Jets." He hung up the phone, beamed at us, and waved to the empty lounge chairs. "Sit down, gentlemen. Just having a conversation with the ambassador. What can I do for you today?"

"The ambassador? Ours?"

"The same."

"He bets football?"

"Oh, no. He just likes to match wits with the odds makers. Merely a hobby of his."

Chief Winkle ran what was, as far as I knew, the only book-making operation for American sports in the Republic of Korea. His busiest time of the year was the pro football season, but he also took bets on baseball, basketball, and boxing. He used the betting line that was published every Thursday in the *Pacific Stars & Stripes.* His trusted customers were allowed to place bets over the phone and he'd collect when he saw them, usually at the Embassy Club or the United Nations Compound Club. If they won, he had a Korean soldier transport their winnings directly to them in a U.S. government vehicle. He was in the perfect spot for running his operation—the transportation hub of the post.

If Burrows and Slabem ever found out about it, they'd bust him for sure, but of course nobody bothered to tell them. My guess was that the first sergeant knew about Chief Winkle but either he placed bets with him or the provost marshal did— maybe both. After all, betting on pro football is the national pastime. Nothing to get upset about.

"What can I help you with, Ernie?"

"I'm looking for a young GI who works here at 21 T Car named Johnny. I realize that doesn't narrow it down much but the girls out in the ville say that his running partners are called Freddy and Sammy."

"What'd this fellow do?"

"Possibly murder."

"Not that little girl they found out in the ville?"

"The same."

The chief sighed. So much corruption in the world. Why couldn't everyone be satisfied with something nice and sedate, like wagering?

"I know Johnny," he said. "I know Freddy and Sammy, too.

They're just young kids. Fun-loving, boisterous. Your typical GIs, full of life. I can't believe that they'd do . . . that."

I asked, "Were they involved in anything, Chief?"

Winkle narrowed his eyes. "Like what?"

"Like your operation, for instance."

"No. Not at all. I doubt that they even know about it. I don't think they were even black-marketing. Just your average kids. Goofing off, pretending they were working to stay out of trouble during the day and then running the ville every night, chasing the girls. That's all they had on their minds. Business girls."

"Where can we find them?" Ernie said.

"They work in the motor pool. Get assigned to different jobs. Hold on, I'll check." The chief lifted up his phone and dialed some numbers rapid fire. "Hello, Joe? Yeah. I need to know where that kid Johnny Watkins is working today. No, he doesn't owe me any money but you do. Okay, okay, okay. Payday. That'll be fine. Now look it up for me, will ya?" The chief drummed his fingers on the desk. Joe came back on the line. "Yeah, yeah. Thanks, Joe. See ya."

Chief Winkle cradled the phone. "He's working for data processing. Been there a couple of weeks."

"Regular duty hours?"

"Yeah."

We thanked him and left. The ringing of his phone followed us down the hallway.

Eighth Army's data is processed in a green cinder-block building fit snugly into a long row of offices in the main headquarters complex of Yongsan Compound. From time to time on Sundays I had walked down the tree-lined lanes with a soft female hand in mine, when the only sound was the rustling of the leaves and the gurgling of the creek that ran through the heart of the compound.

Today the data processing building was full of buzzing and beep-ing and the quick movements of overworked clerks.

"Can I help you?"

She was a buxom thing with flows of red hair piled atop her head and a tight green Army Class-B uniform showing off her figure. I could have flashed her my badge but it always seemed overly dramatic to me.

"We'd like to see the NCO in charge."

"Sergeant Parsons?"

"Yeah."

"He's out right now."

I looked at the freckles across the bridge of her nose and her nice smile and somehow managed to keep my wiseass remarks to myself. Ernie clicked his gum.

I said, "We're looking for Specialist Watkins. I understand he's been assigned as your driver for the last couple of weeks. We just want to talk to him."

"Oh, Watkins. Yeah." She looked down at a chart on the counter between us. "He's out on a run. Probably won't be back until about four or four thirty."

Ernie rolled his eyes. The first sergeant would have a fit.

I looked back at the girl's bosom and then at the chart.

"Where'd he go?"

"He has to stop at a bunch of small compounds—at the PX's and snack bars, places like that—and pick up their Ration Control Data Entry cards."

"Is this his schedule?"

"Yes." She ran a carefully manicured finger down the list. "Right now he should be at ASCOM City. His next stop is Yongdungpo."

"Do you have a sheet of paper so I can write down this schedule?"

"I'll do better than that. I'll make a copy for you."

A minute later she was back and handed me the extra copy.

"Do you have any idea where this guy has lunch?"

She giggled. "Knowing Johnny, it's probably out in the village."

We thanked her and ambled out.

"Not bad for a white woman," Ernie said.

He started the jeep, rolled through the main gate, and jumped into the Seoul traffic. About twenty minutes later we crossed the Third Han River Bridge, heading south, across murky waters churning with ice.

The 362nd U.S. Army Air Defense Artillery Compound fit perfectly into the little village of Heichang-up. There were shops and restaurants and open-air produce markets and then a few feet of red brick wall, a gate, a few more feet of red brick wall, and then more shops and stores.

Air defense. A part of daily life in this country.

The village sat south of the Han River, about fifteen miles as the crow flies from Seoul. Perfect for shooting up those North Korean pilots who'd just dropped all their ordnance on a bombing run of the South Korean capital. The compound had sat there, quietly, since the end of the Korean War. They'd been on alert plenty of times but so far they hadn't had to use their pop guns, except in training.

A Korean gate guard and an American MP checked everyone who went in or out of the one-lane main gate. Rather than go through the hassle, Ernie and I just parked across the street, got comfortable, and waited for Specialist-4 Johnny Watkins to show up.

Old women, resplendent in their *chima-chogori*, their traditional full-length Korean dresses, peered at us curiously. The young people strode by all in a bustle, paying us no attention. One old woman became so intent on trying to figure us out that she stuck her face into the jeep. Not a lot to do in these little towns. Ernie offered her a stick of gum.

She looked confused, her face wrinkled a little more, and then she withdrew and paraded slowly away.

Ernie leaned back in his big canvas-covered seat, his hands resting contentedly on the steering wheel.

"You think Johnny did it?"

"Hard to say. So far we don't have much information. A girl killed. Brutally. Skewered and burned. Johnny knew her. Kimiko knew her. A whole bunch of other customers knew her. I don't see any reason yet to pick this Spec-4 out of the crowd."

"Other than he's a GI and the Korean newspapers are assuming it's a GI and the commanding general has to give them something."

"There's that. But locking him up for a while won't hurt him. And it'll give us a chance to sort this shit out. If he did it, fine, we'll burn his ass. If he didn't, we'll find out who did."

"Better hope so. For his sake."

Ernie spit his gum out the window, crossed his arms, and closed his eyes. "One thing bothers me, though."

"What's that?"

"The interrogations Captain Kim conducted. Nobody saw nothin'. Nobody heard nothin'."

"That's what I'd expect them to say."

"But Captain Kim can be very persuasive. And he's got enough power out in that village to twist the truth out of them. Yet he let them get away with claiming that nothing shit." Ernie sat up and turned towards me. "You saw those hooches. They're all jammed right against each other. And they're not much more than plywood and plaster. If this guy hurt that girl that bad, and held her down and tied her up and then started a fire, somebody must have heard something! You know they did. They probably all know who the hell did it!"

"They heard. For sure they heard something. But they didn't necessarily see anything. People out there have a habit of not poking their noses outdoors at night."

"Well, maybe they didn't actually see the guy but they knew that something was going on. Hell, that's why that landlady called the fire department so fast. She was wide awake. Listening to it all. And when she first smelled smoke, she called the fire department."

I nodded slowly.

"But for some reason Captain Kim isn't beating the truth out of them. He's letting us work on the case in the blind, without any eyewitness accounts, pretending that he can't get any information." Ernie leaned closer and I could smell the spearmint and stale liquor on his breath. "He wants us to collar a GI on this end so he can clear the case. Even if the GI is acquitted. By the time that happens, everyone will be convinced that he did it and just got off easy in the Korean court because he's an American. It takes the pressure right off Captain Kim to find out who really did it."

What Ernie said made a lot of sense. I couldn't see any flaw in his logic, except one.

"Maybe we're not giving Captain Kim enough credit. Maybe he is working on this case and maybe the next time we talk to him he'll have come up with some leads."

Ernie leaned back farther into his chair and crossed his arms. "Don't count on it."

"Why would Captain Kim not want to find the real guy?"

"Because it involves somebody high up. Somebody with power over him."

"I don't know, Ernie."

Conspiracy theories make me nervous. My stomach churned for a while. Evil juices. I got out of the jeep and walked a few yards down the street to a shop with a big red sign over it that said *yak*—medicine. The middle-aged woman behind the counter blinked at me as I paid her for the Bacchus D, and when I got back inside the jeep I unscrewed the top and poured the entire contents of the little bottle down my throat in one greedy gurgle. It tasted like fruit juice—pears and pineapples—and did wonders for my stomach and my newly aroused headache.

I tossed the empty bottle in the backseat (Ernie's boys at the motor pool would clean it out for him) and settled back in my seat to wait.

Twenty minutes later a hard-topped jeep pulled up to the front of the ADA compound. A sign in the window said COURIER, DO NOT DELAY. The gate guard pulled back the chain across the gate and waved him through.

I got out of the jeep and walked over to the guard shack.

"Was that the guy who picks up the ration control stuff?"

The crewcut MP put down his comic book. "Yeah," he said.

I motioned to Ernie and we got into position and waited some more. We didn't wait long. When Johnny Watkins pulled up to the gate coming out, I stepped out of the guard shack and flashed my badge at him.

"Good morning, Johnny. I'm Investigator Sueño. Just want to ask you a few questions about an acquaintance of yours out in the ville."

"Who's that?"

"Miss Pak Ok-suk."

Johnny was a trim guy, blond, and he wore his fatigues loosely, like a pair of pajamas, unwashed and unstarched. He looked more like he should be on a surfboard at Doheny than driving a jeep for the Army in the Republic of Korea.

"Miss Pak? Sure. No sweat."

He reached for his gearshift as if he were going to park the vehicle and then he let out the clutch, the engine squealed, and he leapt forward, just missing my foot.

Ernie was already making a U-turn as I ran towards the road. He slowed down to let me hop in, but not much.

Johnny got a good head start on us and we got trapped for a few seconds behind a three-wheeled truck overloaded with sacks of cement. Ernie jerked the wheel out into the oncoming traffic, stepped on it, and we barely nosed in front of the truck before a kimchi cab had a chance to plow into us, headfirst.

Johnny sped north towards the Han River and must have had the accelerator to the floorboard because his little buggy was moving. I thought I heard a Jan and Dean song in the background: "Dead Man's Curve."

Wasting ourselves in an auto accident wouldn't be good, and losing Johnny and not making the arrest wouldn't be good. What would be good would be for him to pull over and stop this foolishness, but that didn't seem likely.

Ernie leaned forward, like a pointy-nosed demon, and let the little jeep do its thing. We were up to about sixty-five or seventy and I kept hearing little pings and coughs in the engine as if it were clearing its throat.

Up ahead at the river, the road took a sharp turn around a hill and I figured it for the curve that would get him. We heard honking but when we got around the curve ourselves the oncoming traffic was getting back into line and somehow Johnny had increased his lead. He sped past the entrance to the Third Han River Bridge and boogied on down the banks of the ancient River Han.

Ernie seemed to be getting angrier and taking more chances as Johnny increased his lead. He swerved in and out of traffic, his knuckles white on the wheel, and I saw his jaw moving and I wasn't sure if that was his teeth I heard grinding or the gears of the engine.

We ran past the National Cemetery, green mounds rising gracefully up the side of a hill, and somehow I felt that it was appropriate for us to end here.

It was a big gray ox that finally got Johnny. It was on the

road, towing an old wooden cart, an old farmer pulling it forward gently by the rope through the huge, snorting nostrils. The farmer's wife and two children were in the cart, bundled up in quilts.

Johnny wasn't expecting the traffic to slow that quickly. He slammed on his brakes and swerved to the left, but then had to jerk the wheel back to the right to avoid the man on the bicycle with pallets of eggs piled two feet above his head on the carrying rack behind him.

The eggs went down and Johnny lost control. He spun a couple of times and slid sideways into the water-filled ditch in front of a rice paddy.

Johnny wasn't hurt too badly. Just bruised and shaken up. The guy on the bicycle had a broken leg—a compound fracture—and the biggest omelet I'd ever seen in my life. The ox was okay.

Johnny wouldn't be seeing any paychecks for a while. He'd be liable for the claims against the government on the eggs and the leg and the jeep. But that was the least of his worries.

I set him up on the edge of the road. He looked dazed. I slapped him a couple of times. It felt good but I was on duty, so I stopped.

Johnny Watkins blinked and then stared at me with big blue eyes.

"Miss Pak?" he said.

"No. My name is George."

"Miss Pak? Is she dead?"

"Under the circumstances, yes."

Johnny stared straight ahead for a while, along the splotches of frozen ice covering the rice paddy.

"We were going to get married," he said.

I squatted down next to him. "That's nice."

"We already had the paperwork in. It was supposed to come back any day."

I was touched. So was Ernie. But he was busy tiptoeing through the shattered eggs and listening to the cursing of the man with the broken leg.

5

We didn't bother to tell the first sergeant that Johnny Watkins's marriage packet was in. We thought we'd check that out on our own. Besides, he was too busy interrogating Johnny, documenting his every step for the last twenty-four hours, and calling the provost marshal to let him know that we were off the hook—we had the suspect.

Johnny's story didn't do much to help his case. He had gone out to the ville the night before last, like always, with Freddy and Sammy. They'd hit the King Club, the UN Club, the Lucky Seven, all the regular haunts. Just before curfew, Freddy and Sammy had hooked up with their steadies and made it to their hooches for the night.

Johnny had seen Miss Pak when they stopped in the Lucky Seven around ten thirty. She seemed nervous, upset, angry, which wasn't too unusual these days, according to Johnny. She had told him that she was busy that night and that he should go back to the compound. Kimiko had come into the club, policed up Miss Pak, and paraded her out the door.

Since Johnny was getting screwed around by Miss Pak, it's understandable that he didn't let the first sergeant know right away about the marriage paperwork. He felt like a jerk, I guess, letting her run around like that on him. But I've seen stranger things. When a young man is in love . . . He mumbled something about her being a hostess at big parties for rich guys. There was probably some truth in that. But not the whole truth.

After the first brief interrogation session the first sergeant seemed flushed with success. Johnny had no alibi. He also had a hell of a motive. The woman he loved was running around on him, escorted by the likes of Kimiko, the dregs of Itaewon.

While Top was making some phone calls and preparing a briefing for the provost marshal, we slid out of the office, jumped in Ernie's jeep, and went over to the Eighth Army Chapel.

Churches always amaze me. Long clean carpets, polished pine, huge looming windows. So unlike the real world. A guy in clean but unstarched fatigues walked down the aisle towards us, smiling. Private First Class Hurchek. I'd seen him around the compound. At the snack bar, at the recreation center, at the library— every place but the Lower Four Club. He had dark brown hair cut in a shaggy crewcut, heavy eyebrows, and he looked like he was absolutely overjoyed to see us.

"Good morning, gentlemen." He sang the greeting. "Can I help you?"

"We want to see the chaplain," I said.

Ernie flashed his identification at Hurchek, a lot faster than he normally does, like waving garlic at a vampire. Hurchek frowned.

He realized that we weren't there to save our souls. Although Lord knows, and so did Hurchek, that they needed saving.

Hurchek put a finger to his lip and looked down at the well-manicured carpet.

"You don't have an appointment?"

"No."

"I'll see if he has time to receive you."

He walked away and we sat down on a slippery bench in the hallway.

"I don't want him to receive us," Ernie said. "I just want him to answer a few questions."

"Show a little respect, Ernie."

"You're looking at my best act."

We were nervous—out of our environment. Two whores would have felt more at home than we did.

Great soundproofing in these chapels. You can't even hear whispering. After about five minutes, Hurchek opened the big oak door and waved us in. A ticket to see the wizard.

Chaplain Sturdivant rose from behind his huge desk, walked around, and shook both our hands—earnestly. He was a small, trim man, balding, and from behind thick lenses his brown eyes pinned you. If he had grown a goatee and changed out of his fatigues into a black suit, he would have looked like Lenin.

The great socialist leader sat back down at his desk. "What can I do for you, gentlemen?"

"It's about Spec-4 Watkins. He's just been arrested under suspicion of murder. He also has a marriage packet in with Miss Pak Ok-suk, the woman who was killed the night before last out in Itaewon."

Sturdivant's sloe eyes closed and then opened slowly.

"Watkins. Watkins." He thumbed through a box jammed with three-by-five index cards. "I don't remember him. I should. There's just so many of them." He stopped riffling through the box and pulled out a card. "Here it is. Watkins, John B. And Miss Pak Ok-suk. The paperwork's already been logged in, the interview conducted, and the packet briefed at the chief of staff meeting. It should be on its way to personnel." He looked up at us. "If it's not there already. For that you'll have to check with PFC Hurchek."

"Do you remember anything specific about your interview with Specialist Watkins and Miss Pak?"

"Oh God, no. There's just so many I have to conduct. It seems like half of the young GIs who come to Korea are getting married. They're just so impressionable. So easily fooled." Chaplain Sturdivant shook his head. "You can't believe some of the cases I've had. Just last week a young boy, twenty-one, was set to marry an old Korean business girl. Thirty-seven, she said. I wondered if the family register hadn't been tampered with, because she looked older. And the *report* from the Korean National Police! She's had seven abortions. Seven! When I told this young man about it, he didn't even blink. He just said, 'Oh yeah, she told me.' Can you believe it."

We believed it. Sturdivant went right on.

"When they got in here I did everything I could to slam her, make her ashamed of what she was doing, but do you think it had any effect? None. And the simpleminded trooper just sat through the whole thing with his mouth open. It had no effect on him. He's going to take that hideous old creature home to his parents. To his mother! It just never ceases to amaze me. And we've got stacks of paperwork. Poor Hurchek has to stay here late at night just to make sure that all the packets get out to personnel in some sort of timely fashion."

Sturdivant's hands clenched one another; back and forth, back and forth. He sighed.

"And the command briefings. I usually take a whole box of packets over there, brief the chief of staff on the statistics, and show them some of the more unusual cases. I get more attention at my briefing than even your boss, the provost marshal, gets when he briefs the black-market statistics. Like when I told them about that thirty-seven-year-old whore. I asked her what her real age was and she said, 'Me thirty-seven. No bullshit.'"

The chaplain paused, pleased with his anecdote. His grin fell when he saw me and Ernie just staring back. He sat up straighter. I got back to business.

"Would looking at the packet help jog your memory about Watkins and Miss Pak?"

"Miss? Why do you keep calling her Miss? As if she's not just a business girl?"

Ernie leaned forward. "You know, Chaplain Sturdivant, with all due respect to your rank, you're just about the tightest little asshole I've ever met."

The chaplain turned red and stood up. So did Ernie. I grabbed my partner and walked him towards the door. "Thanks for your help, sir. We have all the information we need."

Later that afternoon I slid in the side door of the chapel and found Hurchek alone in his office. He showed me the packet on Watkins and Miss Pak and I leafed through it quickly. There was a tag on it, a routing slip, with some scribbled initials. I asked him about it and he checked his log.

The packet had been signed out a week and a half ago and then returned a couple of days later. The signature was illegible but it had happened after the weekly command briefing. The recipient was someone on the Eighth Army staff.

As he was talking and checking the ledger, I wrote down the names of the people whose packets had been signed out during the last few months, the dates they were signed out, and the initials of the person who signed them out. It took me a while and it was mainly a dodge to make casual conversation while I pumped Hurchek for information. Mostly I got an earful about Chaplain Sturdivant.

He wasn't married, didn't go out much, and the only hobby he had, as far as Hurchek knew, was schmoozing with the general staff and raking marriage applicants over the coals.

On the way out, I heard a woman crying. The door to the chaplain's office was open. Sturdivant, behind his desk, glared at a nervous young GI in soiled fatigues and a young Korean woman. The young woman was bowed as far forward as possible in her chair, her face in her hands, trying to hide her shame.

After work, I changed clothes and went straight to Ginger. She hadn't seen Kimiko and didn't have any new information about Pak Ok-suk. What she did have was the phone number of Miss Lim from Honolulu. Ginger called for me.

Maybe it was the chase that morning or the thumbing through all the names of the young Korean women getting ready to marry GIs, but for some reason I was particularly excited. Miss Lim and I met and only had a couple of drinks and went right to the *yoguan*. This time she washed me and I washed her and everything seemed permissible on the second date.

Outside, the hooting and honking subsided and the city shut down for midnight curfew. She told me about her husband, finally, and her life in the States, and about the person she had been before she got involved with Americans.

"I was a good student, one of the best, and when I decided to marry an American all my girlfriends shook their heads. 'You are too good to marry an American,' they said. 'We thought you would marry a high-class man. A Korean man.'"

She sat up in bed and lit a cigarette. I made her sit by the open window.

"My mother was ashamed at first but then she thought about our future. Two women, alone in Korea, my father dead for three years. Our money was almost gone. I couldn't go to the university and, if I didn't go to the university, I would not be able to find a good Korean husband. So I married an American. So we could get to the States."

I covered myself with the shaggy comforter.

"What's his name?"

"My husband?"

"Yeah."

"Parkington. Enoch Parkington. He sells houses in Cincinnati. After I got my green card, I worked for a little while, saved up some money, and flew to Hawaii."

"Has he divorced you?"

"No. Not yet."

"If he does, you'll lose your visa and have to move back to Korea."

She shrugged her slender shoulders and exhaled a huge puff of smoke. Moonlight glistened across her black hair.

"No sweat. If he divorces me, I will pay some guy in Hawaii to marry me, so I can keep my green card."

She stubbed out the cigarette and walked into the small tile-covered bathroom. When she returned, we resumed.

6

Riley is one of those drunks who is superefficient during the day. His fatigues are neatly pressed, his hair spiffily greased back into an old fifties-style pompadour, and he never stops moving, pivoting his head around, the pencil behind his ear constantly threatening to fly off. Maybe he thinks he's fooling people. Or maybe the concentration he puts into churning out all those neatly paper-clipped stacks of official correspondence helps him keep his mind off the rancid juices that are rotting his gut.

Back in the barracks he keeps a couple of bottles of Old Overwart in his locker, the cheapest stuff they sell in the Class VI store. He hits the vending machine in the hall for cans of Coke and usually by seven or eight in the evening he's completely blotto. He has a girlfriend who shows up in the barracks from time to time, and he's been known to stay up until as late as four o'clock in the morning, chasing her around the showers, trying to lather her down. I don't know if he ever catches her.

Occasionally Ernie and I take him out, usually on the weekends, and try to get him to eat something, listen to music, have a couple of drinks without getting destroyed.

When we suggest dinner he acts as if we're abusing him. I think he eats about one greasy cheeseburger a week. And even then he opens up the burger and grimaces as if he were fighting back vomit, and finally wolfs it down as if hoping that, if he's fast enough, somehow his stomach won't notice it. Skinny isn't the word for him. He makes broom handles look robust.

Riley's from Philly. And he's always going on and on about the tough old Irish neighborhood he grew up in. He uses all the racist jargon: wops, spooks, spics, and a few others I've never heard of. He respects the Italians, though, because they're rich. But for all his bluster, face to face, he's about the sweetest guy you'd ever want to meet. When people come to him with a problem, he adopts them as if they were stray puppies, regardless of their race, creed, or national origins.

When I point out the inconsistency in his position he looks at me as if I'm mad. "Of course I don't like spooks," he'd say. Then I'd say, "Well, what about that time you helped Ricky Hairston get that compassionate reassignment when his mother got sick?" Riley would shrug. "That's different. Ricky's a fine human being. You just don't understand, George." And then he'd launch into a long, detailed story about how he and his buddies back in Philly used to kick ass.

Riley's position in the CID Detachment was one of great responsibility. He was the personnel sergeant. As such, he was responsible for not only all the personnel actions for the people assigned to the detachment but he also had the additional duty of running the Admin Section. Which meant he had to log in and distribute all incoming messages and he was responsible for maintaining all classified documents. It was a hell of a job. But with Riley's manic dose of daytime energy, he somehow handled it. His only help was Miss Kim.

Miss Kim was one of the finer acquisitions the CID had ever made. She was so fine that guys from other offices throughout the thirty- or forty-acre headquarters complex would make a special trip just to say good morning to her. Ernie always found time to sit on her desk and look at her for a while, and usually he offered her a stick of gum, which she gratefully accepted. For some reason she put up with him. She wasn't so tolerant of Burrows and Slabem although she was always polite and efficient in her official dealings with them.

Maybe she resented Burrows's birdlike gawking or Slabem's sly little porcine eyes. I couldn't tell. I have a policy with gorgeous women. I leave them alone. When business calls for me to deal with them, I don't flirt, I just get the job done. That's not to say I'm grim. When the time is appropriate, I smile and say good morning or good evening or whatever. But I don't harass them. I don't believe in it. I know I wouldn't like fending off a bunch of clumsy oafs all day, not on the pay Miss Kim receives. Besides, if a woman likes you, she'll let you know. No sense pressuring her.

The way she reacted to Ernie added a somewhat demented corollary to my theory. He didn't speak to her much at all, he didn't touch her, and he didn't pressure her in any way. He just stared at her, with pure unadulterated appreciation. Miss Kim seemed to come alive under his attention, like one of those plants that blooms when you think good thoughts at it. Ernie's version of charm.

Riley treated her as a colleague. A full partner in the mission they had to accomplish. During working hours he didn't seem to notice her attractiveness, only her mind. When we mentioned to him that he was lucky to be working with such a fox all day, he nodded agreement. But it was an intellectual acknowledgement, not visceral. A woman just didn't have all that much appeal to him if he couldn't lather her down and chase her around the latrine.

"Top's been looking for you guys," Riley said, as we sauntered in.

"Isn't he always?"

"It's about this KPA bullshit again."

Ernie wandered over to Miss Kim's desk. She stopped typing and looked up, smiling. He sat down on the edge of the desk and looked at her. Then he offered her a breath mint. She accepted it, smiled, and turned back to her typing. Ernie just stayed there, staring at her. Sometimes I wondered if they weren't autistic.

Riley shuffled through some papers and handed me one.

"It's one of those guys from KPA. He put in this written complaint and now he wants to talk to the first sergeant. Top wants you and Ernie to sit in."

"He's here now?"

"Yeah. His appointment's in ten minutes."

I sat down to read the complaint. The Korean Procurement Agency is the civilian arm of the Eighth Army that uses American taxpayer money to buy local goods and services. Stuff that we were not going to go to the trouble of shipping over. Anything from a head of lettuce to a new command bunker extending three stories down into the ground. It was a huge operation with millions of dollars' worth of contracts flowing through it every year. Most of the monitoring was done by accountants sent out by the Army Auditing Agency, but corruption and influence peddling was not always reflected in the credit and debit ledgers.

The guy who was making the complaint was an American, of course, hired from the States, and judging from his manic drive to get everything straightened out, he probably was on his first tour in the Far East.

I figured Top mainly wanted Ernie and me in the office as

witnesses, so the guy couldn't make accusations against him later. Most of this sort of work was done by Burrows and Slabem, but they were out at the Yongsan District Police Headquarters, monitoring the ROK activities on the Pak Ok-suk murder case. They were the experts at handling this KPA kind of situation. Not me and Ernie.

I read over the complaint. Routine. Korean businessmen were turning in bids on U.S. government contracts. Okay so far. But the Americans required three bids from three different companies on each contract. The businessman making the bid, of course, already had a connection with one of the Korean career bureaucrats within KPA so he knew exactly how much money was budgeted for a particular project. What he did was get three different stationery letterheads and put in three bids, ostensibly from different companies, and each signed by a different executive, with all three bids hovering right at or just below the budgeted appropriation.

The bidding was open to competitors, but through the network of Korean power brokers they would be warned off if they seriously tried to butt in. It was a syndicate, in effect, milking the American government. Nothing new. They'd been doing it for years.

And the work they did was not shoddy. It was efficiently produced and, for the most part, brought in on time. That's why the U.S. Army lived with the system. It got results. Of course, they still went through the charade of all the regulatory purchasing requirements. The Koreans didn't mind this. They liked paperwork: It produced jobs. And they understood the need to save face. Over the years there'd been a number of attempts to reform the system but in the end the Koreans had always patted the petulant American reformer on the head as he headed back to the States.

The American who was complaining this time only knew that someone was turning in three bids under three different cover companies and that the guy was buddies with one of the Koreans in the agency who let out the contracts. He saw only what looked like corruption to him. He didn't see the cultural machinery that had evolved over four thousand years that kept disputes to a minimum and allowed for the smooth running of a society.

I had no plans to explain all this stuff to the bean counter or to the first sergeant. I would just keep my mouth shut and go through the motions, which was all, I figured, Eighth Army really wanted me to do. Mainly, I wanted to get back to the murder of Miss Pak Ok-suk and I didn't need to waste a lot of time on some silly diversion.

The first sergeant plodded down the hallway in his big wingtips and peeked in the door of the Admin Section.

"Bascom. Sueño. Come on down to my office."

Miss Kim stopped her typing and gave Ernie a goodbye look. He got up, adjusted the buttons on his jacket, and marched down the hallway after the first sergeant. I followed.

In his office, the first sergeant introduced us to Mr. Tom Kurtz. We all sat down: the first sergeant behind his desk, me and Ernie sort of off to the side, looking at Mr. Kurtz, seated in front.

"What can we do for you, Mr. Kurtz?" the first sergeant said.

"I thought Inspectors Burrows and Slabem would be here."

"They're on a high-priority case and I'm afraid I couldn't pull them off it."

"Ah, well. They were so helpful and so concerned about getting to the bottom of the corruption at KPA."

Kurtz was young, like maybe just out of college, with curly brown hair and a tailored blue suit covering his frail body. He kept pushing his glasses back up his pug nose.

He bent forward, as if to confide in us. "You know I can't stand working with people who aren't totally honest. I don't know how Eighth Army could have allowed the situation to deteriorate so much. I've recommended that a few of the people who work for

me be fired, but all that happens is they get transferred, sometimes into better jobs, and the people who take their places are no
better than the ones that left."

Kurtz sat up in his chair. "But I'm not here to complain. Not
this time. I'm here to thank you for all your help. Since I put in
my complaints and your investigation started, things have really
changed for the better at the Korean Procurement Agency."

I had been starting to doze off but this woke me up. A little
anyway.

"For the first time we're getting real competition during the
bidding for contracts. Just last week an entirely new company
won a major contract to build a recreation center at Camp Carroll
down in Waegwan. And it wasn't just one of those shifting-letter-
head deals either. I met the man who got the contract. He was
delighted to be doing work, for the first time, for the U.S. government. What convinced me that the whole thing wasn't some sort
of sham was how upset my Korean employees were at the whole
thing. And that's not the only contract that has gone to new vendors. The winds of change are sweeping through KPA and I have
you gentlemen to thank for it."

"Just doing our job," the first sergeant said. "You played a big
role in this, too, Mr. Kurtz."

The first sergeant didn't want all the blame.

"No, no, no." Mr. Kurtz waved off the compliment. "It's you
fellows. And especially Inspector Burrows and Inspector Slabem.
Please give them my thanks."

"Write them a letter of appreciation, for inclusion in their
personnel folders."

"I'll do that, said Kurtz enthusiastically.

That's Top. Always looking out for his troops—when it
doesn't cost him anything.

Kurtz got up, we shook hands all the way around, and he left.
Ernie and I stood, grinning.

"What was all that?" I said.

"I haven't a clue. Go on," Top said. "Get out of here. Get back to work."

We clomped down the hallway. Ernie was chuckling but all I could think about was that there must be something terribly wrong at the Korean Procurement Agency. All that money wouldn't have slipped away without a fight.

But that worry belonged to Burrows and Slabem. I put it out of my mind and tried to figure how I could find the elusive Kimiko, as we drove off toward the ville.

Itaewon during the daytime is sleepy and wonderful. We found a back alley parking spot for the jeep, Ernie chained the steering wheel, and we wandered up the street, past the shuttered shops, the noodle stands, and the black gaping maws of the few clubs that had their doors open this early.

An old woman accosted us. "You want nice girl?"

"No thanks, *mama-san*. I only want bad girls. Nice girls always make me feel guilty afterwards."

We pushed past her and headed up the hill towards the hooch where Pak Ok-suk had been murdered. The burnt-out room was surrounded by white police tape.

The landlady squatted in front of a large pan filled with laundry, occasionally reaching up to the rusty old pump handle to draw more water.

"*Anyonghaseiyo*," I said.

She looked at us, took off her rubber gloves, and stood up.

"We're looking for Kimiko."

The woman twisted her head towards Kimiko's room. "She hasn't come back."

I walked towards the room. The woman followed. Ernie stayed back, next to the gate.

I slid back the paper-covered latticework door. There was a small plastic armoire in one corner, some rolled-up bed mats, and a six-inch-high makeup table with a small mirror and about twenty pounds of multicolored goop in various bottles. I took off my shoes, entered, and rummaged around. There were a few dresses hanging next to a couple of empty hangers. No wallet. No money. A few spaces on the makeup table were vacant, as if some small jars of this or that had been plucked up. I turned to the landlady.

"She hasn't been back?"

"No."

"Not since Captain Kim talked to her?"

"No."

I put my shoes back on and thanked her. Ernie and I bent over as we ducked through the small door in the gate.

Kimiko had disappeared after being interrogated by the chief of the Itaewon Police Box concerning the murder of Pak Ok-suk. She had added nothing to Captain Kim's investigation and she had not been identified as a suspect. And she still wasn't, as far as I knew. Why had she taken off? Maybe because she had information that she didn't want to divulge. Also, why had Captain Kim allowed her to go? Maybe because he, too, didn't want any information she had to be divulged.

Or maybe I was wrong. Maybe she knew nothing and had merely gotten spooked and left the ville to ply her trade elsewhere. Maybe.

We walked up the hill towards the Roundup. If anybody knew where to find Kimiko it would be Milt Gorman.

Gorman had been living in Korea since returning from a tour in Vietnam. He and his Korean Army buddy had set up a couple of small joints on the outskirts of Itaewon, expanded their operation, sold them, and used the money to renovate an old building and open the biggest country and western club in Korea, right in the heart of Itaewon. On the side, Gorman did a little import and export, but most of his money came from selling the beer and the hoopla and the little taste of home to the lonely country boys from the States. Most of the CID agents assumed that he was crooked. I knew he wasn't. He was one of the most honest men I'd ever met.

The Roundup was dark and it took our eyes a while to adjust. We heard the slap of playing cards before we could see them.

The little girl behind the bar stopped her cleaning long enough to serve us a couple of beers. We wandered over to the table. It was Milt Gorman and three other old reprobates, Army retirees with nothing better to do on a Wednesday afternoon than play pinochle for a penny a point, ten cents a set. All four men were riffling through their cards and crinkling their eyes. Pinochle gets expensive at those prices.

"George! Ernie!" Gorman looked back to his cards. "What brings you enforcers of the law out to Itaewon at this hour of the day? And drinking on duty yet."

We sat down at a couple of bar stools near the card table. Beer, sandwiches, and ashtrays competed for space with the stacked playing cards and the score sheet next to Gorman's elbow.

I said, "We came to talk to you, Milt."

"Shoot! What can I help you with?"

A young woman shuffled out of the latrine. She emptied the ashtrays, checked the beer bottles, and asked everyone if they wanted another. She got a couple of grunts in reply and, carrying the refuse, scurried off to the bar. She had a nice tight little figure and wore the brief blue uniform of the waitresses at the Roundup. Must be nice to afford such attractive help for your personal card games.

I waited until the woman disappeared behind the bar.

"I'm looking for Kimiko."

Milt snorted. The other old guys looked up from their cards, mildly interested.

"You want what?" Milt said.

"Kimiko."

He took a sip of his beer. "You and Ernie can do better than that. Unless you're getting into perversions that are just not becoming to men as young as you two. For these old farts"—Milt waved his arm around the table—"I could understand. But not you guys."

"We're not looking to get laid, Milt. We're looking for information—concerning the murder."

All four lowered their cards and the table got quiet.

Milt spoke: "And you think Kimiko might have it?"

"She knew her. Worked with her, you might say. And she lived right next door to the hooch where the murder took place."

"Haven't the KNPs already checked her out?"

"Yes, they have." I was going to be patient but I wasn't going to go away. Ernie sipped his beer and kept his eye on the door and the young waitress who was refilling the beer order.

Milt sighed, put his cards down, and got up from the table amidst a round of grumbling. "Come on over here, George. We got to talk."

I followed Milt through the rows of tables and across the small dance floor. At the far wall, he ducked through a small door that led into the deejay's room and I popped through after him. The sky was suddenly purple, and the universe was full of small blinking lights. Milt fondled the headphones and looked away from me. Otherwise we'd have been belly to belly. How could that deejay stand working in here eight hours a night, spinning that cowboy crap?

"George, the last few weeks have been some of the craziest I've seen since I've been in Itaewon. Somebody's trying to muscle in. I don't know who, but all the Korean bar owners are nervous."

I paused to think about it. "What about the guys the bar owners pay for protection?" I said.

"They've been pretty calm so far. But they've got to be on edge, too. They don't want to be replaced, any more than the bar owners do."

"Who's trying to replace them?"

"I don't know for sure. Some sort of consortium, with connections of its own. I've never met any of them, thank God, but the one name I've heard bandied about is Kwok."

"Kwok?"

"Yeah. Mr. Kwok."

"He's leading the move on Itaewon?"

"As far as I can tell."

"How about you, Milt? Are you all right?"

"Yeah. No sweat. I'm small potatoes. And an American to boot. Besides, my partner's family has its own pull around here. We'll be all right."

"What's all this have to do with the murder?" I said.

"I'm not sure. All I know is the gossip I hear from the Koreans. The word is that the police aren't going after the case as hard as they usually do. They're not too anxious to find out who really killed that little girl."

"Why?"

Milt shrugged. "Somebody is lacking enthusiasm."

"Who?"

"I don't know. Maybe somebody involved in what's going down around here."

I shook my head. "How did this little girl, just in from the country, get caught up in all this shit?"

"Hell if I know, George. The citizens out here don't really want to talk about it. And they're not too excited about hanging a GI for it. I know the Korean papers and TV are playing that up big, and the general populace is all pissed off about it, but here in Itaewon people know better."

"We've arrested a GI for the murder."

"I heard," he said.

"That didn't take long."

"Out here, nothing takes long."

I handed Milt my card, paid for by the U.S. government. I wouldn't shell out any of my paltry paycheck for that sort of stuff.

"If you need help, Milt, call me."

"From what I hear about you and Ernie, you're not in the office much."

"Leave a message."

On the way back to the compound I briefed Ernie on what Milt had told me. We were both quiet. First a young girl had been hideously murdered, maybe by a GI, and the Korean police hadn't gone after it in full force. Then the decades-old networks that had been formed to maximize profits from U.S. Army contracts had begun to break up and be replaced with new ones. Now somebody with muscle was putting a move on Itaewon, going after the millions of dollars that flowed through the village every year from booze, women, and black marketeering.

And then there was Miss Pak, an innocent who hadn't understood such things. Of course, Ernie and I didn't understand them either.

We zigzagged through the traffic and finally popped through the gate and into the relative calm of the Eighth Army Compound. It was an oasis, like a piece of Kansas in the middle of a bustling metropolis.

"You know what I wish, pal?" Ernie said.

"No. What's that?"

"I wish things weren't getting so interesting."

7

The first sergeant had already finished his report on the interrogation of Johnny Watkins and the frightened young man had been transported, under heavy MP escort, down to the Eighth Army Stockade at the Army Support Command in Bupyong. There he would await the paperwork that had to be done before the U.S. authorities could turn him over to the Koreans.

The U.S. government would pay for a Korean lawyer for him but the trial would be decided primarily on the basis of public opinion. If somebody had to pay the price for the murder of Pak Ok-suk, and the public thought it should be a GI, then whoever happened to be in custody would be it. It was like the government minister who had to step down when a typhoon destroyed a couple of cities. Everybody knew he didn't have any control over the weather but he had the responsibility. And somebody had to be sacrificed to restore the harmony.

If the judge determined that Johnny was probably innocent they'd go easy on him. The last GI Ernie and I had tried to keep out of a Korean jail only got four years. Not bad for murder. He would have gotten a lot more if he'd actually been guilty.

All this somehow made sense to me. Maybe it's my Mexican genes.

I didn't see how we could make much progress in this case and keep Johnny Watkins out of jail unless we found Kimiko. The best way to do that was to run the ville, which was no problem because it was always on my program anyway.

After the retreat bugle sounded, Ernie and I turned in the jeep, changed out of our coats and ties, and showered, shaved, and popped a couple of wet ones. We were parading through the alleys of Itaewon, OB bottles in hand, when we heard the squawk of a radio in a parked MP jeep. The two uniformed MPs had their feet kicked up and they were laughing.

"What's so funny?"

"The Officers' Club. They're asking for MP support. Some old gal named Kiko something is raising hell. Apparently she kicked the chief of staff in the balls."

Ernie and I looked at each other, jumped in a cab, and headed for the compound. We were both thinking the same thing: Kimiko. Who else would be nuts enough?

We paid the driver and, flashing our identification, ran through the gate heading towards South Post. We trotted along the placid avenue until we saw red lights flashing atop MP sedans in front of the canopied entranceway to the Eighth Army Officers' Club. Doors slammed and more sedans raced past as we ran towards the commotion.

The members, mostly officers in tailored dress blue uniforms and a few ladies in evening gowns, wandered back into the club.

The master-at-arms was a burly black NCO by the name of Bosun. He wore a baggy Hong Kong suit and looked like he'd just lost the main event in a wrestling match with the Magnificent Destroyer.

I didn't need to show him my badge. He'd seen me around.

"Who was it?"

"Some old bitch." He patted the scratches on his forehead with a handkerchief. "Crazy."

"Kimiko?"

He looked at me suspiciously. "Yeah. I think."

"What'd she do?"

"Tried to corner General Bohler. When he told her to get lost, she went berserk."

"Kicked him in the balls?"

"How'd you know that?"

"The news is already in Itaewon."

The big guy just shook his head and walked back towards the door.

"Who escorted her in?" I said, following.

"I don't know. Let's look in the log."

At the raised desk just inside the glass doorway, Bosun opened the big ledger marked Guest Register. He didn't have to look too far. Most of the people who entered the O Club were authorized. At the NCO Club, dozens of business girls were brought in every night and the guest registers had to be ordered by the bushel full, but here not too many officers brought their Korean girlfriends. Bad for the career.

"She was brought in by a Lieutenant Leibowitz. He brought in two girls. A Miss Ahn and this old broad, Kimiko." The master-at-arms looked up at us.

I said, "See if you can round up this lieutenant and his girlfriend. Do you have a place where we can talk to them?"

"Yeah. Back here in the MA's office." Bosun was happy to

cooperate because he was pissed and wanted to see Kimiko get
burned. We waited. When the lieutenant came in, all decked out
in dress blues, I showed him my badge.

He put his hands up in front of his chest. "Hold on, now. I just
brought a couple of girls to the O Club."

"To a commander's call?"

"Yeah. It's sort of formal but Miss Ahn is such a nice person,
and so well dressed. I never figured anything like this would
happen."

Ernie stuck his nose through a crack in the door and peered
out. Apparently Miss Ahn was worth looking at.

"Where'd you meet her?"

"I've known her for a long time. She's never been any trouble.
And she's—"

"Where'd you find her, Lieutenant?"

"Outside the gate."

"On the street?"

"Well . . . not like you mean. She was just *standing* outside the
gate and she needed somebody to escort her on post to the O
Club."

"So you signed her in at the gate and then into the club?"

"Yeah."

"How long ago did you first meet her?"

"A couple of months ago. And she's never been any trouble."

"She stays with you sometimes on the compound?"

"Sure. But that's never—"

"How did Kimiko get into the act?"

"I'd never seen her before tonight, she's just a friend of Miss
Ahn's, and when I went outside the gate to pick her up, this
woman Kimiko was there, and Miss Ahn asked if I could escort
her, too. I figured one more wouldn't hurt, so—"

"Did Kimiko say why she wanted to come to the O Club?"

"No. She didn't say much of anything."

"Why do you think she wanted to come to the O Club?"

"Just to have a fun evening, I guess."

"She had that. And didn't you think she wanted to meet some-one here and maybe make a few dollars?"

Leibowitz straightened his shoulders. "That is no affair of mine."

"You've paid Miss Ahn before, haven't you?"

"That's none of your business."

I knew the answer. A few of the classier girls stood outside the gate that led to the Officers' Club and made arrangements with someone, usually young officers, to escort them on post. Sometimes they had someone who would meet them out there and sometimes they just took their chances, smiling and asking a likely-looking young man to help a lady in distress. There weren't too many women because the pickings were slimmer at the Officers' Club, but when they made their rare strike the payoff was better. And most of the women who went that route were good-looking and highly presentable in the more sedate confines of the Officers' Club. Not like the droves of old hags and young floozies who crowded the front gate, waiting for someone to take them into the Lower Four Club. Of them all, I preferred the old hags. They weren't trying to be something they weren't.

I thanked Lieutenant Leibowitz for his time. He straightened his jacket and strode off in a huff. Your typical infantry officer. All spit and polish. No brains.

"She's out here," Ernie said. "Miss Ahn."

Bosun and the MPs had her behind the MA's desk. She was tall and wore a low-cut blue-patterned dress that was guaranteed to draw every man's eyes. Her hair puffed out in a short bouffant and surrounded a face that had been very pretty and was still holding up well.

I spoke to her in English.

"Why'd you bring Kimiko on the compound?"

"She is a Korean woman. She asked me for help, so I helped her."

"How much did she pay you?"

Miss Ahn reached in her handbag and pulled out a pack of American cigarettes. She tapped one free and lit it without waiting for any of us to offer.

She said, "How much doesn't matter. But yeah, she paid me." She exhaled the smoke past the cheap artwork that lined the walls.

"How long have you known her?"

"Long time. Everybody knows Kimiko. But is she my friend? No. And did I ever take her to the Officers' Club before? No. I was surprised she wanted to go. Usually she works in Itaewon."

"Why did she want to go in?"

"I don't know. Make money, I guess."

"Did she sit with you and Lieutenant Leibowitz?"

"For a little while. Then she go."

"Where'd she go?"

"I don't know. I didn't pay attention. Next thing I know, big fight."

"With who?"

Miss Ahn's eyes opened wide. "General Bohler. You know."

I thanked her for her help. No sense making enemies. These business girls can be a lot of help to an investigator, and she was looking good in that long blue dress. Near thirty, though. But my standards were getting less stringent.

"You give me a ride off compound?" she said. Apparently, Lieutenant Leibowitz had abandoned her.

"We don't have a car."

"Shit."

She puffed rapidly on her cigarette. There were plenty of men inside the club and plenty of booze. Someone would help her.

An MP stepped over. "Sueño?"

"Yeah," I said.

"General Bohler's aide, Major Zaronsky, wants a word."

"Can you point him out?" I said.

"Sure can," he said. "He's the one making all the noise over there."

Five young officers were sitting at the table. One of them was waving his hands in the air, dominating the conversation. He was prematurely balding and cropped blond hair fringed his dome. His look was pugnacious. I couldn't tell from this distance but I felt certain that Major Zaronsky's eyes would prove to be blue and vacuous. I thanked the MP and walked towards their table.

The major was in the middle of a dissertation. The other officers, all junior to him, were staring with exaggerated attentiveness, making sure they'd max their efficiency reports.

I interrupted him in midsentence: "Are you Major Zaronsky?"

The major stopped talking, both hands in midair. Keeping them there, he turned his upper body around slowly. "Who wants to know?" he asked, eyes wide, feigning amazement that anyone would have the temerity to interrupt.

"You wanted to see me?" I said. "I'm Sueño."

"Sergeant Sueño?" Zaronsky spat it out, his hands still in the air. "You're not in my unit," he said, his voice rising. "What unit are you in?"

"Sir. Maybe we could go in the game room."

"The game room?" Zaronsky asked in mock astonishment. "I don't want to go in no fucking game room." His arms came crashing down. "Now I asked you a question, Sergeant. What goddamn unit are you in?"

"I'm with the CID," I said, in a forced monotone. "I'm here on official business, and I'd like to keep it confidential."

"The CID?" Once again Major Zaronsky was astonished. "What in the *world* would the C-I-fucking-D want here? There ain't nothing wrong here. There ain't nothing wrong that *everybody* in the club can't listen to!"

Major Zaronsky was shouting. He was right about one thing: Everyone in the club was definitely listening. What the hell was his problem?

"Well, sir," I said, "if you insist on discussing it here, I'll tell you—" I could see Ernie out of the corner of my eye, he was facing us, standing next to his bar stool, with no beer in sight.

"If you had done a thorough shakedown of the guests tonight," I said, "you might have prevented an attack on a general staff officer." I hurried my speech, so the loudmouth major wouldn't be able to interrupt. "And that unaccountable lapse in security has turned out to be deeply unfortunate."

Major Zaronsky's face was changing. The feigned surprise was gradually becoming genuine anger.

"But," I said, "since you're so sure that there is nothing wrong with your procedures, Major Zaronsky, I won't bother you any further."

I stared into his empty blue eyes. For the first time he was quiet. I turned and started to walk away but the major was up and red with rage.

"Now hold on, *Ser*-geant," the major said, dragging the word out a few extra syllables. "I'm the security officer here and I'm sure as hell not going to let you come in here and cast aspersions and insults."

The major got up real close and stuck his nose right in my face.

"You asked me to tell you, sir." I struggled to keep my voice even.

"Don't argue with me!" His foul breath wafted up against my closed mouth. "And stand at attention when I'm talking to you."

I wanted to punch him and he knew it. And the more I showed it, the more he enjoyed it. I came slowly to attention.

"Who's your commander?" the major barked.

I hesitated and then answered. "Captain Daily."

"And your immediate supervisor?"

From the corner of my eye I saw Ernie moving slowly away from the bar. He held a glass ashtray in his hand; the sharp, jagged point protruding from between his thumb and forefinger.

His movements were languid—zombie-like—and his head was tilted back, lifting his nose high into the air. He peered down from this vantage point and moved toward us as if his mind had retreated to some higher plane.

I ran at him, hit his shoulders with my forearms, and got him moving back towards the exit. He allowed his body to be guided towards the door but his head swiveled back at the offending officer. Behind his glasses, his bulging eyes were fixed on Zaronsky, who had fallen uncharacteristically silent.

By the time we arrived at the PM station it was too late.

"What'd you do with her?"

"Turned her over to the KNPs." The desk sergeant was working the crossword puzzle in that day's *Pacific Stars & Stripes*. It seemed to be much more interesting to him than the Kimiko incident.

"But she just kicked a major general in the balls."

"He decided not to press charges. Public relations, you know. Who wants to admit that an old, worn-out business girl got the best of a warrior like General Bohler? Don't press charges, turn her over to the Korean National Police, that's the best route. They'll work her over good. That's what the man wanted. Otherwise he'd lose face."

"Which police station did they send her to?"

"Itaewon."

Ernie and I headed towards the door.

The desk sergeant glanced up from his puzzle. "What's a ten-letter word for 'a destroyer of sacred images'?"

"Ball-breaker," I said.

Ernie and I trudged back to the Main Supply Route and this time it took twenty minutes to flag down a taxi.

Ernie said, "If I'd known we were going to be working on a case tonight, during our off-duty hours, I'd have checked out the jeep."

"No sweat, Ernie. You can afford it."

"It's your turn to pay for the cab."

"Like hell. I got a family to support."

"The King Club bartender and Miss Oh don't count. They're only Class B dependents. Me, I got the Nurse."

Nobody could accuse the Nurse of being Class B. I paid the cab fare.

We got off about a block before reaching the Itaewon Police Station. I wanted to sneak up on the place. In case we heard screaming.

She clutched the bars, spread-eagled; her long black hair in mad, sweat-matted disarray. Her dress was hiked up to her waist and her facial muscles were bunched in knots across her face as she grunted and held on.

The two policemen trying to pull Kimiko out of her cell were getting nowhere and when they sensed the presence of two large Americans they pulled harder, cursed, and first a brass button and then an epaulet popped off of their uniforms. Finally one of them let go, Kimiko's body recoiled towards the bars, and then he was pummeling her.

She swung back wildly but it was no contest and, while she was protecting herself from the blows, the other policeman grabbed her under her arms and jerked her through the doors and down the hallway to the interrogation room.

Captain Kim came up behind us, red faced, waving his hand in front of my nose.

"No. No. No. You go! You go!"

He put his head down and pushed me and Ernie back towards the front desk.

When we had come in, no one was paying too much attention to us so we decided to slip back into the cell block and see how Kimiko was doing. Now we knew.

"We want to talk to her," I said.

"Not now. She is in our custody. First we will talk to her. Later you talk to her."

"When?"

Captain Kim paused and looked around the room, catching his breath.

"Tomorrow. Tomorrow you come back."

There was nothing else to do. She was in their jurisdiction and, as far as the United States was concerned, no charges had been filed by us against her.

As we were escorted out of the police station, we heard more guttural cursing down the hallway and what sounded like a slap.

We walked until we were out of sight of the police station and then we hopped across the street to the Hamilton Hotel. We found a narrow alley running off the Main Supply Route that gave us a clear view inside the police box, and there we stood in the shadows. I doubted that they'd spot us, primarily because they weren't looking.

"Well, we're here," Ernie said. "We got a great view of the Itaewon Police Box. My next question is, why?"

"I want to make sure they don't take Kimiko anywhere."

"Hold on a minute, pal. I'm not going to stand outside here all night just to protect the human rights of some poor innocent bar girl."

"We won't have to stand here all night. Just until Captain Kim leaves. He's the honcho. Nothing important happens unless he's there to supervise it."

"Why would they want to move her?"

"I'm not sure. She seems to be at the center of this whole thing. I just don't want to lose tabs on her."

"And when Captain Kim leaves?"

"We take the rest of the night off. And then come back here before he returns to work."

"Holy shit, George. You always get like this. Taking these cases too personal. If Kimiko knows anything about the murder, the KNPs will get it out of her tonight, and if not, at least they'll give her a block of instruction on the importance of not kicking general officers in the *cajones*. Nothing to worry about."

"I want to talk to her."

"And you're worried about losing her trail?"

"Right."

Ernie sighed. "All right. I'll get the beer."

In a few minutes he was back with a big frosty liter of OB. The cap had already been popped off. He took a swig and handed the bottle to me. I was hot and thirsty from all the running around and the beer tasted delicious. I gurgled about half of it down.

We waited.

By the time we were thinking about buying another bottle, Captain Kim walked out of the police box. He had changed into a dark blue business suit and carried a briefcase. Korea, for all its modernity and contacts with the Western world, is still a Confucian society. Scholars are esteemed while people who work with their hands, like policemen, are lower on the social ladder. So it's not uncommon for people to change into suits on their way to and from work, hoping they will look like your average professor of nuclear physics. Even my houseboy did it.

Ernie watched him go. "Just another day at the office."

"And now we're off duty, too."

"Where to?"

"Where else?"

We walked across the Main Supply Route, up the hill, and into the glittering heart of Itaewon.

The King Club was packed and Miss Oh was busy serving drinks. Ernie and I wedged ourselves into the crowd at the bar so as to stay as close to the source as possible. She spotted me, gave me a half smile, and then let it drop. Trouble.

The band wailed away. They were a little better than the one the club used to have. I figured two or three more beers and then I might be able to fool myself into believing they were on key. The last combo had required a six-pack.

I leaned towards Ernie. "Who's it going to be tonight? Miss So or the Nurse?"

"I sort of gave up on Miss So. The Nurse is all right. She takes care of me."

Like the time she took the butcher knife to you, I thought. And threw your mattress into the well.

Miss Oh walked by, balancing a tray full of drinks. She sidled her way through the tables and served a group in front of the dance floor. When she was finished, she stopped in front of me.

"I can't see you tonight," she said, and started to walk off.

I grabbed her by the arm. "Why?"

"Somebody's having a big party tonight. I have to go."

"Who?"

She swiveled her head and stared at me. Her narrow eyes flattened a little. "Why you ask me?"

"Is it the new honcho in Itaewon? Mr. Kwok?"

Her eyes widened for a moment and then her lips tightened. "Yeah. That's him," she said. "Mr. Kwok. So what?"

I let go of her arm, we glowered at one another for a moment, and then she tossed her hair back as she walked away. I watched her hot pants sway as she teetered down the crowded aisle.

Ernie took a swig of his beer, looked at me, grinned. "Miss Lim?"

I thought of something coarse to say but instead just slammed my empty beer bottle down on the bar. "Yeah." I said.

It was against my principles but there I was in the American Club, after already spending the last two nights with her, looking for Miss Lim again. I didn't ask but Ginger told me that she hadn't been in yet. After serving us a couple of beers, Ginger slid off, back to the telephone. If I hadn't known better, I might have suspected that she was doing something devious. Actually I didn't mind, and I was fuming about Miss Oh. In my opinion she was the best-looking woman in Itaewon and she had to be on everybody's list of the top ten. If the honchos have a big party, they will staff it with the best-looking help available and Miss Oh was sure to be in on it. This guy Kwok—she hadn't flinched when I mentioned his name, so maybe she didn't actually know him. Or maybe she would have agreed with whatever name I gave her just to make me jealous. If so, it was working.

By the time Miss Lim arrived, I had calmed down and was delighted to see her. We had a few beers and then a few more and the band started to sound great. I even danced with her one time: a slow dance, to be sure.

I have a theory about fast dancing, that it's intended to make men look ridiculous. And the more ridiculous a woman can make a man look, the more power she has over him and the more she affirms her own attractiveness. It makes me want to barf to see all those guys out there shucking and jiving with big smiles on their faces, as if they're really enjoying themselves. I don't believe it. Why don't they admit that they'd rather be in the sack with the woman and stop pretending that they love the rhythm and the sounds of the movement? Give me a break.

Once, at the Lower Four Club, I was somewhat less than sober and a girl Riley had picked up somewhere coaxed me into fast dancing with her. When they saw me on the dance floor, Riley and Ernie had apoplectic fits that ended up with them both rolling on the carpet, holding their stomachs. But there was nothing wrong with slow dancing with Miss Lim and it made me remember what had gone on last night and made me want to repeat it again tonight. I even came up with some new ideas.

By the time we left, Ginger was pleased with her handiwork and Ernie and I walked out into the cold air, Miss Lim held firmly between us.

Ernie hailed a cab and guided him down the MSR a couple of blocks, up a steep hill, and around a few alleys until we pulled to a halt in front of the Nurse's hooch.

She stood in the doorway, nightgown fluttering, silhouetted by the stark light behind her. We all took off our shoes, sat down on the warm vinyl floor, and the Nurse put on some music. Ernie slipped her some money, and in a few minutes she was back with beer, unhusked peanuts, and strings of dried cuttlefish. We drank and feasted and laughed and when it got too late, we turned off the music and turned off the light and Ernie slept with the Nurse in the bed and I slept with Miss Lim on the floor.

At dawn I shook Miss Lim awake. She seemed confused, and embarrassed about being there. I helped her find her clothes and then walked her out to the street and hailed a taxi for her. If I were more of a gentleman, I would have paid the cab fare.

Ernie was up by now and the Nurse had prepared a large pan of warm water for each of us. I squatted outside, washed my face, and borrowed one of Ernie's razors to shave. Without a mirror. When we were presentable we sat cross-legged in the hooch while the Nurse served us steaming cups of freeze-dried coffee.

By the time the first rays of sunlight were warming the narrow lanes of Itaewon, we were back in our alley, watching the police station. Passersby, scurrying on their way to work, squinted at the two big Americans loitering in the cold shadows. I didn't mind. I just hoped the police wouldn't notice.

Captain Kim worked late but he also arrived late and it got real uncomfortable waiting for him. I sauntered over to the Hamilton Hotel once and used a public phone to call Riley at the office. I told him to let Top know that we were following up a lead on the Pak Ok-suk murder case. The less details the better. Of course, Top might get sort of peeved at us being out here, since they already had a suspect and the case was ostensibly wrapped up, but he hadn't told us not to continue working on it and, anyway, I'd worry about that later. Ernie wasn't complaining. He'd hung with me through worse shit.

Finally, when it was almost nine o'clock, Captain Kim, in his neatly pressed blue suit, strolled into his place of business. It was nice to have the waiting over but then we had to wait again. There was no telling if, or when, he would release Kimiko. Waiting's the worst part about being a CID agent and Ernie swore if he ever got out of this shit, he'd never wait for anything again. If he needed a cavity filled, he'd go to the emergency room.

"Yesterday he said we could talk to her," Ernie said. "So why don't we just Bogart on in there?"

"He'd probably stall us and then hold on to her until we cleared the area. If we hold tight here, Captain Kim might decide to let her go early, before we arrive to start asking questions."

She came out just then, into the sun, blinking like a bruised rat, looked around, and then stepped gingerly onto the slippery ice. She was still wearing her short dress, her hair was gnarled and matted, and all traces of makeup had been smeared off her face. She must have been freezing. She teetered down the sidewalk and then up the hill to Itaewon, heading for hearth and home.

We followed, one of us on either side of the street, stopping occasionally in doorways to make ourselves as inconspicuous as possible. There was a fairly healthy crowd of pedestrians but when you're over six feet tall and Caucasian it's sort of difficult to put an effective tail on someone. Maybe not in New York but definitely in Seoul.

But anyway, Kimiko wasn't looking. She was exhausted, beat up, defeated. When she turned up the narrow alley leading to her hooch, we hesitated a while to give her a head start and then we turned the corner.

What we saw didn't exactly make our day although it did confirm my paranoid suspicions.

The two guys looked very tough, and when we stopped moving forward they just stared at us.

Kimiko couldn't see us. One of the guys held her arms behind her back and with his free hand he pushed the back of her neck down so her long hair dangled, brushing the ground.

I was getting sort of tired of people pushing her around. Ernie took the first steps forward. And then me.

The bad guys didn't move.

I did have one comforting thought. One of the great things about living in Korea was that the country had total gun control. You didn't have to worry about getting shot in the back by some hoodlum looking for a little target practice. Only the police and the soldiers had guns, and for a private citizen to get caught with a firearm was a major offense.

Of course, sometimes the local soldiers got out of line. Every now and then one of them went berserk and holed up in a hotel with hostages. Just didn't want to sign in off his pass, I guess. Even in the line of duty, they could make you a little nervous. Like at a roadblock when some American got the bright idea that he didn't have to show his identification, since he was one of the heroes from the Land of the Brave, and an ROK Army soldier leveled his weapon at him. Still, they're very reluctant to shoot Americans.

We didn't have to worry about guns, but we did have to worry about the men. They were both tall for Koreans, close to six feet, thin but not skinny, with knots of muscle at various strategic points around their bodies. I noticed the calluses on their knuckles and the stances they were in and, by the looks of them, the years of practice that went into such familiarity.

Ernie took a few steps off to the side of the alley and got his back up against the stone wall. An old habit from Vietnam. If they decide to waste you at least you'll see them coming.

The hoodlums had turned their attention to us but still held Kimiko, who was muttering vile curses through her constricted throat.

I thought of turning around and walking away, pretending we were just innocent bystanders who happened to stumble on this scene and didn't want to get involved in any trouble. But that wouldn't do Kimiko much good. And I didn't want to lose her after all the trouble we'd gone through to find her. Anyway, my guess was that these guys had probably spotted us following her, because they hadn't seemed too surprised when we rounded the corner.

I decided to go for one of those lines, like you hear in the movies, that gets everybody's attention and puts the fear of God in your enemies. My brain churned but all I came up with was, "Why don't you leave the girl alone?"

Ernie tried to strengthen it some. "Yeah," he said. "Leave her alone."

The guy with his hands free had a square face, stubbled whiskers, and a short, thick scar along the side of his neck. I don't think he understood me. Just as well.

Instead, he looked at us for what seemed a long moment, and then he said, slowly and distinctly, as if he'd rehearsed it, *"E yoja dala kamyon dangsin ae jamji chalubkeita."*

Most of the words were familiar to me but I was too nervous to put it all together. Something about what would happen if we continued to follow her. I tried to remember the sentence as a whole, and the noun *jamji* in particular because that was a new one to me.

Finally the man got impatient and he waved his hand at me. *"Ka! Bali ka!"*

I didn't have any trouble with that one. "Go!" he said, as if he were talking to a dog.

He shuffled another step towards us. *"Bali ka, sikya!"*

Fighting words.

I felt the old fear rise within me. The fear of bullies, the fear of gangs, the fear of the mean, pitiless, sun-seared streets.

The fear made me angry.

I returned the insult—*"Yoja manjijima, sikya!"*—speaking to him as if he were dirt.

He understood that. Like a scorpion he was on me, stinger raised. The bottom of his foot slammed my chest and I hurtled back against the stone wall.

He was a little too confident about his own expertise and let the foot linger on my chest, knee bent, while he leaned forward to punch me in the head. I twisted left, covered. The punch landed on my arms. He was much quicker than me but the road was slippery and I was now above him, on the incline. I pushed forward and his footing gave. He slid down the hill and landed on his butt. Bounding across the alleyway, I pulled the other guy off Ernie and heaved. Kimiko snarled and missed him with a snap kick as he twisted down the alley. He careened into his buddy and for a second they both lay on the road.

The one with the scar sprang upright, reached out and yanked his comrade to his feet.

We were like three glaring musk-ox—Ernie, Kimiko, and me—rump to rump, defending the herd.

By this time a small crowd had gathered on the main road and was starting to gawk. The scarred guy sneered and said, *"Ka ja,"* to his friend, and they both walked away, dusting themselves off.

I suppose I could have gone after them and tried to arrest them, but for what? Given her track record, I doubted Kimiko would have testified against them, so it would have been Ernie's word and mine against theirs. And I'm not so sure Captain Kim would have been enthusiastic about the whole thing. Besides, I was afraid of them and not at all certain that we'd come out as well in the next round. I was happy just to see them go.

Kimiko straightened out what little there was of her dress and tried to dust it off, pulling the hemline down below her soiled panties.

"Why you help me?" she said.

"Lady in distress."

She stared at me for a moment, her face lined with little creases, the nose rounded and slightly protruding, the lips fleshy, her hair like a snarled black mop. Fifty, at least. But her body was trim and her bosom soft and round. Her stock in trade.

Kimiko squinted. "You CID?"

Cover in Itaewon lasts for about five minutes. We'd been here for months.

"Yeah."

"So you follow me? Cheeky, cheeky."

"Yeah."

"Why?"

"To find out about Miss Pak."

Kimiko searched my face and then slowly turned away. "Yes. Come on."

The three of us trudged up the hill, and about halfway up the block Kimiko turned right through the open gate and we followed her into the courtyard with the charred remains of the rented home of Miss Pak Ok-suk.

The landlady stood in the courtyard, arms folded.

The doors to Kimiko's hooch were open. Ripped open. Splintered wood and tattered strips of white paper lay strewn across the narrow wood-slat porch. Kimiko stood frozen for a moment, then spoke quickly to the landlady.

The men had come here about an hour before curfew, searched the room, and then waited all night. In the morning they tore the room apart, searching everywhere, under the vinyl-covered floors, behind the wallpapered plasterboard. Apparently they had found nothing that satisfied them.

None of this seemed to faze Kimiko. She wasn't the type of woman to place a lot of value on possessions. She didn't even carry a purse, at least I'd never seen her with one, and her room was as spare and utilitarian as it was possible to be. Now it was a shambles.

She stepped into the room and I followed. The plastic and wire armoire had been smashed, and the few dresses within were shredded, carefully—with a knife. The bottles on her little makeup table had been crunched, making a sweet reeking smear across the floor. The mirror was splintered into a million shards. She rummaged through the mess, calmly, but found nothing that she wanted to keep.

The landlady brought a short broom and a dustpan and together they set to work cleaning up. In a few minutes everything was out in the trash and the cement floor, splotched with vinyl, started to look like home again.

Kimiko told us to come in. We took off our shoes, crouched to pass through the doorway, and sat down cross-legged on the floor.

"I no have coffee," she said.

"Yeah. That's all right," I said.

"You got cigarette?"

"No. I don't smoke."

She looked at Ernie. He shrugged.

Kimiko frowned but let it pass and then started talking, without preamble, about Miss Pak. She talked for maybe twenty minutes and when she was finished she just stared at us.

"That's it?"

"That's it."

"And what about you? What will you do now?"

Kimiko lifted her shoulders and let them drop. "I will do what I always do. Make money from GIs."

We got up.

"Tonight," she said, "you see me, you buy me drink."

"We'll see. Who were those men who attacked you and did all this?" I waved my arms around the room.

"I don't know." Her face showed no more emotion than the bottom of an empty *soju* bottle.

"What were they looking for?"

Kimiko didn't bother to answer. She just shook her head.

At the bottom of the hill Ernie pulled out a stick of gum, unwrapped it, and popped it in his mouth.

"Did you believe her?"

"Some, yes. Some, no."

"I think she's holding a lot back," he said as he waved down a cab.

It was sort of hard to argue with that.

8

After showering and putting on fresh clothes back at the compound we went to the snack bar. I got a cup of hot coffee and a copy of the *Stars & Stripes*. The sports page I didn't read, the front page was beyond belief, and I thought the editorials were a bunch of drivel. I don't know why I bought it every day. Just that stray article, I guess. About the little girl who had been missing in San Diego for two weeks and then was found and reunited with her father, or the old people confined to their homes in Pittsburgh, who were brought food and companionship by the local kids in the elementary school. I liked to read about people doing the right thing and I wondered how I so often ended up doing the wrong thing.

Ernie plopped into the seat in front of me and clinked down a plate of scrambled eggs, bacon, and hash browns.

I said, "Worked up an appetite last night, eh?"

"The Nurse. She keeps me healthy."

Now that the table was guarded, I went to the serving line and ordered a bacon, lettuce, and tomato sandwich with a tall glass of cold milk. After I got back, we ate breakfast quietly for a while, amidst the clinking of glassware and the murmur of shuffling customers, both of us thinking about what Kimiko had said.

Miss Pak had been an excitable girl: alive, barely able to contain herself in anticipation of all the wonderful things that were bound to happen to her in life. Her eyes sparkled, according to Kimiko, and she loved to laugh uproariously, eyes wide, even at the mildest joke casually thrown out by some GI who was unaware that he was such a comedian.

She loved men and trusted them, and it was Kimiko who had set her straight. Get the money first. No matter what they say, no matter how much they like you, in the morning they will see things differently. And they'll start thinking of how many days it is until payday and how much they could do with that ten or fifteen dollars' worth of freshly minted Military Payment Certificates.

Miss Pak had listened but she'd faltered a couple of times, especially when the guy was young, like her, and made her laugh.

She was pretty, and when she strutted out on the dance floor with her short skirt and her tight blouse, all the men watched. There might be twenty girls on the floor but everyone kept their eyes on Miss Pak Ok-suk.

Kimiko had borrowed some pungent Korean cigarettes from the landlady and she told us about Miss Pak with a clinical detachment as the room filled with smoke. It was a purely professional analysis from an experienced observer.

Kimiko had contacts, and she felt that Miss Pak Ok-suk was wasting herself running from GI to GI in Itaewon when she was young enough and pretty enough to make some serious money. So Kimiko hooked her up with some of the older Americans around, the kind who don't want to be seen running the ville in Itaewon, also a few rich Koreans and even the stray Japanese tourist. Miss Pak was making good money but, like so many young girls, she had to go and screw it all up.

She got hooked up with Johnny and they put in their marriage paperwork. Kimiko told her not to trust that. The whole process took six months or more and usually, after talking to his immediate supervisor, his commanding officer, the chaplain, the legal officer, and the personnel officer, and after whatever new hurdle the Army bureaucracy had cooked up, the young GI would change his mind.

Kimiko knew. She'd had marriage paperwork put in on her a half dozen times and it had never gone through. She told Miss Pak not to fall for it, but the girl had stuck with Johnny and this is how it turned out.

I asked her if she had seen Miss Pak on the night she died. She said she had. Briefly. She tried to talk her into going to one of the big hotels and finding a couple of rich tourists. Miss Pak refused. The last Kimiko had seen of her was when she left Miss Pak on the front steps of the Lucky Seven Club. She had no idea where she'd gone after that, back into the club, or elsewhere.

I was about halfway done with my BLT, and I was already finished with my cold glass of milk so I got another one. Ernie pushed his empty plate away, sipped on his coffee, and read the *Stars & Stripes*.

I wondered how much justice we'd done that girl. So far, we didn't have much more than when we started. We knew that she'd been murdered, but exactly how, we still weren't sure. The Korean medical examiner's report had been vague. Asphyxiation. That could have been from strangling or from the smoke of the fire. And if it was from the fire she must have been knocked out or drugged or something. No one was too interested now that a GI was in custody. My guess was that the family had fallen under the wing of a lawyer who specialized in claims against the U.S. government.

No one had any particular interest in proving that Spec-4 John Watkins hadn't been the one to commit the murder. Certainly not the family. They didn't want to blow a bundle. And not the Korean National Police, who were glad that, once the GI suspect was turned over to them, they'd get the press off their backs. Even Eighth Army was ambivalent about the whole thing. With Spec-4 Watkins as the sacrificial lamb, their public-relations problem was solved and they could go back to business as usual.

Of course, maybe Johnny Watkins did kill her. I couldn't be sure that he hadn't, but it didn't seem to fit. He just wasn't mean enough. But who knows? I'm wrong about people more often than I'm right.

Then there was Kimiko. No one in Itaewon had known Miss Pak Ok-suk better than Kimiko. Not even Johnny. But why would she want to kill that young girl? Was she stepping on territory Kimiko considered to be her own? Or maybe it was jealousy engendered by years of bitterness and ridicule in the oldest and toughest of professions.

And why had those guys come looking for Kimiko? They had been after her for something. Only what? Kimiko didn't appear to have any money at all. Or had she been squirreling away a little bit at a time over the years, with a big stash somewhere? Or maybe they were looking for something else.

Kimiko hadn't seemed too concerned about the whole thing. She'd relaxed right away, as soon as they left, and she didn't seem worried that they might come back.

The Korean National Police? They hadn't gone at this case aggressively. Like Milt Gorman said, they must be protecting someone, or something.

Those two guys we'd seen this morning—were they members of the local syndicate? Sent by Mr. Kwok? If so, why? If Mr. Kwok wanted to kill one of the girls in Itaewon, he could do it a lot more efficiently than Miss Pak's assailant had. Why would he want to ice some bar girl anyway? Even if Miss Pak was a little money machine, getting married and backing out of the business was routine in Itaewon. Hundreds of girls married GIs every year. No sweat, there were plenty of replacements.

I looked down at my plate and realized I had finished my BLT. I hadn't tasted it. Not that there was much taste to an Army snack-bar sandwich.

I felt a chill. Or maybe it was just that I knew we had to go into the office and face the first sergeant.

"Where the *hell* have you two guys been?"

Ernie cracked his gum. "Doing what you told us to do, Top. Trying to get a line on who murdered Pak Ok-suk."

"More evidence on Watkins?"

"We're not so sure he did it."

"Then who did?"

"We don't know that either."

"You got any evidence?"

"Nothing new."

He looked at us long and hard. "Dicking off again, eh?" Neither of us moved. "Let the Watkins case be," he said. "The Korean courts will take it from here."

Ernie clicked his gum again, wandered over to the big coffee urn, and started fiddling with the cups and the spoons and the non-dairy creamer.

"There's no reason in the world," I said, "to think that Johnny Watkins murdered that girl."

"Other than that he was going to marry her," the first sergeant snarled, "and she was messing around with other guys."

"I'm talking about physical evidence. Sure, maybe he had a

motive. But we got no direct evidence putting him near the scene of the crime."

"But we got no evidence putting him anywhere else, either. A strong motive and the lack of an alibi is enough for the Koreans."

"Because the newspapers and the locals want blood?" I said.

"Yeah. But I wouldn't worry about him too much. The judges are fair. They won't give him too much time if they can't pin it on him. And they'll probably let him ease on out of jail quietly, after about eighteen months, and deport him back to the States."

"And kick him out of the Army."

"A general discharge. No sweat." The first sergeant shrugged.

"And if all this happened to you and you were innocent?"

"I wouldn't let it happen to me," he said, softly.

The first sergeant leaned across his desk and picked up a manila folder. He probably wouldn't; he was a very cautious guy. But you never know.

I rubbed my eyes. "And what about the real killer? What happens to him?"

"If it isn't Watkins, the Korean police will find the real killer."

Ernie snorted. Some of his swirling brown coffee splashed onto the counter and the dingy brown carpet below. The first sergeant waited while Ernie sopped it up with a brown paper towel, then started again.

"Besides, I need you two for yet another load of shit that's come up at the Korean Procurement Agency."

We waited.

"There's a guy named Lindbaugh—Fred Lindbaugh. According to Tom Kurtz, our snitch over there, he's been approving a lot of the changes in contracts. We want you to follow him, find out a little more about his personal life. He's single. Other than that, we don't know much about him."

"I thought Burrows and Slabem were going to handle this KPA thing."

"They are. The paperwork part. But their faces have been seen in the main office. Lindbaugh knows them."

"Does he run the ville?"

"Probably. He's single."

"Which is why you want us to follow him?"

"Yeah. The experts."

"What are we looking for?"

"A flamboyant lifestyle. He's only a GS-7. We want to find out if he lives above his means."

"GS-7. Single. That's a lot of loot for Korea."

"Yeah. And we understand he's very popular with the ladies."

"He doesn't have to be on the take to be spending pretty free."

"Just watch him. Burrows and Slabem will be checking out his bank account." The first sergeant gave us a long once-over. "You two look sort of haggard. Take the rest of the day off. Lindbaugh gets off at five. Be there."

On the way out, we turned into the Admin Office. Miss Kim had on a bright green dress that clung to her figure and when she smiled my nerve endings flared like flower buds triggered by the sun. Ernie offered her his customary stick of gum, she took it, unwrapped it, and they fell into their customary monosyllabic conversation punctuated by grunts and giggles.

Riley was out. I sat down behind his desk and pouted. Over Miss Kim and over the Watkins case—I wasn't happy about being taken off it. On the other hand, I really didn't know what else to do. The only lead I had was Kimiko and she wasn't the type to spill much of anything. If this guy Lindbaugh was a ville rat, though, we could still keep an eye on her. And also I had my free time. Top couldn't say anything about that.

I wondered why I gave a damn about the fate of Johnny Watkins and, to be honest, I probably didn't. Top was right. He would be okay. A little jail time—max. Unless they actually proved that he did it. It wasn't him that I was worried about. It was the late Miss Pak Ok-suk. She would never be okay. Maybe she wasn't a saint but she wasn't the worst person in the world either. She didn't deserve to be murdered that way and none of us who were still living deserved to have her killer walking around free.

Back in the barracks I took out a pencil and paper and wrote down as much as I could remember of what the Korean thug had said to us that morning.

The first part was clear. *E yoja dala kamyon* meant "if you follow this woman." The second part was a little more difficult. *Jamji chal-uhkeita.* This meant he was going to cut something. Something of mine. Something called a *jamji.*

I got out my little plastic-bound Korean-English dictionary and thumbed through it, humming to myself. Happy to have something academic to do for a change. My humming stopped when I found the definition.

Jamji was the diminutive reference to the male member: the penis of an infant.

The offices of the Korean Procurement Agency were in a small compound off by itself, away from the main Eighth Army Headquarters complex, near Samgakji. The buildings were the familiar two-story red-brick jobs built by the Japanese Imperial Army during the occupation prior to World War II.

The parking lot was small and almost full. A lot of the American civilians who worked here had cars. The Koreans, without exception, took the bus. We were sitting in Ernie's little jeep, wedged between a beat-up old Chevy Impala and a quarter-ton delivery truck.

"We should be off by now," Ernie said, getting ready to run the ville. "Not waiting around for some overpaid civilian asshole."

Ernie, when he wasn't raving, was usually a pretty calm

person. One of the calmest people I've ever met in my life. Almost comatose. But don't mess with his Happy Hour.

People started to pour out of the offices, as if a whistle had gone off. Then we heard the distant bugle call and the blast of a howitzer on the main post. The flag-lowering ceremony was under way. Nobody stopped for it here. The Korean men in suits and ties and the women in smart office outfits shrugged on their overcoats on the steps, wrapped mufflers around their necks, and headed purposefully towards the bus stop just beyond the gate, manned by two Korean security guards.

A roly-poly rascal bounded down the stairs. Tom Kurtz trotted to keep up with him, almost tugging on his sleeve, and finally got him stopped in the parking lot, chatting quickly. The fat guy looked around, trying to make a getaway, totally uninterested. Kurtz had promised to show us Lindbaugh by glomming on to him at the end of the workday. The fat guy was our boy.

Finally Kurtz smiled a goodbye and let Lindbaugh go. With a sigh of relief, the fat man waddled towards a green Army sedan on the other side of the parking lot.

Lindbaugh was average height, maybe five nine or so, but he must have weighed about two hundred pounds, most of it lard. His hair was straight and black and parted, so it had a habit of sliding down across his forehead into his eyes. He kept brushing at it with his pudgy fingers. He wore a three-piece suit and the vest was stretched so far beyond its limits that it rode up a couple of inches above the overloaded belt, exposing white shirt.

He bundled into the sedan, fired it up, and pushed his way through the crowd of Korean co-workers. Ernie started up the jeep, rolled slowly forward and, after watching the thick calves of a pair of nice-looking female office workers, he popped us into the Seoul rush-hour traffic.

Lindbaugh seemed to be in a big hurry so he fit right in, because everybody was. Kimchi cabs swerved in and out of one another's way, straining for that extra few inches of advantage over their competitors. Lindbaugh swerved, accelerated, slammed on the brakes, and seemed to be cursing a lot. Ernie sat back in his canvas seat, hands lightly touching the steering wheel. Relaxed. And he had no trouble keeping us an almost constant fifteen or twenty yards behind the erratic Lindbaugh.

Lindbaugh turned right at Huam-dong, ran up the long straightaway between Camp Coiner and the ROK Marine Corps Headquarters, and was waved through by the gate guards at the back entrance to Yongsan Compound. We followed him in and past the barracks and the gym and the main PX and the big Army Communications Center, back out through Gate 5, across the MSR, back to the sedate environs of Yongsan South Post. He turned left in front of the Officers' Club, raced past it, turned right down a tree-lined avenue, and stopped in front of one of the small houses that served as BOQs—Bachelor Officers' Quarters. That's what the civilian workers get: their own private rooms, a communal living room, kitchen, and latrine with an old *mama-san* who did the laundry and the cleaning. Pretty convenient lifestyle really and, other than the monthly tips for the cleaning woman and the aged houseboy, free. All part of their pay and benefits.

Ernie rolled on past. Lindbaugh was struggling to get his chubby body out of his car, not paying any attention to us whatsoever. Ernie cruised around the block, came back, and parked under a tree where we had a clear view of the sedan and the front of Lindbaugh's BOQ.

We could have busted him for unauthorized use of a government vehicle. The sedan was for use during the day, for official business, not for running back and forth from your hooch. Lindbaugh seemed pretty brazen about its use, not caring how many of his co-workers saw him using it to get home at the end of the workday. Small wonder Kurtz had fingered him.

Ernie drummed his fingers on the steering wheel. "We could be here all night."

"No way, pal. If he doesn't go out in an hour or two, we'll just figure he's going to stay in for the night."

"Any place to get beer around here?"

"There's a Class VI store back by the Officers' Club."

Before we could decide whether one of us should walk over there or if we should take the jeep, Lindbaugh left his quarters. He wore a pullover golf shirt that fit him like Saran Wrap. His blue jeans were baggy and faded and his white sneakers scuffed. Just a regular guy kicking around the neighborhood. He drove off. We followed.

"He can't be going to the village dressed like that."

"No way," I said. "Got to be a local run."

We followed him down a narrow lane that led up around the rear of the Officers' Club to a small back parking lot where most of the food and beverage deliveries were made. Off to the side was the Class VI store, a PX Shopette, and the Steam and Cream.

The Steam and Cream was known officially as the Army and Air Force Exchange Service Steam Bath and Massage Center. Lindbaugh parked out front, popped from his car, and ambled through the door as if he'd been there a million times.

Ernie parked the jeep between some other cars in the lot.

"Now I know it's going to take a while."

"Five dollars for thirty minutes or seven-fifty for an hour."

"At least he brought us to the Class VI."

Ernie got out of the jeep and came back in a few minutes with a six-pack of cold beer. We popped open a couple of wets and waited.

In the Army you get used to things like this: not really being in charge of an investigation, not knowing all of what's going on, just being told to watch somebody and report back. People think of the Army as being demeaning. In a lot of ways it is. Though I think many civilian jobs have the same demands: don't ask questions, just do it.

The one thing the Army has going for it is that you can't be fired. Not easily, anyway. You have to do something wrong, almost commit a crime. Of course the Army's standards for what constitutes a crime are a little less stringent than those of the civilian world. For instance, being late for a formation or not showing up for work—in the Army those are crimes. But if you avoid the obvious stuff, the things they can nail you for under the Uniform Code of Military Justice, then you have a lot of latitude. If your boss doesn't like you, he can make your life miserable but he can't fire you. Not without specific charges. And being a smartass isn't good enough. In fact, if he brings it to the attention of his higher-ups, they'll probably wonder why he isn't capable of handling the situation himself.

So in a lot of ways the Army offers more freedom than the civilian world. I don't have to worry about whether or not the company I work for is making a profit or if the wife of the boss doesn't like the way I look. I can mostly count on having a job as long as I don't get stupid.

Besides, who else would send me to Korea and pay me to drink beer outside of a Steam and Cream?

We had gone through the entire six-pack and both taken a leak in the bushes behind the parking lot by the time Lindbaugh came out. A young lady in a blue steam bath uniform held the door open for him and waved goodbye. He looked like a pink new baby—pampered, powdered, and now patted on the butt on the way out. He walked next door to the PX Shopette and emerged again with a shopping bag full of groceries and a magazine wrapped in cellophane. Then he drove back to his hooch. Ernie and I parked outside for a conference.

"He ain't going nowhere." Ernie said.

"Naw. Tomorrow's a workday. He's had his fun." I checked my watch. It was still early. Nineteen thirty. "Time to head out to the ville."

"You got that right."

When Kimiko spotted us she strutted across the King Club, brown OB beer bottle in hand, and reached for my crotch. I jumped back spasmodically, barely avoiding her grasp.

"How's it hanging, GI?" she said.

"It's hanging just fine, Kimiko," I said, "all by itself."

"You buy me drink?"

"Hell no. You're supposed to buy us a drink, for saving your *kundingi*."

The same beige dress she had had on this morning was now washed and pressed and her long black hair had been shampooed and combed. She had scrounged some makeup from somewhere. The oldest business girl in Itaewon was back in town.

She considered my proposal about the drinks. "Okay," she said. "I buy, you pay."

Ernie and I elbowed our way to the bar. I ordered three OBs and ceremoniously handed one to Kimiko. She curtsied, her knobby knees flared slightly to the side.

The joint was busy, as usual for this time of night, and Miss Oh hadn't noticed our entrance yet. She served a tray of drinks and was heading right for us when Kimiko, with that incredible sense of timing that women have, threw her arms around my waist and buried her face in my shirt.

I tried to pull her off but she had a tight grip and Miss Oh walked by, increasing her speed as she passed, glowering at me for the loss of face I was causing her.

If she didn't have time to see me, because she had to party with a bunch of big-shot Koreans, did I get mad? No. But some old broad throws her arms around me, without invitation, and she acts as if I've just broken a sacred vow.

I pried Kimiko's biceps away from my ribs. She looked up at me, her face clouding.

"Whatsamatta you? You no like Kimiko?"

"Yeah, I like," I said. "Just don't break my back, okay?"

She pouted and lifted her beer bottle to her lips. Tilting it straight up, she let the bubbling hops gurgle and swirl down her pulsating throat. My kind of chick. Then she burped. Me and Ernie too. Three-part harmony.

Miss Oh was snapping quick looks at me from the waitress station. Hell with it, I thought. Ernie had commandeered a bar stool and sat down, his back to the bar, knees pointing towards the crowd. He was chortling. I said, "Pretty hilarious, eh, pal?"

"You're a riot, George. Better than Dobie Gillis."

We decided to get into some serious drinking and ordered shots and another round of beer. When we had finished, the three of us paraded out into the streets of Itaewon, not really sure where we were going, letting the surging pedestrian masses lead us. Shortly, we found ourselves in front of the American Club. Ernie dragged us in. I was worried about running into Miss Lim but the lust for more booze kept my feet moving.

Ginger saw us and her face brightened. She started her charge down the planks behind the bar when she saw Kimiko and, slowly, her face hardened. She sauntered down to us at the open bar stool we had found. Kimiko jumped up on it and Ernie and I wedged ourselves close to the railing on either side of her. Ginger filled our order and gave us our change without saying anything. I hadn't spotted Miss Lim. Then I noticed Ginger on the phone, face grim.

Some of the old retirees at the bar knew Kimiko, and soon she was glad-handing around as if she were running for mayor.

Ernie and I leaned into the drinks heavy—who knew when

the stuff could run out?—and then the C&W band started and all of my thought processes stopped. During a particularly hideous cowboy lament, Kimiko returned and at the same time Miss Lim walked in the door. Kimiko's beer bottle was empty and she tried to get me to refill it for her. Miss Lim sashayed past without looking at me and joined one of the more presentable retirees at the end of the bar. He smiled so broadly I thought his cheeks were going to pop. Then he stood up and offered her his bar stool. Offering someone a bar stool is the greatest sacrificial gesture a retiree can make.

Miss Lim took off her coat, assisted by the ex-lifer, sat down primly, and ordered a drink from the concerned and attentive Ginger. When the drink appeared, she *dupshida-ed* with the guy, took a sip, and glanced at me.

Yeah, I was riveted to her every move. And kept trying to brush Kimiko off. Finally, Kimiko realized what was going on, stared for a while at Miss Lim, and then turned back to me.

"She married. Why you mess around with married woman?"

I didn't answer, just ordered another round of straight shots. Morality lectures from Kimiko, yet.

After a while Ernie and I both got tired of standing so we took a tiny table and Kimiko followed us. We were working our way through Ginger's liquor storehouse at a pretty steady clip; the table started to pile up with empty beer bottles.

Kimiko turned her attention towards Ernie since I was beginning to slow down on the generosity angle. They were warming up to a major public display when a woman materialized from the crowd. I didn't recognize her at first but when I realized it was the Nurse, I knew this just wasn't our night.

The Nurse wore soft-soled shoes, blue jeans, a black turtleneck, and a black bandana around her forehead. Her small knotted fist brandished a four-foot-long cudgel. Actually, I think it was a broom handle but at the moment it looked like a cudgel.

She floated towards us, taking small steps, arms raised high, and then she whacked the broom handle across our small cocktail table. Beer and shattered glass flew everywhere. The crash stopped the band and the talking. The only sound was me and Ernie scuffling back our chairs, and then she was advancing, jabbing the stick at Ernie, screaming at him in incoherent Korean.

Kimiko salvaged a full bottle and scuttled off to the side, hiding herself in the crowd.

Ernie twisted and dodged, hands outstretched, trying to ward off the stick, stumbling backwards over chairs and tables as people jumped out of the way, drinks and glassware smashing. Finally he crashed into the amps of the band on stage. Ernie grabbed the broom handle, trying to pull it out of the Nurse's grasp. They grunted and cursed at each other. She let go of the stick with one hand and clawed at his face, screaming.

"You go out every night! Play with woman! No take care of home! No take care of rent! No take care of food!"

Ernie ripped the stick from her grasp and just stood there panting, not knowing quite what to do with it. The Nurse lunged again. He dropped the stick and threw his hands up to protect his face.

She screamed and clawed and slavered, and Ernie backed closer and closer to the main door. I tried to pull her off but she elbowed me in the ribs, stomped on my foot, and went after him some more. Locked arm in arm, they went out the swinging doors of the club. A crowd gathered.

They strained against each other, muscle on muscle, and then the Nurse let go, all at once, and Ernie had to hold her up to keep her from collapsing.

She was crying, pulling away from Ernie. And Ginger was there, comforting her. Other women stepped forward to help.

Both the Americans and the Koreans in the crowd turned their attention to Ernie and me. Their comments became progressively uglier. I tugged on Ernie's elbow. He seemed to come out of his trance and he followed me as I pushed our way through the crowd, heading for the welcome darkness of Itaewon's back alleys. And then we were running.

Heels clicked behind us. Kimiko.

When the light from the street lamp hit her face, she stared at us. Deadpan, she said, "You buy me drink?"

Ernie looked like chalk. I stifled a laugh.

I turned back to Kimiko. "Sure. Why not?"

I dragged both of them to Milt Gorman's place, the Roundup. Ernie went to the latrine to rearrange his ripped shirt and his scratched face. Kimiko stuck close by me while we ordered our drinks. Ernie returned. He sipped listlessly on his beer. He paid no attention to our conversation, and my efforts to cheer him up were useless. After he drained the last of his suds, and without a word, he got up and left.

Milt Gorman stopped by and asked me how the investigation was going. I told him it was over. He smiled and had one of his waitresses bring us a couple of beers. The nice-looking young woman gave us some strange looks as she poured our beer and tidied up the table. Kimiko ignored her. A lot of the GIs were giving us strange looks, too. I was a little uneasy about the attention but I ignored it.

Something made Kimiko decide to tell me her life story. I didn't have anywhere to go so I listened.

Her father was a very rich man, rich enough to own large tracts of land in North Cholla Province, land that was worked by tenant farmers. He had a main wife and second and third wives, but Kimiko's mother wasn't a wife at all. Just a scullery maid. And her earliest memories were of running through the pigpens and the open fields and the orchards ripening with pears and apples. There were plenty of children to play with and most of them were related to her in some way, but as she got older and started school, her place was made clear to her. She was not a real child of a real wife and as such she would be allowed six years of schooling and then must go to work, like her mother.

There was a large household to feed, the biggest burden being the noon meal, when Kimiko's father was obligated to feed the day laborers who were so often working in various of the fields. She and her mother packed up wooden carrying boxes with rice and bean curd soup and cabbage kimchi, and her mother would head in one direction and Kimiko in the other.

After Kimiko finished her sixth year of schooling, she noticed changes in her body and, much sooner than the other girls her age, she started to turn into a woman.

It was her breasts that caused her the most grief. They were large and pointed and she strapped them in tightly, hurting herself every morning when she put on her *chima* and *chogori*, hoping they wouldn't get any bigger and cause her any more shame. In Korea large-breasted women were considered to be stupid, and her body seemed to be betraying her, confirming everyone's already low opinion of her.

I asked Kimiko about her first experience with love. It must have been on a beautiful spring evening, I said, under the blooms of a cherry tree in the orchard.

She shook her head. No one touched her at her father's house. "No can do. Not supposed to."

As Kimiko reached her thirteenth year her mother's health started to fade. More and more of the chores in the big kitchen fell to her, and her father would allow no new help. Finally, after months of hacking and spitting up blood, in the heart of a cruel winter, Kimiko's mother wasted away and died. Her father buried her, without excessive ceremony. The snow was too deep and the watching eyes of the first, second, and third wives too critical to allow for much in the way of mourning. Only Kimiko grieved.

And now the full weight and responsibility of the kitchen fell upon her and she threw herself into her work.

As she lay dying, her mother had given Kimiko a small brooch, a gift from her father when they had first started meeting, late at night after the first wife had gone to bed. It was made of jade, a finely etched design of white cranes rising from their nests.

In the spring, when the orchards burst back into life, Kimiko packed a small bag and walked through the fragrant fields, away from the life into which she had been born. She walked for three days, sleeping on the side of the road, begging handouts from strangers, until she arrived in Chonju, the capital of North Cholla Province.

There she sold the brooch, for much less than it was actually worth, and bought a new skirt, new blouse, and a ticket on the steam vehicle to the capital city of Seoul.

When she arrived in bustling Seoul Station she had no money, just her wits and her burgeoning young body.

Kimiko wandered, trying to find employment. She wheedled information and food but after a few days she was profoundly hungry and tired of sleeping in the street, huddled under the clay-shingled alcove of a temple or a large house.

In a wine shop, an old woman with a brazenly made-up face looked Kimiko over.

"Do you speak Japanese?"

"Only what they taught me in school, ma'am."

The woman laughed a harsh laugh. "That's enough. The Japanese soldiers don't expect too much talk from you. You can get a full-time job, food, and a place to stay. In Itaewon, the Japanese village."

Kimiko's eyes widened and her throat convulsed. She was unable to speak.

"Well, what do you say, girl? I have a friend there who owns a wine shop. A large, grand wine shop. Not like this little hovel."

Kimiko nodded, and in a few minutes the woman had bundled her into the back of a pedicab and they were heading south, past Namsan Mountain, into the sloping Han River lowlands of Itaewon.

The wine shops were large, made of wood and concrete, and signs with Japanese lettering were everywhere. Some of the buildings were two or three stories high, and young women looked down at the urchin in the pedicab from their balconies above the puddled dirt street. Kimiko felt small and alone.

The woman who had brought her got out, went into the largest of the wine shops, and was gone for what seemed a long time. She came out all smiles, and another, even older woman came out and took a good look at Kimiko. She was led into the bowels of the darkened shop and she realized now that she had been sold.

It was hard to adjust. Many of the other girls hated her immediately, just because she was new and younger. But slowly she made a few friends and they washed her up and gave her new clothes and taught her how to wear her hair piled up in the Japanese style and how to put on makeup. Soon she was entertaining the Japanese soldiers who came to the wine shop every night to eat and drink rice wine and clap their hands and sing. The work was much easier than that in the kitchen at her father's house and soon the men started to notice her. They noticed her shyness and her youth and quietly they began whispering to the old proprietress. One evening Kimiko was sold to an older balding man who, it was said, was a very important officer on Yongsan, which was the headquarters of the Japanese Imperial Army in Korea.

She didn't mind so much, it didn't hurt, and the next morning the old woman gave her a share of the money. It was more than Kimiko had ever seen in her life.

After that, she began to make her own friends, and have her

own customers, men who would vie for her attention, and the jealousies of the other girls grew greater.

Then suddenly the war was over. The emperor had surrendered Japan. The cruel forty-year reign in Korea was ended. That day, the soldiers stopped coming to Itaewon. They stayed in their barracks, fortifying themselves for the vengeful onslaught of civilians that they expected before the Americans or the Russians could arrive. But the Koreans had no arms, and those of heroically rebellious spirit had died long ago.

The old woman brought all her girls together and gave them each some money and told them they must go. She could no longer afford to house and to feed them. Kimiko did not know what to do. That night there was a great fire and men ran through the streets yelling curses at the girls of the Japanese quarter. They grabbed them by the hair and pulled them into the street, calling them traitors. The fire spread rapidly, and Kimiko put on her old clothes and bundled all her money and her few possessions into an old rag.

The village of Itaewon was reduced to charred rubble, and Kimiko was back on the streets of Seoul, where she stayed for five years, until war again came.

"During the war, not so bad," Kimiko said. "I had to move a lot but there were many soldiers and they gave me food or soap or cigarettes. Other people were very hungry, but I did okay."

"And after the Korean War, you came back to Seoul?"

Kimiko spat on the floor. "No. I was sick of Seoul people. Too cold heart. I stayed up in the country. North. In the Second Division."

"What made you come back?"

"I got in some trouble. Went to the monkey house. So after, I come back here."

By then she was too old to compete with the young girls farmed out to the Second Division area. Guts and sheer hustle could get you further in Seoul.

It was almost curfew. Nobody else was left in the club. I sent Kimiko home in a taxi and walked halfway back to camp before I hailed one myself.

9

When we gave our report on Lindbaugh, Ernie did most of the talking: "We sat in the parking lot behind the Officers' Club while he got a steam job and a blow bath. Then he bought a bunch of groceries and a cock book and went back to his hooch."

"What time did you end the surveillance?"

"Close to nine."

Seven thirty is close to nine—not very close, but close.

"Our man Kurtz," the first sergeant said, "is keeping an eye on him during the day but I want you guys to hang loose in case Lindbaugh decides to go anywhere unusual. Tonight, be at his hooch before five. Stay with him at least until curfew. It's Friday night so he might have someplace to go."

So did we. But my stomach was churning too violently to mouth off.

The first sergeant rubbed a speck from the gleaming surface of his immaculate desk. "I want you out at the parking lot at KPA watching his sedan during the lunch hour and then back at his hooch before he gets off work. Any questions?"

"Yeah," I said. "What's for chow?"

"Get out of here, Sueño."

We got up.

"Keep an eye on him, Bascom. He's going to kill himself out there running the ville."

Was I that obvious?

Ernie drove me back to the barracks. He said he'd be back at about ten thirty to pick me up for the noon surveillance. I went to my room, took off my coat and tie, and lay down on my bunk. Carefully, so as not to wrinkle the synthetic material of my suit pants too much.

It was good to lie down. Mr. Yi, the houseboy, brought two pairs of glistening black low quarters into the room and placed one pair under my bunk and the other pair under the bunk of my roommate, Pederson.

Pederson worked rotating shifts at the communications center, had a lot of hobbies, and hung out mostly at the arts and crafts center. I didn't see much of him. He was cagey, though. On the weekends he'd strap a camera over his shoulder, take a bus down to Ewha Women's University on the outskirts of Seoul, and ask the best-looking young ladies he could find to take photos of him standing by a fountain. This often led to conversations in a coffee shop and occasionally much more.

Freebies.

Pederson was smart and also thrifty. He let them buy the coffee and didn't bother to put any film in the camera.

I tried to go over the Pak Ok-suk case but it was a struggle.

There were so many people involved. Something was missing but maybe whatever was, was only something that I had failed to notice. Maybe all the pieces were there but what was left out was my ability to put it all together.

I had yet to see a photograph of Miss Pak but I had acquired a picture of her in my mind. She was lovely, with soft round thighs and long black hair, and every time I thought of her she was dancing for me and smiling. I reached out to her and something shook me. My eyes popped open. Ernie.

"Time to hat up, pal."

I washed my face in the latrine and then we jumped in Ernie's jeep and drove over to the KPA compound. We found a little parking spot in the shade of one of the big red-brick buildings and waited. Ernie looked me over.

"What's happening, man?"

"Not much."

"Did you spend the night with Kimiko?"

I turned and stared him down.

"We talked."

"That's one worry off my mind," Ernie said.

"What'd you do last night?"

"Hit a few bars. Then I went back to the compound. On the way in I checked Lindbaugh's sedan. Cold. Hadn't been moved."

"And then you went back to the barracks?"

Ernie's hands squeezed the bottom of the steering wheel. He looked straight ahead and for a moment I thought he hadn't heard me.

"Naw. I went to see the Nurse."

I let out a whoop. "I knew it! You can't stay away."

Ernie grinned a sheepish half-moon filled with well-brushed canines. "It's the tears. They do it every time."

We heard a door slam and a heavy rhythmic pounding as someone raced down the metal stairwell. Lindbaugh.

"Here he comes."

Lindbaugh zigzagged his big frame through the parking lot, reached deep into his suit pocket for a wad of keys, and piled into the green Army sedan. He screeched off in a cloud of slush. Ernie started the jeep and we followed, about thirty yards behind at first. Steadily Ernie closed the gap to about ten. There were still two or three kimchi cabs between us at any given time as we threaded our way through the rushing flow of traffic.

Instead of turning right at the Camp Coiner intersection, Lindbaugh turned left, towards the sedate, leafy neighborhood of Huam-dong. About two blocks down the road he took another left into a narrow alley and parked. We continued up the main road, Ernie made a U-turn, doubled back, let me out just in front of the alley, and continued down the street, hung another U, and positioned himself across the street where he could see as far down the alley as possible.

Shops lined the narrow lane: a bicycle repair shop, a small fish market, a florist. Down the road a few yards a huge red banner waved in front of a small restaurant. The banner said PO SHIN TANG, "Body Protection Soup." A nice way of saying dog meat.

Lindbaugh's car was parked a few yards down from the restaurant but he was gone. I pretended to look at some of the flowers at the open-air florist. An old man, in rolled-up gray slacks and sleeveless T-shirt, shuffled over towards me. I smiled and waved him off. He seemed convinced that I was harmless and returned to his chores.

I walked a little farther down the street, until I could see through the window of the restaurant. It was dark but I could make out the big girth of Lindbaugh and the outlines of two Korean men sitting across from him at a table. I went back to the florist and waited.

Apparently, they were having lunch. I wondered if Lindbaugh could read Korean—I doubted it—and whether or not he knew what the specialty of the house was. Lunch was mercifully quick.

Lindbaugh broke through the beaded curtain and looked both ways. I faded deeper into the stall of orchids. He walked down to his car alone and got in. After he drove past, I waited until the two Koreans came out. They paused in the alleyway, as if to make sure he was gone. Then they went back inside. Maybe they had a big weekend lined up and needed some more body protection soup, since it was believed to be an aphrodisiac.

Ernie drove us back to the KPA compound. Lindbaugh's sedan was there.

I told Ernie about the dog-meat restaurant and the two Korean men sitting with Lindbaugh while he slurped his soup. Ernie nodded, bored. Just another clerk taking bribes. He didn't show any interest until I told him the two men were the same two guys who had jumped Kimiko in Itaewon.

We had four more hours until Lindbaugh got off work so, on the way to the CID Detachment, I had Ernie drop me off at the base library. They've got a few shelves there dedicated to Korean culture and history and language. I scrounged around until I found the fat Korean-English dictionary and sat down to look up Miss Pak Ok-suk's name.

The family name, Pak, was a clan name and literally millions out of the country's forty million were named that, the three major clans in Korea being Kim, Lee, and Pak. The Koreans say that if you climb to the top of a tall building in Seoul and throw a pebble off, chances are that it will land on the head of a Pak, Kim, or Lee.

At one time people with the same family name were not allowed to marry but that was done away with: It just wasn't practical. There are too many unrelated people with the same last names.

Her given name was more interesting. As I had thought, *ok* meant jade. In the Orient, jade is the most highly prized of all precious stones, and up until only a few decades earlier it had been considered more valuable than gold. Women often wore it in rings to signify that they were married.

Ironically, the second half of her name, *suk* meant virtue. Feminine virtue. Purity.

I made notes on the case and tried reading the Seoul papers. After a while, I put the dictionary back on the shelf, crumpled my notes, and threw them away.

When we got to Lindbaugh's quarters, his sedan was parked in front. After twenty minutes he appeared, nattily dressed in dark slacks, sports shirt, gray sweater, and a black windbreaker with ITCHEY FOOT BAR AND GRILL, TOLEDO, OHIO on the back. Two big fluorescent footprints framed the bar's name and seemed to step forward rhythmically as Lindbaugh waddled to his sedan. We were out of our suits and ties, too, the things that advertised us as CID agents. I wore sneakers, blue jeans, and a nylon jacket with dragons embroidered on the back—just your typical GI.

We followed him over to the Officers' Club, where he parked the Army sedan out of the way, up against the tree line. He walked to the entranceway to wait for a cab. He got one in less than ten minutes and went directly to Itaewon.

Ernie dropped me about twenty yards behind where Lindbaugh was paying the driver. I leaned back against a door across the street from the UN Club, hands in my pockets, trying to look bored, as if I were waiting for someone. Lindbaugh glanced around but not very carefully. He didn't seem to notice me. I followed his waddle up the hill.

He headed towards the King Club and for a moment I thought he was going to go in, but instead he passed the big wide steps of the entranceway and continued up the hill. Little hole-in-the-wall hostess bars lined the way. Music blared. The girls were out like they always were, in front of their respective alleys. Like trapdoor spiders, they would drag you back to their hooches, for a price. Lindbaugh got propositioned a couple of times but showed admirable restraint. At the Sloe-eyed Lady Club he went in.

Great name. They'd probably looked it up in the Korean-English dictionary not realizing that most GIs would understand slant-eyed but sloe-eyed would sort of throw them. They had a good sound system, I could hear it from ten yards out, also a lot of bright neon, and some snappy-looking ladies milling around. So who cared what the name meant?

I stopped and talked to one of the girls who had propositioned me and she dropped down to five dollars real quick since it was still early and there wasn't much traffic yet. I thanked her anyway and walked in front of the Sloe-eyed Lady Club so I could get a good look at Lindbaugh through the plate-glass windows.

He was gone.

I tried to act unconcerned, walked up a few yards, talked briefly to another girl—this one started at five dollars—and then crossed the road to get another angle on the windows of the Sloe-eyed Lady Club. The joint was empty, except for the girls. No customers. Lindbaugh must have snuck out the back.

Maybe he had someone to meet out back—a girl?—or maybe he had spotted his escorts and decided to ditch us.

I followed the road as it swerved around Itaewon. Ernie was walking down the hill towards me.

"Watch the front of the Sloe-eyed Lady Club. Lindbaugh must have slipped out the back." I pointed to the narrow alley running off through the high cement-block walls. "I'm going to check back here. If we get separated, meet me at the King Club at"—I checked my watch—"eight."

Ernie nodded and sauntered down the road. I crept into the narrow alley.

The stone and cement-block walls were so high that they blocked most of the light. I had to stop a moment and let my eyes adjust. There were wooden gates set into the stone walls but most of them were shut tight.

I walked down to about where I figured the back of the Sloe-eyed Lady would be. The gate was open. Light shone out and I heard voices, feminine voices. I peeked in. There was a small open area, mostly cement spotted with a few wilted plants. Two rows of wooden hooches extended to the two- and three-story buildings that fronted the main road of Itaewon. There was plenty of light coming from the hooches, illuminating a central path, and a few girls shuffled back and forth, shouting to their friends and busily getting ready for the night's work.

I ducked through. One of the girls noticed me, stopped in the center of the walkway, and shouted, *"Sonnim wa!"* A guest.

A couple of girls slid back their wood slat doors as I walked into the center of the hooches. Some squatted on raised vinyl platforms in front of makeup mirrors, meticulously stroking and rouging and brushing. Others, still half undressed, casually put on clothes as I watched.

I could see clearly the back of the building that housed the club. It was two stories. An old rusted stairwell rose to the second floor. Light shone in the window on the second floor and I thought I saw shadows passing across it.

Buildings in Itaewon had a club on the first floor and either apartments or professional offices on the second and third floors. The village had dentists, OB-GYN clinics, passport and visa offices, and even a travel agency—all the things the girls might need for a toothache, a pregnancy, and for when they found a GI who wanted to marry them and take them home.

I couldn't figure what function the second floor above the Sloe-eyed Lady Club served. I hadn't noticed any signs.

"You come early, GI."

"Yeah, I'm early." She was short and cute, and a few years ago, I would have said that she was too young for this business.

"You want nice girl? I have many beautiful sisters." The girl slowly waved her arm towards the entire colony of hooches.

"How about you?" I said.

"Sure. Why not?"

"Maybe. I got to go to *byonso* first."

The girl took my hand and led me towards the back wall. I could smell it before I saw it. It was nestled in the darkness between the last hooch and the wall that separated this real estate from the buildings out front.

"Is this the Sloe-eyed Lady Club here?"

"Yeah," the girl said. "I think so."

"You don't know?"

"All club same same. I don't go small clubs."

"You only go to the big clubs?"

"Yeah."

"Which ones?"

"King Club. Lucky Seven."

"Why don't you go into the small clubs?"

"*Papa-san* say no can do."

The small clubs already had their own hostesses, hand-picked girls, girls they could keep tabs on, and they didn't want the hassles of having stray business girls hustling on the premises. The big clubs, on the other hand, had a lot of floor space and a lot of seats to fill. Sometimes on paydays, when the clubs were packed with GIs, the owners made the business girls stand up along the walls to save the seats for paying customers, and to display the flowers better.

I braced my nostrils and walked into the foul-smelling latrine. It was nothing more than a rickety old closet made of rotted wood.

The floor was cement with a rectangular hole in the center that led directly down into the cesspool below. I took a leak and came back out quickly.

There didn't seem to be any way, other than climbing the fence, to get into the opening behind the Sloe-eyed Lady Club. I was going to ask the girl, when I heard a door open high above me and the creaking of metal as someone stepped out onto the decrepit stairwell. I stepped back into the latrine and closed the door. There was a small window in the wood and I could see out without being seen.

Lindbaugh was walking down the steps, his chubby face pinched with anxiety. Following slowly behind him was a swarthy Korean man, solidly built, with a square head, and my first impression of him was that he had a lot of hair for a Korean. It was hard to tell for sure, though, because of the dim light. Not that his hair was bristling out, it was short-cropped, but he was one of those guys whose beards and growth of hair are so thick that they make their complexions look darker than they actually are.

They reached the bottom floor and I popped out of the latrine, gratefully.

The little girl held onto my wrist and I almost had to drag her down between the hooches to the front gate.

"Where you go?" she said.

"Maybe I'll see you some other time," I said.

"When?"

"Soon."

I shook her loose. She was cursing and I could hear the stomping of her small feet on the pavement as I went through the gate and sprinted back to the main road. Ernie trotted up the hill and slowed when he saw me.

"I think they're waiting for a cab," he said. "Keep an eye on them while I get the jeep."

I crossed the main road of Itaewon and took a few steps into a dirt-floored alley that led off into the gradually deepening dark. A girl followed me and I talked to her, pretending to be interested, while I kept an eye on Lindbaugh and the Korean man with him.

They stood away from the main entrance of the Sloe-eyed Lady, but there was still enough light to confirm my first impression of the Korean. His black hair was short and brittle, almost kinky. His clothes were casual: a windbreaker, sports shirt, slacks. Expensive, the kind of stuff that was made in the Korean textile mills for export only. He was calm but his eyes surveyed the area carefully. They looked at me, then, seeing the girl, moved on.

Lindbaugh, on the other hand, seemed exceedingly nervous. His pinball eyes bounced everywhere, and he kept talking, and gesturing with his hands, but the Korean didn't seem to hear.

A cab chugged up the hill, made a U, and stopped in front of them. A young Korean bounced out of the passenger seat and held the back door open as the two clambered into the back. Then they were off.

Ernie squealed around the corner, spotted me in the alley, and screeched the jeep to a halt. I jumped into the passenger seat and the open-mouthed business girl didn't have time to move before we were off in a cloud of dust.

"Orange cab," I said. "The Kei In Company. It just hung a left at the MSR."

The traffic on the big road was bumper to bumper but Ernie didn't slow down. Breaks squealed, horns honked, and savage cursing marked Ernie's plunge through the traffic. He swerved, downshifted, and cut around cars and pedestrians.

I spotted the cab. It hadn't gone far because it was waiting to turn about a block further down the road. The cabbie found an opening and punched through the traffic. Another guy was waiting to make a left but Ernie swerved around his flank and edged out into the oncoming flow, making people stop. More screeching tires and curses, but we were through. Their taillights were at the top of the incline ahead. Ernie floored it and put some serious gas to the old jeep. It sputtered and responded and pretty soon we were doing about fifty. If I hadn't been watching the sides of the road we would have missed them.

"Hold it! We passed them!"

Ernie slowed, pulled over to the curb, and this time waited for the traffic to clear before making a complete turn.

We cruised on by again. They were getting out of the cab in front of a big modern two-story house with a cement-block fence around it.

Greeting them and bowing were two beautiful Korean women in full-length traditional *chima-chogori* dresses. The entranceway was bathed in yellow light from the sign above the gateway.

"Chinese characters," I said. "*Ok Lim Gong*. The Palace of the Jade Forest."

"A *gisaeng* house?"

"Got to be."

"They're giving old Lindbaugh first-class treatment."

Ernie turned into a dirt alley and found a place to park. I toyed with the translation: The Palace Amidst an Orchard of Precious Gems. Any way you sliced it, it sounded like a fun place.

Ernie stayed in the jeep while I got out and walked to the mouth of the alley. The cab was gone but now there were two more vehicles, short black limousines, and businessmen types in dark blue suits were getting out. More girls appeared, also dressed like something out of the sixteenth century. They smiled, bowed, and escorted the men inside.

I went back to the jeep. "Looks like it's going to be a big party. I'm going to try to get a better look."

Ernie started the engine. "I'll turn around."

I went back out to the alley. The buildings lining the street were brick, two and three stories high. A teahouse was advertised on the second story of the building next to the *gisaeng* house and I figured that was my best shot. I climbed the narrow cement stairwell to the teahouse and pushed through the beaded curtain.

A young woman in slacks and blouse bowed as I came in, her eyes wide with surprise. Not too many GIs came into these kinds of joints. She waited for me to do something. Korean men were scattered around the room in pairs, smoking, drinking coffee, and receiving attentive care from the hostesses seated next to them. I found an open table next to the windows facing the *gisaeng* house and sat down. My hostess stood at attention in front of the table, her hands clasped across her stomach, and her head cocked, waiting for my order.

She wasn't a bad-looking girl but was too thin and had on too much makeup and anyway I really didn't have the time. I asked her how much a cup of coffee was. She seemed relieved that I spoke Korean. Two hundred and fifty won. Fifty cents for a little porcelain thimbleful of espresso. I could buy a twelve-ounce bottle of OB for three hundred won. I asked her about ginseng tea. That was three hundred and fifty won. What the hell. At least it would kick my metabolism into high gear. I told her to bring me one.

While the hostess was gone I fumbled with the metal screw that latched the two sliding windows together. The windows were opaque, made of some sort of heavy plastic. I loosened the screw and slid the window open a crack. Bitterly cold air rushed into the warm room. People turned around and looked at me, stared for a moment, and then turned back to their coffee.

My hostess returned with a porcelain cup on a metal tray. I slid the window shut. Using two hands, she placed the tinkling cup and saucer in front of me. I pulled out a thousand-won bill and she left to get the change.

I sipped the tea. The production of ginseng root has been a Korean monopoly since ancient times. Proper ginseng grew nowhere else on earth except this mountainous peninsula. The tea was light brown and tasted bitter. There was no caffeine in it, but I knew from past experience (when Ernie used to carry a raw root in his pocket and would break off a chunk for me every now and then) that it would get your body churning until you actually developed a slight fever.

The waitress brought me my change. I smiled, thanked her, and pocketed it all. She stood there for a moment, waiting to be asked to join me. I played the stupid GI until she bowed and walked away. I took another sip of the biting herb—it grows on you—and cracked the window open.

There was an outside stairway on the *gisaeng* house. Guys in suits walked up it, escorted by women in brightly colored formal dresses. When the double doors were slid back and everyone bent over to take off their shoes, I could see inside. Lindbaugh and the Korean who brought him were seated cross-legged on the floor in front of a large table filled with plates of food and bottles of clear rice wine. Two girls sat next to them, smiling while another, off to the side, fiddled with some musical instrument that I didn't recognize.

More men came up the stairs. All bowed and shook hands with Lindbaugh first and then bowed more deeply and shook hands with his Korean comrade.

I felt a soft hand on my shoulder.

"*Yoboseiyo. Nomu chuwo.*" My hostess hugged her arms around herself, chilled, and looked at me pleadingly.

I glanced back at the *gisaeng* house. The big sliding doors had been closed. I smiled at the girl, slid the window shut, and finished my tea. When I got up and walked out, the patrons of the tearoom were no doubt relieved to see the dragons on my back.

I heard the steady crunch of feet moving up the narrow alleyway. I leaned back farther into the shadows protecting me. When the footsteps passed I poked my head out. It was Kimiko. She was bundled up in a warm coat.

She followed the alley and was quickly out of sight. I followed. Her footsteps were outlined clearly in the dirty snow. She had gone into the *gisaeng* house.

All the gates lining the back were shut tight and no lights shone in the houses behind them except the one.

I had to get closer. The cement and the brick walls blocked the sound of her steps. The ground was unpredictable. Not the flat, hard pavement on the roadway but bricks and stones placed haphazardly in the frozen earth like cobblestones.

I held my breath and stood perfectly still. She was just a few yards away from me. I knelt down carefully and lowered myself so my chest was just above the ground and, like a huge, cloth-covered salamander, I slowly inched forward until I could see. It was a double wooden door. Kimiko was rapping on it and calling out softly, "Ajima. Ajima."

Finally a piece of wood slid aside and the back door opened. An old woman held it for her, she entered, and then the door was shut again. I heard the wooden crossbar slide into place. I stood up and waited a moment, then went to the gate and tried to find any openings in the wooden slats that I could see through. There were none. It was well built and heavy and sat flush up against the brick wall. The wall was about eight feet high and shards of jagged glass, imbedded in the mortar, stuck up along the top. Coiled and rusted barbed wire wound through the glass, completing the compound's defenses.

I carefully placed my hands atop the wall, between pieces of glass, and pulled myself up until I could just see into the courtyard. It was set up like a typical Korean house. Four hooches were arranged in a U shape against the back wall facing out toward the front gate. In the center of the courtyard was an old hand pump with a lot of plastic pans and two rickety-looking wooden benches nearby. A small circular planter held the stems of what was left of a few sturdy bushes. Earthen kimchi pots lined the walls on either side of the house, most of them covered with a small inverted cone of snow. Directly below me and to the left was a small solitary building. The odor left no doubt as to its function.

The old woman puttered around on the wooden porch running the length of the four hooches. Finishing her chore, she padded along in her stocking feet and entered the small hooch off to the right.

There were lights on in the two central hooches and I could see a shadowy figure moving back and forth behind the paper windows of the wooden panel doors. From the height and general size there was no doubt in my mind. It was Kimiko and she seemed to be very busy.

I looked beneath the porch to see how many pairs of shoes were down there, and what type. There were outlines of shoes in the darkness. I couldn't make them out.

I stayed there hanging from the wall as long as I could, but my muscles were beginning to give out. I was just starting to lower myself when I saw a shadow walk toward the open door. It was Kimiko. She stood there for a minute directly in front of the opening and I could see her face clearly. She was looking up at the sky, at the stars, or maybe something even farther away. She turned suddenly, as if she had been startled out of her reverie by a sound and, without looking back, she slammed the door shut.

My arms were cramping up and I wasn't even sure I could unfold them. I just let go of my grip on the cold brick and dropped back down to the slippery pavement. I lost my footing, gyrated for a moment, arms flailing, and then fell flat on my ass.

I hit flush and wasn't hurt but I just sat there for a moment, taking inventory of my chilled limbs and slowly unfolding the knotted muscles of my forearms and biceps. When the cold moisture began to seep through the seat of my pants I jumped back up and swatted the snow off my rear end.

I walked back to the recessed doorway across the street and stood in the shadows to think for a while.

Kimiko had been wearing black silk stockings with a black garter belt and a black brassiere. When she looked up at the sky,

I had been staring at her jet black pubic hair. Further back in the room was sprawled Mr. Lindbaugh in equally scanty attire.

Two hours later she came out and hailed a taxi on the main road. We followed it back to Itaewon and the Lucky Seven Club.

Inside, Kimiko wore a bright blue low-cut dress and sat by herself at a table near the stage. She ordered a big liter bottle of OB and a bottle of Suntory whiskey with a small bucket of ice. A young boy arrived carrying a square metal box. The boy squatted next to Kimiko's table and slid back the walls of the box, revealing two steaming plates of food. One was *mul mandu*, boiled meat dumplings, and the other was *chapchae*, rice noodles mixed with beef and vegetables. The boy placed the plates on Kimiko's table, along with a few small side dishes and a short bottle of soy sauce. He closed the box up, bowed, and trotted through the half-full tables and out of the club.

Kimiko split apart her wooden chopsticks, rubbed them together to get off all the splinters, and dug in. She didn't notice Ernie and me standing in the back of the room.

"She's rich," Ernie said. "A catered feast."

"Didn't take long."

"And she couldn't have made it entirely on her charm. What's she celebrating?"

We backed out of the club and I almost jumped when I saw him but managed to keep my eyes straight ahead. At the bottom of the hill, we turned towards the King Club.

"Did you see him?"

"Who?"

"The guy in the alley."

"No."

"One of the pair who jumped Kimiko. Smoking a *tambei*, in the alley next to the Lucky Seven."

"What a coincidence," Ernie said.

"Yeah."

The King Club was packed: wall to wall with GIs, business girls, and a few American civilians. Ernie and I shooed a couple of business girls away and took a small table back in the darkest corner. A couple of waitresses came by to serve us but I waved them off until Miss Oh came close and then I grabbed her wrist and pulled her over and ordered two OBs.

She was still pissed but, after all, we were two customers in desperate need of beer and, as a cocktail waitress, it was her sworn duty to provide.

When she brought the beers back I made her wait for the money.

"The only reason I walked out of here with Kimiko last night," I said, "is because of my job."

She glowered at me.

"We all have to do things we don't want to do sometimes. And I'm sorry if I made you feel bad. Let me buy you a drink, any kind you want."

The sullen expression of her beautiful face didn't change but her eyebrows lifted just slightly. She flounced away.

"You're in for it now," Ernie said.

A couple of minutes later she brought back something big and red and full of tropical growth.

"Two thousand, two hundred won," she said. Over four bucks.

GIs at other tables and business girls gazed at us. Smirking. Imagine me, Itaewon's number-one Cheap Charlie, buying something ridiculous like this. But it was the price I had to pay to restore Miss Oh's face. I forked over the money.

She bounded away happily. In a few moments she came back, put her metal cocktail tray down on our table, lifted the big tumbler, and sipped her drink. I was certain there wasn't an ounce of hooch in it. She put the drink back down, smiled at us, and then went back to her appointed rounds.

"Looks like you're back on the sleeping mat, pal."

"At what a price."

Ernie shrugged. "A few bucks."

"It's not the money. It's the self-respect. Nobody but a dildo spends money on those sweetheart drinks."

"Maybe you can join Dildos Anonymous."

"You're a world of help, you are."

Later, when Miss Oh had returned, I asked her about the man I had seen with Lindbaugh.

"The man at the Sloe-eyed Lady Club," I said. "He has an office upstairs or maybe he lives upstairs. I think he's the honcho."

She ran her fingers over my cheeks. "A lot of hair? Black?"

"Yes."

"Kwok," she whispered, her voice soft, as if she were in church.

Before Miss Oh told me about Kwok, she made me promise not to repeat the story to anyone. "If anyone talks about his daddy," she said, "he gets *taaksan* angry."

She held her forefingers to her head, as if she had grown horns.

Although Kwok didn't like the subject discussed in his presence, apparently the demimonde of Itaewon was well aware of his mixed ancestry. His mother was a farm woman, seeking refuge with the rest of the country during the Korean War, when she and her family had run into a small, bedraggled contingent of Turkish soldiers. They were part of the United Nations forces sent over to protect the South Koreans from the attacking Northern Communists and their Chinese comrades. Kwok's mother was raped. The result was the man who was now trying to take control of all the rackets in Itaewon.

After the war, when things had settled back to some sort of normalcy, the young woman with the half-Turkish baby didn't have a chance of finding a husband. War had left young men in short supply and the Koreans can be sticklers on little items like racial purity. But the family of the young mother loved her, and they pooled all their money for a dowry. A charcoal carrier, whose tuberculosis and gimpy leg had kept him out of the war, was finally persuaded to accept the dowry—and the young woman and her half-Turkish baby who came with it.

His name was Kwok and he turned out to be a drunk. A vicious one. He squandered the dowry on rice liquor, gambling, and fancy women, and began to vent his rage on the young boy who had taken his name. He beat the boy for imagined offenses and made him do most of the work at the *yontan* yard and carry the charcoal briquettes to customers throughout the rural village. The boy carried them on a wooden A-frame strapped to his little back. His mother tried to protect him as much as she could but it was of little use.

Young Kwok grew up tough and immensely strong. He worked and cursed and drank like a man before he was ten years old. His mother contracted tuberculosis from his stepfather and by the time her son was thirteen, she had succumbed.

By now the young man was approaching his full growth and the gimpy elder Kwok had begun to fear him. Fear made him drink more and made him more vicious until, it was said, the young Kwok simply strangled him.

The official police report said that the elder Kwok had drowned in his own vomit. The police figured the young man had suffered enough, but he had brought shame on the village so they forced him to leave. Young Kwok hopped on a train and went off to Seoul, to receive his higher education on the streets. He was sixteen.

His strong-arm exploits, unorthodox in Korea, were terrifying and soon brought him to the attention of racketeers. They considered having him killed. He was affecting their operations. Instead, they decided to discipline him, and keep him on a leash, like an attack dog awaiting his master's bidding. He acquiesced but ended up turning on a few of his immediate masters, gradually working his way up to the top of the syndicate until he was in a position to make a grab for control of Itaewon.

I said, "Do you think he will eat all of Itaewon?"

Purple light caressed Miss Oh's body. "Yes," she said. "He will win." She stared off into the din of the bar. "You should see his eyes."

10

I had told Ernie to meet me at the coffee shop of the Hamilton Hotel at six in the morning. He hadn't been happy about it since it was Saturday and we were supposed to be off, but he had promised. Now he was late.

It was already 6:20 and I was sipping my second cup of instant coffee. I'd already paid the teenage girl in the waitress uniform over four hundred won. Miss Pak Ok-suk was beginning to get expensive and I wondered if she was worth it. I could have been asleep back at the hooch with Miss Oh. Certainly Lindbaugh had crashed, probably with one of those girls at the *gisaeng* party.

Last night I had answered Ernie's grumbling with a conjecture. For all we knew, the guy waiting in the alley for Kimiko had been planning on killing her, and early this morning, when we went to check her out, we might stumble on a corpse.

But I didn't think so. I figured if these hoodlums had wanted to waste Kimiko, they could have done it long before this, and if they had planned to kill her last night I doubted that they would have waited around in alleys to do it.

They were following her. For the same reason they had roughed her up before and searched her hooch. The problem was that I didn't know what that reason was.

But the harassment had stopped, it seemed, and somehow Kimiko had come into money. We'd seen evidence of that. She was enjoying herself, putting on the dog at the Lucky Seven, a place that had barred her in the past and had just had one of its employees killed—Miss Pak Ok-suk. Kimiko had to hustle every night just to keep afloat. Suddenly she was flush and coasting.

Perhaps the old crone who ran the club didn't feel like tussling with Kimiko any longer and let her come and go as she pleased.

Had Kimiko been paid for murdering Pak Ok-suk or for setting her up to be murdered? But why would anyone want to kill a simple business girl?

The first night after the murder, when Kimiko disappeared, where had she gone?

Her friend is murdered. She disappears. When she returns, thugs search her room and keep her under surveillance. Then she comes into money.

She's got something they want. The only way to find out what is to do the same thing the thugs are doing. Follow her.

Tires screeched in the parking lot outside the coffee shop and somebody leaned heavy on their horn. Ernie.

I got up, pocketed all my change, and pushed through the turnstile doors.

"You're late."

"The Nurse wanted me to practice my injection technique."

We sped up the hill towards Itaewon and Ernie pulled to the side of the road before we got to the turnoff to Kimiko's hooch. I walked up the road while he waited, the engine idling for a quick takeoff. I stayed across the street from the entrance to the alley-way, hoping I wouldn't be noticed. I walked up, past the alley, waited a couple of minutes, and then made another pass going downhill. I returned to the jeep.

"He's still waiting, in a doorway across from her hooch."

"She's probably still asleep."

"Probably."

"What now?"

"We wait. Hide the jeep."

Ernie groaned, jammed the gearshift into reverse, and whined down the road and then back into an alley out of sight.

In a few minutes he came around the corner walking towards me.

"I need some coffee."

"Me too."

Everything in Itaewon was closed. This part of Seoul was reserved for the night.

The shutters on a market up the road rattled and then one of the panels fell back in. A middle-aged Korean man, in sleeveless T-shirt and pajama bottoms, methodically unlocked and pulled back the protective partitions. We waited until the front of the store was completely open and then sauntered towards the little one-story building. I bought a small bottle of orange juice and Ernie bought some gum. I talked to the old man about coffee. He said they didn't have any. I told him about how bad we needed it and finally he relented and yelled something to his wife, who was just getting up from her bed on the floor in the room directly behind the store. Two children, about ten and twelve years old, were still asleep under the blankets.

We waited outside, keeping an eye on the alley, while his wife boiled water. I shook my bottle of orange juice and drank it down in one gulp. I returned the empty to the man, who was sweeping behind the counter. His wife, with a robe on now, came out with a tray and poured two glasses full of boiling water and then mixed in generous portions of instant coffee, Maxwell House spelled out in Korean characters. I offered her money. She waved it away and went back to her room.

Outside we sat on stools at a metal table with a big OB beer umbrella over it. The coffee was good. I had been so busy last night that I hadn't been able to get too drunk.

I felt better than I had in a while. And grateful to the store owner and his wife who had made the coffee for us.

In so many ways we were so different from the Koreans, and sometimes the GIs resented them a lot. But in a thousand small ways the Koreans were extremely generous and friendly. I imagined it was that way with all the people who had misunderstood each other over the centuries. Hatred in war and then friendship, and even love, when you had time to get to know them.

Last night's booze and this morning's caffeine were getting to me.

A gnarled stick poked over the wall of the hooch on the corner across the street. I elbowed Ernie. We took our coffee with us and walked back into the store.

A hand reached up on the wall and then another and then a head followed, hooded by gray material. The top of the ten-foot-high wall was studded with various colored shards of broken bottles but the person behind the wall placed a straw mat atop the glass and gingerly pulled herself over. It was a woman. A Buddhist nun. The hood turned into a gray cape and beneath it was a long dress of the same material. She wore soft-soled black shoes and black stockings that disappeared beneath the dress.

She clung to the top of the fence like a cat. Carefully, she lifted the straw mat and threw it back into the courtyard she had just left. Then she dropped herself to the street, hit, and rolled smoothly onto her buttocks and back. A jumpmaster at the Fort

Benning Airborne School couldn't have done better. She popped up, dusted herself off, and tiptoed to the mouth of the alley. She peered around the corner. The hoodlums were half-asleep, their faces turned away from her. She glanced around in our direction.

That's when I saw her face.

She darted across the alleyway like a large gray mouse. Then she trotted down the hill and slowed to a brisk walk, looking back occasionally, and straightening her shoulders when she realized that no one would be following. She brandished her polished walking stick in front of her and looked for all the world like a proud representative of a religion that had preached peace and mercy for the last twenty-four hundred years.

We put our half-empty glasses down on the counter and waved our thanks to the owner. And then we were running. Ernie had the jeep started and moving before I could climb all the way in.

After Kimiko.

Kimiko knew the hoodlums were waiting for her outside and they had underestimated her. She had put on the Buddhist nun outfit, climbed over the wall that surrounded the cluster of hooches among which she lived, crossed the neighbor's courtyard, and then climbed the wall that led to the main street running through Itaewon.

She was more careless now because she hadn't counted on a second set of pursuers.

The jeep hummed through the frigid Korean countryside. The rice paddies were brown and frozen, and most of the trees had long ago dropped their leaves for the winter. Smoke curled from straw-thatched houses, sturdy oxen pulled wooden carts, and heavily bundled children skated on smooth fields of ice.

Ernie had the heater on full blast but it was still cold in the jeep.

"That must be her plan," Ernie said. "Freeze our balls off before we get to wherever she's going."

Kimiko had walked a couple of blocks down the Main Supply Route and then caught a local bus that took her to the Central Seoul Bus Station. It had been a little rough tracking her there. Ernie kept the jeep idling while I scouted around, trying to keep my big six-foot-four body from being too conspicuous. Luckily, it had been easy to spot her from a distance in her Buddhist nun outfit. Unless I had gotten her confused with another nun, in which case we were screwed. But I didn't think I had. She bought a ticket and boarded a bus heading north. We followed at a respectable distance. There were a number of stops—it wasn't an express—and at each one Ernie held back a little, keeping the jeep across the street on the blind side of anyone getting off the bus, while I trotted across the road and hid behind whatever was available to see if Kimiko got off.

So far she hadn't.

I also kept an eye on the back windows of the bus to see if anyone was showing any curiosity about the jeep that was following them. So far no one had.

If the bus driver was anything more than somnolent he must have noticed that we were following. We weren't trying to be subtle about it because we couldn't afford to lose her. There was no indication that it bothered him, though.

As we traveled north it became increasingly obvious that this road, known as the MSR, the Main Supply Route, had been built by, and for, the military. Small compounds appeared with greater regularity as the bus drew inexorably closer to the Demilitarized Zone.

I read the signs in Korean: "SLOW, COMPOUND AHEAD." As we passed, the armed soldiers blew their whistles and waved us on. Every half mile or so there seemed to be another installation.

One small compound was American. The tall guard at the gate wore a fur-lined winter cap. Its upturned bill made him look like a cossack. Over the guard shack a large sign read: INFORMATION ON NORTH KOREAN INTRUDERS WELCOMED AT THIS GATE.

Then came the roadblocks. Korean soldiers with M-14 rifles peered suspiciously into the bus and then motioned the driver forward to continue the northward journey.

And then the tank traps. Huge cement blocks, weighing tons each—formed enormous overhangs across the road. Loaded with explosives, they would be blown by the last retreating South Korean units—the final attempt to block the advance of the onrushing North Korean tanks.

The bus swam upstream against a river of Korean soldiers. Most had huge packs on their backs, some humped commo gear, and some had machine guns balanced like scales across their shoulders. But they all had a somber and weary look, as if they'd been on this road for years, centuries, a never-ending stream of young men going off to cram their bodies into the insatiable maw of an impervious history.

They were on maneuvers; they had left their base camps and they were moving out. Behind them the deep rumbling of tanks came toward us, the sound carrying like tremors through the cold, packed earth. They lined both sides of the road, and when Ernie followed the bus to a turnoff, he had to flash his lights and wait until there was a break in the endless files to make his left turn.

And then there were no U.S. military compounds, no signal sites, no antiaircraft artillery batteries. Just flat farmland with a few rolling hills between valleys.

In a few more miles we'd come to the foothills of the mountain range that ran along the Korean peninsula like the jagged spine of a long-dead dragon. Where was she going?

The road through the wooded hills narrowed, and gradually there were fewer villages and fewer stops for us to worry about. When the incline really steepened, the road started to twist like a snake as the bus climbed the mountain out of the misty valley. There must have been only a few people on the bus now and Kimiko had to be one of them. Kangnung sat on the other side of the mountain range near the coast of what the Koreans call the East Sea. The rest of the world called it the Sea of Japan.

Suddenly, the bus stopped. There was no village nearby that we could see. Nothing.

Ernie reacted quickly. He zipped past the bus to an outcropping of rock beside the road, and backed the jeep up behind it. We were concealed. He shut off the engine.

The bus idled but not for long. The driver shifted gears and the big powerful diesel groaned slowly up the side of the mountain, picking up speed as it went. We chanced a look.

Across the road, a grove of poplar trees rustled in the breeze, but there were no buildings and no one there, only a wooden sign and a small footpath that led off past the poplars into the evergreens.

Ernie looked at me for a decision. We could always catch up with the bus but we were taking the risk that Kimiko would get off while we weren't watching. I told him to wait while I investigated.

The sign was painted with an inverted swastika, the ancient symbol for a Buddhist temple that predated the Nazis by about two and a half millennia. The sign, sharpened at one end like an arrow, pointed up the path. The fresh imprints of two small feet led away from the bus stop. Soft-soled shoes. I trotted back to the jeep feeling particularly proud of the Indian blood of my ancestors from Mexico.

Of course, the pathway had been carefully raked and any idiot could have followed those tracks. The Apache trackers didn't have to worry about their place in history.

Ernie chained the jeep and we started after her. A few yards up the footpath we heard it. It wasn't just a sound but a long low reverberation that passed through the brush and the forest that surrounded us and then entered our bodies, seeping into our bones and our innards, lifting them gently on a slow wave and then passing serenely by.

A gong. It was calling supplicants to prayer.

That was us, a couple of supplicants. The kind who sit on a stool waiting for the bar to open, hoping the bartender won't be upset at the intrusion and will slam a cold one down in front of us, like some sort of nugget of holy wisdom.

From the low timbre of the gong I figured we weren't very far at all from the temple. I didn't want to stumble upon someone too soon, so I motioned to Ernie for us to get off the footpath, and we crashed straight up a hill through the underbrush until we found a good vantage point.

The temple was made of wood that must have come from the surrounding trees. Except for its enormous size and the smooth, finely shaped slats, it would have looked something like a log cabin. There was a gateway, a large courtyard of raked gravel, and then the main hall. The roof of the hall was shingled and turned up slightly at the ends like the raised toe of a young girl in a traditional dance. Life-size figurines of monkeys lined the roof, protecting the holy place from demons. The foundation of the big hall was made of squared stones neatly fitted together.

Out back were what appeared to be living quarters and to the left, offices or study halls. Fallow but neatly outlined fields stretched out for a couple of acres until they were overcome again by the forest. The place was simple, elegant, and Spartan.

Shaved-head monks in blue robes floated towards the main hall.

"Looks like boot camp," Ernie said.

A large wooden mallet swished through the air just inside the open doorway of the main hall and the gong sounded again.

"Must be chow time."

"Prayer time."

"For me," Ernie said, "it's chow time."

We hadn't eaten all day and it was almost noon. Sacrilegious. I hadn't expected to shadow Kimiko all the way out here. And there weren't any Burger Kings in this neighborhood—or on this continent, for that matter.

"We'll get some chow in one of those villages we passed."

"They better uncork another pot of kimchi because I'm half starved."

Gray robes fluttered amidst a sea of blue. Her arms were entwined with two monks who walked on either side of her.

"That Kimiko sure makes friends easy," Ernie said.

Once everyone was inside the temple they bowed, knelt down, and started chanting. After it had gone on for about twenty minutes I paced around the edge of the hill, trying to find a better vantage point to view the layout of the monastery. The stone foundation beneath the main hall was about four feet high and there were a couple of buildings directly behind it and attached. My guess was that there was a basement or some kind of underground storage beneath the main hall, otherwise the foundation wouldn't have been as large and sturdy as it was.

A cliff dropped off behind the monastery. It looked sheer from where we stood and opened onto a panoramic view of the valley below. The hills surrounding the monastery, including the one we were on, were steep and enclosed the monastery grounds in a cozy little basin. The open fields between the ground and the hills provided plenty of time for the monks to spot anyone approaching. All in all, the monastery was the perfect place to stash something.

Maybe that's why Kimiko was here. And maybe that's why those hoodlums who searched her room had found nothing and Kimiko had seemed unconcerned that they would. And it would explain why she had been so careful to shake her pursuers before setting out for this fortress in the woods.

When the chanting was over, Kimiko came out into the courtyard, bowing to the two monks who had escorted her in. They bowed back deeply.

"She must have laid it on heavy when they passed the contribution plate," Ernie said.

The monks escorted her to the open gate and bowed once again as they separated. We waited until she had passed our position and then we scooted quickly around the waist of the hill.

Kimiko led us up a narrow path and in a few minutes we were on top of a small hill covered with a neatly tended lawn and a few benches facing out toward the huge valley below. Vegetable fields and small clumps of fruit trees reached across the valley, and in the distance gradually rose the magnificence of the mountains.

The hills on the sides of the valley were covered with saplings, barren now except for the pines. The large rounded slope to the right of us was spotted only with shrubs and four large white placards evenly spaced. Each placard had a neatly printed word written on it in Korean script.

The signs were a warning to keep away. Like many other spots in Korea, this hill had been so laden with undetonated bombs, mines, and explosives of all kinds, that the government had not even bothered to clear it but had just decided to keep people out—a lethal reminder of the war that had so devastated the peninsula. There were also small burial mounds scattered all around it. Each mound was about six feet in diameter and four feet high. Some of the richer families had built small cement pagodas and even statues of the deceased atop the mounds. We heard the clanging of cymbals and the wailing voices of mourners. Two monks with shaven heads and purple robes led the procession, each swinging a censer filled with incense. Behind them walked the chief monk. Behind him were six men carrying a huge red palanquin. It was engraved with gold dragon's heads, and elaborate Buddhist symbols. A bell atop it rang discordantly.

Behind the palanquin came the mourners. They were wailing and moaning and all of them were dressed head to toe in clothing made of drab yellow sackcloth. Among them was Kimiko, now wearing a sackcloth hat.

The procession continued down the dusty pathway to the

other side of the hill and we followed. There was a long chanting ceremony led by the monks, and finally they lifted a body out of the palanquin and lowered it into a waiting hole cut into the side of a mound. Kimiko stood rigid.

The body was placed in a stone sarcophagus, and two scruffy-looking grave diggers began to shovel dirt to rebuild the mound.

The procession reformed with the now empty palanquin and returned along the hill, curving down toward the main road. They trudged silently for some minutes. At the bottom of the hill, the mourners filed on to a large gray bus. There was a generous square door at the rear that was just wide enough for the palanquin. Once they got on the bus, the mourners whipped off their hats and began laughing and talking and lighting up cigarettes.

Kimiko pulled off her hat and handed it to one of the professional mourners. She got into the front seat of the bus. We waited in the tree line. The bus took off, leaving a cloud of dust in its wake. It swirled in the chill wind.

We trotted across the road towards the boulders that concealed our jeep.

Ernie got there first and let out a groan.

The jeep had been jacked up on piles of flat rocks and the wheels were gone. Ernie walked around the vehicle, cursing as he went. The spare tire and the can of mo-gas strapped to the back hadn't been touched, and neither had the chain that immobilized the steering wheel. The innards of the engine also seemed to be intact.

We stared at the useless vehicle for a while, both of us wondering what to do next.

"How much money do you have?"

Ernie checked his pockets. "Twenty bucks."

"I got a little over ten. I'll catch a ride to one of those villages back there and see if I can find us some tires."

"Without 'em it's going to be sort of hard to explain this shit at 21 T Car."

"We were on official duty."

"The first sergeant took us off the case."

"They couldn't hold us to that. Even the first sergeant wouldn't be that much of an asshole."

Ernie looked at me.

I turned my head.

"Well, maybe we just better get some tires."

It would be a long wait for the next bus. I was fidgety. Something was bothering me. I walked back to the jeep and saw the lug nuts. Six on each brake drum. We'd been had.

The monks came out of the woods, laughing. They rolled the four tires towards us, and Ernie and I had to jump and dodge so as not to be hit.

Ernie's neck and face turned bright red until I could even see crimson beneath his light brown hair. He sprang across the road at the monks.

All of them had their heads shaved and wore the same blue robes and leather sandals as their brethren in the monastery. Three of them were very young. Maybe teenagers. But I realized that with a shaved head and fresh complexion, an Oriental man was liable to look much younger than he actually was. They were probably in their early twenties. About the same age as me and Ernie. But they were acting silly. They thought rolling the tires down the hill at us was the greatest joke in the world. Cosmic, I guess you could call it.

The tallest of the monks looked as if he was in his mid thirties. He smiled and remained calm as Ernie charged.

Ernie let loose a big roundhouse aimed at the monk's bulb head, but the guy just lowered his body slightly by flexing his knees and moved his right foot back. The blow missed his nose by no more than an inch and Ernie stumbled forward, tripping. He went down. Before Ernie could get up, the monk was on him. He twisted Ernie's arm behind his back and braced a knee on his spine, then lowered his weight. Ernie couldn't move. He sputtered and cursed. I stood in front of the monk, waiting for him to let Ernie go.

Ernie calmed somewhat when he realized that he was helpless and that I was there. The monk stood up quickly, like a crane rising from a swamp, and stepped back.

I helped Ernie to his feet and he cursed some more and dusted himself off. The monk's face was calm with just the hint of a smile, but there was no anger at being attacked and no smug flush of victory at having bested Ernie. The young monks behind him were smiling. No malice there. Just sheer . . . enjoyment.

The older monk spoke. "I am sorry we took your wheels. We will be happy to put them back on for you."

His enunciation was precise. He must have studied English at the university level.

"Why did you take them off?"

The monk remained perfectly still. "It seemed the easiest way to delay you. You have been following our friend. We thought it best if you didn't."

"Kimiko?"

"Yes. I think that is her professional name."

"You know her profession?"

"Oh, yes. Her life has been very hard. But she is a great soul. I think she is making progress—spiritually—and will probably achieve a more rewarding life in her next incarnation."

"No nirvana yet?"

"Who can tell?"

Ernie adjusted his clothes, trying to get the dirt off the back of his shirt, and glared at the erudite monk. "The closest she ever got to nirvana was when somebody overtipped her."

The monk glanced at Ernie but his expression didn't change. "She has been a great supporter of our temple for many years."

"How many years?"

"Since the war. The temple and outbuildings were completely destroyed during the fighting. Both sides saw it as a stronghold and a vantage point from which to track enemy movements. After they left, our sister helped us rebuild."

"She gave you money?"

"Yes."

"Because of her devotion to religion?"

"Yes. But also because of our master."

"Your master?"

"Yes. He reestablished the temple and died a few years after the war, after the work was finished."

"Why would Kimiko want to use her hard-earned money to help him?"

"Because he was her husband."

Ernie continued his cursing as we sped down the road.

"Take it easy, GI. It's not every day that you get a free Zen lesson."

He glanced at me. "You talking about the tires?"

"Yeah."

His knuckles whitened on the steering wheel. "Fuck a Zen lesson!"

Quick learner.

After keeping us in conversation for a few more minutes the young monks had put our tires back on. The elder monk had offered us lunch at the temple and I would have loved to check the place out but I declined since Ernie was still fuming.

The story he'd told about Kimiko had just heightened the mystery of the woman for me. After World War II, when she'd been chased out of Itaewon along with all the other *gisaeng* girls who catered to the Japanese, she'd wandered for a long time and almost starved to death.

When the Korean War broke out she was on the road, as most everyone was, streaming south to evade the Communist North Korean invaders. She fell in with a young man, a fellow refugee, who was as broke as she but very generous and very kind to her. When the frontlines solidified somewhat, Kimiko was able to go back to plying her trade near the bases of the United Nations forces that had flooded into Korea. The young man stayed with her, still doing any kind of coolie labor he could find during the day, and pretended not to notice Kimiko's nightly assignations.

After MacArthur's landing at Inchon, and the second retaking of Seoul, the young man told Kimiko that he must return north to refurbish the monastery from which he had fled. All the monks had been killed by the northern Reds; only he had escaped. Kimiko wanted to go with him, he wouldn't let her. He did tell her where the monastery was and how to find him if the war ever ended. Eventually it did. And Kimiko found him. He was the head of a fledgling Buddhist monastery. She came as a simple suppli-cant, not advertising the fact that she and the master had lived as man and wife.

The master wasn't ashamed of her, though, and told all the monks how she had helped him and how they had been one dur-ing the disruption of wartime. Kimiko continued to visit and make contributions for years afterward. A few years after the master had died, Kimiko got in trouble up north in Yongjukol and was sent to jail.

Who had she buried, I had wanted to know, even though the answer seemed obvious.

"Miss Pak," the monk replied.

11

Yongsan Compound on Monday morning was bursting with energy. I bundled up and walked out into the cold air, past the deep reds and browns of the old brick buildings and past the leaf-less trees, shivering like skeletons in the morning breeze, past the soldiers and civilians scurrying to their posts.

First I went to the snack bar and got a warm cup of coffee. I didn't bother with a copy of the *Stripes*. I had too much to think about.

I wanted to get out to the ville and talk to Ginger, but I would be lucky if the place opened by noon. Meanwhile I had to kill some time.

The Lower Four Club opened at eight on weekdays. I fin-ished my coffee, went for the free refill, and by the time I was good and hopped up on caffeine, I walked up the hill to the club. It was 9:05.

I tried to figure why I kept pressing on this case. Everybody else was happy. The first sergeant was happy, the Eighth Army provost marshal was happy, the chief of staff was happy—so why did I keep going after it?

Part of the reason was Miss Pak. Someone had denied her the rest of her life. She wasn't happy.

There was also Spec-4 Johnny Watkins. He was about to become a bitter young man.

Why did the damn Army make me take an oath if they weren't serious about it?

The wind whipped in sudden gusts down the road. The Lower Four Club loomed up ahead.

My reasons for wanting to solve the case went even deeper. When I had been moving from home to home, handled as just another number by an overburdened bureaucracy, it had been the odd individual who had taken an interest in me that had saved me. They had kept me from drowning in despair.

I owed something to Miss Pak Ok-suk and Mr. Watkins. Not because they were friends or relatives but just because they had been assigned to me: my responsibility. I'd be damned if I'd take the easy route and not do my best for them.

Kimiko was another matter. I'd developed a grudging respect for her. Just a few days ago I had thought of her as the sleaziest short-time trick-turning artist in the village. Knowing something about her had made me realize how she had ended up here, how she had struggled to stay alive, and what her hopes had been. I was starting to like her.

But the problem was that Kimiko was standing between me and doing my duty for Miss Pak and Johnny Watkins. I was either going to find a way around her or I'd bust through her.

I had three days before Johnny Watkins went on trial.

The cocktail lounge of the Lower Four Club was open. The light was dim, glassware tinkled, and the place reeked of sliced lemon, disinfectant, and stale booze. Home again.

A few of the stools were already taken. Retirees. Gravelly-voiced Merle, cheerful Kenny Burke, somber old Hermann the German.

"How's it hanging, George?"

"Straight down, Kenny. How are you guys?"

"Gradually getting rid of the shakes." Kenny lifted his glass as if to demonstrate. Ice rattled.

I ordered a beer. Mr. Pyon, the bartender, served me and then went back to his station by the cash register. My eyes adjusted to the dim light. Across the bar, slot machines blinked on and off, waiting for the crowd of inveterate gamblers that would filter in before noon. Two pretty young Korean waitresses, in bright red dresses, chatted quietly with old Mr. Pyon: a grandfather making mild jokes with his granddaughters.

None of the business girls had made their way into the club yet. Still too early.

Two husky Korean men clad in cooks' white uniforms wheeled a huge metal cart back to the kitchen laden with various sized card board boxes. Stocking up for the day's business. One of them brought Merle and Kenny an illicit breakfast.

With the food in front of them, Merle and Kenny got busy. They buttered their rolls and then started in on the condiments. Merle must have put half the contents of the pepper shaker on the various items on his plate. Kenny, meanwhile, covered his scrambled eggs with a puddle of Louisiana hot sauce. Then they traded.

Maybe Vietnam had done it to them.

The Lower Four Club was the hub for certain of the American expatriates: electronics technicians making extra pay for the "hardship tour," insurance salesmen thriving in a sea of uninsured young bachelors, and the occasional representative for a distributorship zeroing in on the PX market.

Many of them were veterans, military retirees living on their pension checks, former NCOs who'd finished their twenty years and now got a check every month for fifty percent of their former pay. Most of them held part-time, horse-shit jobs on the compound. Almost to a man, the retirees had a Korean wife or mistress who they lived with down in the village. A lot of them had kids. Often it was their second set; the first kids, by an American wife, were grown and on their own.

They were a strange lot. A few of them had lived through the Korean War and couldn't get away from it. Most of them didn't really understand why they lived in Korea. They only understood somehow that they would never go home.

I sipped the cold hops. The beer tasted good against the film of coffee still on my palate.

Five minutes later Ernie walked in. He had the Nurse with him. We walked over to the dining room and each ordered the ninety-five-cent breakfast special: two eggs, bacon or sausage, hash browns, toast, and coffee or tea. I had two of them. With beer. Ernie had one. And then he ate half of what was on the Nurse's plate.

She spread jam on his toast and seemed very happy.

By the time we got out to Itaewon we were all half looped. I had talked them into going with me to the American Club and I had told Ernie about the information I needed.

"Why didn't you find that shit out before?"

"In all the excitement, I forgot about it."

"What excitement?"

Sometimes I wondered if Ernie wasn't suffering from brain damage.

The American Club was completely empty. All the chairs were upside down atop the tables and someone had just finished a thorough mopping of the floor. The Lower Four Club, by contrast, was jumping by the time we left. People spend their days on the compound and their nights in Itaewon.

I pulled a line of stools off the bar and we sat down. Ginger came out of the back room, her hair tied up with a heavy-duty barrette, her hands in long yellow gloves.

"*Aigu! Watkun a!*" You're here.

We ordered three cold OBs from Ginger and she called back to one of her boys, who hustled out and started putting all the chairs down on the floor. She dimmed the lights and turned on the stereo system. Gordon Lightfoot. Ginger was a genius. She remembered everything, including her customers' favorite musicians. No memory loss there.

She took off her rubber gloves, wiped some sweat from her brow, and fussed with her hair for a while. When Ernie and the Nurse became engaged in conversation, she leaned toward me.

"Why you no come, Georgie? Miss Lim she been looking for you."

"I thought she was mad, about the last time she saw me with Kimiko."

Ginger shook her head. "Yeah. She was mad. But I told her you CID. Sometimes you have to hang around with people you don't really like. To get information. She thought about it. She calmed down. She's okay now. Pretty soon she go back to the States. You be nice to her, okay, Georgie? Don't make Ginger lose face."

She sliced her chubby hand across her round face.

"Okay, Ginger. Don't worry. You call her now. Tell her I'm sorry."

Ginger's face brightened and she trundled off to the phone. When she came back, she was smiling.

"Did you get that information you were going to get for me, Ginger?"

"What's that?"

"About the girl who used to be Kimiko's friend. Before Pak Ok-suk."

"Oh yeah, I got." Ginger crossed her arms on the bar and leaned close. "She was young girl. Pretty too, like Miss Pak. Kimiko take her, introduce many men, make a lot of money. One day this girl gone. Nobody know why. Some people say she went back to country. Back to her family."

"What was her name?"

"Li Jin-ai."

I made a motion with my hand as if I were scribbling. Ginger brought me a pad and pencil. I wrote the name in English and then in Korean, but I misspelled the Korean so Ginger wrote it for me correctly.

"Did she have any friends here in Itaewon? Other than Kimiko?"

"I don't know. Not many, I think. She wasn't here long."

"How long?"

"Maybe three or four months."

"Which club did she hang out at?"

"The Double Oh Seven Club."

Another boy came in and Ginger got busy shouting orders to him about more cleaning. She kept a very clean club. No stale booze smell, just the lingering fragrance of ammonia. I liked jaded old places better. Where the liquor and the sweat and the burnt tobacco has seeped into the pores of the leather and the wood and the cement.

The wheels in Ernie's mind were churning, I could see, as he leaned in at the bar rail.

"Aw," he said, "we might as well face it. When you figure all we got to do and then add the time to do it, we sure as shit aren't going to get much time down in the ville. All this because some broad got herself killed," Ernie said.

"Remember, the mortician's report said Miss Pak had been sexually abused just prior to her death," I said, trying to interest him.

Ernie lowered his beer and looked at me in open-mouthed incredulity. "Sexually abused? Every girl in this country has been sexually abused." Ernie turned and stared intently at the vacant wall. "A crusade," he said, and let out a dramatic sigh. "There goes our time in the village."

"Not necessarily. I might be able to wrap this thing up quick." I gave Ernie my best sly smile but it never has seemed to work very well. "I got an idea."

"You're full of them." But he couldn't resist. "What is it?"

I took a quick drink of my OB. "We could solve this case."

Ernie's head swiveled. "You must have been mainlining rice wine again."

"No," I said. "I'm serious. I mean, we're investigators, aren't we? We're highly trained dicks for the greatest investigatory agency in the world, aren't we? The Criminal Investigation Division of the United States Army. That's the C-I-fucking-D! I mean, after all, we could just *solve* the son of a bitch!"

Ernie clutched the edge of the bar and took a deep breath.

"Shit, pal. I never thought of that," he said sarcastically.

"Yeah, we could just do it."

"Fuck." Ernie scowled. He checked his watch. "Mount up."

The first sergeant was busy, getting briefing charts ready, while Riley stoked piles of paperwork into the big bureaucratic furnace that was the Eighth United States Army. They were too busy to mess with us. I pulled Ernie away from Miss Kim to review again the list I had made of the chaplain's marriage packets signed out to the Eighth Army staff during the last few months. Each entry had the name of the service member, the prospective spouse, and the initials of the staff member who had taken a packet.

"Who do you know up at the headshed?"

"Strange."

"What?"

"Strange—he works right there in the distribution center, in charge of the paper shuffle and the classified documents. You remember him. Receding hairline, dark glasses, cigarette holder."

"The guy who hangs out on the MSR trying to pick up little girls?"

"That's him, Strange."

I shook my head. A pervert in charge of top-secret documents. The more I thought about it, the more it made sense.

We slid out of the office and wound through the old brick buildings of Eighth Army Headquarters, past brown squares of frozen lawn and short rows of naked trees. Just inside the back door of one of the Eighth Army Headquarters buildings was a snack stand with stale cellophane-wrapped doughnuts and a steaming urn of coffee clouding the windows. We turned right down the hallway and passed the sentries at the broad entranceway, one British and one Korean. Both were in their dress uniforms and armed with .45s—members of the United Nations Command Honor Guard.

Halfway down the corridor we stopped at a wood-paneled room with large metal-barred windows. An empty cigarette holder peeped through the rods.

"Had any strange lately?"

Ernie pinched the cigarette holder and pulled it slightly forward. The pursed lips behind it seemed to be cemented in place.

"No strange, Harvey. No strange. What we came for is to get some information from you. On the QT."

I slapped the list, palm down, on the narrow counter.

Strange glanced down at it but his lips were still cemented to his cigarette holder. Ernie noticed and let him go. Strange stood up slowly, slightly offended but unruffled. He glanced down at the piece of paper and then a bony claw flashed out and snatched it, wadding it quickly into his left pants pocket. He said nothing

JADE LADY BURNING

but turned away from the window. Then we saw a door open on the paneled wall along the hallway and the cigarette holder and then Strange peeped out. He looked both ways down the long plush carpet. The hallway was deserted. He crooked a finger and we followed him about five yards behind. He kept looking back over his shoulder, snapping his head back and forth.

His shoulders were narrow and his hips were just slightly wider than his waist. He was flabby. Unused. Like sliced suet sweating in the sun.

When he reached the men's room he pulled the door open slightly and stepped through sideways until he disappeared. If I had blinked, I would have missed it.

"Why are we going in here?"

Ernie shrugged. "He feels most at home near a sewer."

Strange waved us over to the sink in front of the last stall. His clawlike hands held the rumpled list and his cigarette holder traveled back and forth along his thin lips as he studied it.

"List of names," he said. "GIs. And Korean women. But what's all this shit?"

He pointed at the row of letters written next to the names.

"Initials," I said. "Of the people who signed out marriage packets from the Eighth Army chaplains office. Do you recognize any of them?"

Someone walked into the latrine. An officer, in a dress green uniform.

I pretended to wash my hands in the sink. Ernie combed his hair in front of the mirror. Strange shoved the list back into his pocket and jumped into one of the stalls. The officer finished his business at the urinal and then frowned at us as he splashed a little water on his hands. When he left I knocked on the door of the stall that Strange was in.

"All clear."

No answer. I opened the door. He was sitting on the

commode, pants still up, studying the list. His cigarette holder was waggling furiously. He pointed to one of the entries.

"This one's gotta be Ida up at Protocol. That old bitch likes to get into everybody's business. No reason for her to be signing out marriage packets. And this is Major Hardy from the G-2 office."

"Security?"

"Yeah. Some of these guys must have clearances."

I stepped further into the stall, almost completely blocking the light.

"What about these entries here?" I pointed to the letters behind Pak Ok-suk and Li Jin-ai. "Do you know whose initials these are?"

"KMH. It doesn't jerk my chain."

"Maybe if you looked at some of the signatures back at your office you'd be able to find it."

Reluctantly Strange got up from the commode and waddled out of the latrine and down the hallway. We waited outside the barred window as he shuffled through various ledgers and logs and piles of paperwork. He came back to the window shaking his head.

"KMH. I can't find anyone in the headshed here with the initials KMH. Nobody who picks up distribution anyway."

"Do you have a complete list of employees?"

"No. No reason to break it down that way. The Civilian Personnel Office would have a complete list but that would be of all the employees at the Eighth Army Headquarters. The whole complex. Not just this building."

"People from other buildings sign stuff out here?"

"Sure. A lot of them."

"Will you keep looking for this KMH for us?"

"Yeah. But don't expect me to stay here late. I got to go out tonight and find some strange."

Ernie gave Strange his card and told him to call if he figured out who this KMH was. We left the building. The brisk air outside seemed life-giving after the claustrophobic tension that pervaded the Eighth Army Headquarters.

"He seemed awfully helpful," I said. "He'll do anything for me."

"Why?"

"Because I tell him about the strange that I get."

"What strange?"

"I just make it up. He lives in a fantasy world anyway."

We strode back to our own little dreamland at the Eighth Army CID Detachment.

Investigators Burrows and Slabem were in the first sergeant's office. Slabem had his shirt off and Burrows was taping wire to the soft flesh of his pink body.

"I know," Ernie said. "Don't tell me. You're going to pop out of a cake at an electronics convention."

The first sergeant growled. "Knock off the bullshit, Bascom. Slabem here's going to get the goods on this guy Lindbaugh so we can bust him for taking kickbacks from this Mr. Kwok out in the village."

Burrows finished the taping job and Slabem put on his shirt. The first sergeant told them to leave and then he glared at us.

"If you guys got something against Burrows and Slabem I want you to just keep it to yourselves."

"All they care about is statistics, Top," Ernie said. "So they'll look good at the briefing and have a better shot at getting their next promotion."

"Which you two guys probably won't get."

"I didn't join the Army to get rich," I said. Actually, I joined to eat regular, but I didn't tell him that.

"Well, you're off the Lindbaugh case now. Burrows and Slabem will wrap it up."

"You mean, make sure it doesn't explode and involve too many people."

The first sergeant's face twisted, as if something rotten had suddenly decided to take possession of his intestines. He held his breath for a while and then slowly exhaled, getting it under control.

His voice was calm and precise: "I'm putting you guys back on the black-market detail. Eight to five. Get out there and get me some arrests."

"Mayonnaise and instant coffee," Ernie said and shrugged. "Ya gotta do what ya gotta do."

Beneath the dingy, unlit neon, a beaded curtain drawn across the open door, stood Mama Lee's.

It was a nightclub, but there were a series of rooms in the back. The girls who worked here lived here, on display in the front but making their real living out back.

I clattered through the beads into the large main room. The bar was against the far wall and there were about twenty cocktail tables arranged neatly around the room. I went through the back door toward the hooches and heard some murmuring. Mama Lee was in the first room.

Sitting on the floor, she was ensconced comfortably next to a twelve-inch-high table heaped with PX goods. The inventory was typical: freeze-dried coffee, Carnation creamer, Nestle's hot chocolate, Tang, Jergen's lotion, almond butter facial cream, maraschino cherries, olive oil, honey, strawberry jam, peanut butter, four bottles of Jim Beam, two cases of Falstaff, and eight cartons of Kent cigarettes.

Two old ladies sat across the table from her, puffing madly on American-made cigarettes, bargaining and waving their hands.

They stopped talking and looked around when I appeared.

"Oh, Geogi," Mama Lee said, looking relieved. "It's you."

The women were well-known black marketeers and old enough to be my mother. I had occasionally been involved in raids in which they had been arrested by the Korean National Police. The raids were just a face-saving gesture for the police. The old women would open up shop in a new location the next day—after splitting some of their profits with the KNPs. Only the GIs caught doing business with them would be shafted: court-martialed, fined, kicked out of the service.

"She back room *isso*," Mama Lee said, waving her thumb toward the rear of the hooches. "You try new girl? *Taaksan* number one." She beamed at me with a gold-toothed grin and held her thumb straight up in the air.

"No," I said, looking at the pile of goods.

The old woman cackled and stared at me. Smoke rushed through her craggy teeth.

"Number ten no sweat," I said. "All GI *taaksan* number ten."

"Yeah," Mama Lee said, leaning back in mirth and slapping both her knees. "You right, Geogi. You right."

I winked at the old women and walked down the hallway to the last room, where Kimiko waited. As Mama Lee had promised when I called, she was there.

We sat on the woven mats, a small table between us.

"You must have spent all your money on the funeral," I said.

"It was important."

"Yes," I said. "It was very important."

There was an awkward silence. I nodded.

"Miss Pak have no family. Like me. When little, other children make fun sometimes, because we didn't have . . ." Kimiko looked at me and groped for the word. "Old people?"

"Ancestors," I said.

"Yes, ancestors," she said. "We didn't have graves of ancestors to visit on holidays. My mother made me promise that someday I would return to the graves of our ancestors in North Korea. When everyone else is with their ancestors, I will visit with Miss Pak."

"That will be good," I said in Korean.

Kimiko smiled.

"Kimiko," I said. "I have a secret. But if I tell you, you must tell no one else."

"Yes," she said. "I promise."

I reached out my hand to hers and we hooked our small fingers together in the Korean gesture of affirmation.

"There will be more Miss Paks, more girls who will suffer, unless you give me the thing you have."

She was stone white. Silent. "Yes," she said, finally. "I know. I used it to get what I wanted from them. A burial place for Miss Pak, a nice funeral, and a little money for myself. But they will tire of this arrangement soon. They will demand it from me."

"That's why they've been following you."

"Yes."

"Where do you keep it? Where is it hidden?"

"Here," she said, and rose to her feet. She padded over to the improvised shelf on which Mama Lee had stacked a cache of her bounty, and from among dozens of green and white little boxes she took one. Back at the table, she extended it to me and I accepted the box of Fuji film.

"You'll be on your own now," I told her.

"Yes. I know."

"*Anyonghikeiseiyo*," I said to her. Stay in peace.

"*Anyonghikaseiyo*," she replied. Go in peace.

12

At the Moyer Recreation Center on Yongsan Compound I signed some paperwork for the middle-aged doughnut dolly working the front desk and she gave us the key to one of the darkrooms and a thick tome of instructions on how to develop film. We had to buy the various chemicals from the supply room and the entire procedure was almost as difficult as the time Mrs. Aaronson taught me how to bake unleavened bread when I was twelve.

After we figured we had everything mixed right and we were waiting for the first prints to come out, Ernie got antsy.

"I'll go next door to the snack stand at the bus station and get us a couple of beers."

"Not supposed to open the door. It could expose the film."

"You stand in front of the tray. I'll just crack the door quick and slide out."

"You sure they got cold ones?"

"Positive."

"I'll take two."

I held my coat open around the film tray and Ernie slid out. The prints were gradually starting to come alive with images.

By the time Ernie got back the prints were clear. We popped our Falstaffs and admired them.

"Holy shit. The old creep."

"Yeah. Yeah."

Miss Pak Ok-suk was tied up, and the naked Major General Clarence T. Bohler was performing various acts upon her body. Miss Pak's face looked variously worried and twisted in pain. She was withstanding the abuse like a trouper, though: part of the price she figured she had to pay.

There was one shot where the look of resignation had left her eyes and had been displaced by panic. Bohler was bent over and manipulating something down near her backside. His forearm was around her neck. The photo was slightly blurred; she must have been struggling. From the grip he held her in, it appeared that she was having trouble getting air.

A couple of the photos showed some sort of medallion around Miss Pak's neck. I went to the front desk, talked to the doughnut dolly, and managed to scrounge up a magnifying glass. Once my eyes had readjusted to the light in the darkroom, I took another look at the print. The chain appeared to be made of gold and the medallion of carved jade. It was a circle surrounding a Chinese character. *Ok*—jade. Part of her name.

In all, there were nineteen photographs. The rest of the film was blank. Three of them were so blurred as to be useless. The other sixteen were clear. Something had gone wrong. She had died.

There was no way of dating the photos. They could have been taken prior to the night of her death but I doubted it. Bohler's driver could place him in the vicinity of Itaewon, and these photos would prove his intimate, abusive relations with Miss Pak Ok-suk.

We had enough to arrest him. And once formal proceedings were started, I knew we could get the evidence that would nail the case down. Kimiko would have to testify. It would be the only way for her. Her only chance was to take away the rationale for Bohler needing to silence her.

Ernie finished his beer and opened a second. "So now we know why Kimiko's been so well paid lately, and getting all those fancy jobs."

"Sure. Probably through Bohler."

"And the night she went to the Officers' Club, that was to let him know what she had on him?"

"And to give him a kick in the balls for good measure."

"Now we know why he didn't press charges."

I popped my second can of beer and we hung the prints up to dry. Using some wrapping paper and an envelope I folded the negatives away and put them into my coat pocket.

We finished our beers, put the eight-by-twelve glossies into a manila envelope, and returned all the equipment we had checked out to the front desk.

The woman said, "I'm glad you boys are getting yourselves a hobby. Every soldier needs one."

Milt Gorman's residence wasn't very far from The Roundup. The fortress he called home was illuminated by the glare of a flood-light. A ten-foot-high stone and mortar wall framed a huge metal gate and the entranceway to a small garage, locked tight behind a roll-down shutter made of corrugated metal.

Ernie rang the buzzer and shouted, "Bobby *ohma!*" A few seconds later someone opened the front door of the house.

"It's George," I yelled. "Here to see Milt." The front door

closed and a pair of slippers shuffled toward the gate. A metal bar slid free and an old Korean woman held the gate open as we entered. She relocked it and led us toward the house.

We took off our shoes in the entranceway and Milt ushered us into a big warm living room equipped with everything money could buy from the PX. Bulbs blinked at us from mounds of stereo equipment. A huge blank faced Japanese-made TV was mercifully turned off. Four or five kids in an adjacent bedroom were watching cartoons on another TV set. One of the boys was bigger and chubbier than the others but somehow he looked younger. His hair was light brown and his nose slightly pointed but his eyes were heavily lidded ovals.

"Some of the neighborhood kids like to come over and watch cartoons with Bobby," Milt said. "Hell, I enjoy the damn things almost as much as they do."

The old woman had disappeared into the kitchen. "*Ajima!*" Milt yelled. "*Mekju seigei.*" He held up three fingers to no one in particular. We sat down in the comfortable armchairs and in a moment three frosted cans of Falstaff and a large bowl of mixed nuts were in front of us on the coffee table. It and all the other furniture was done in black lacquer with inlaid mother-of-pearl designs. Traditional Korean stuff.

"The place looks great," I said.

He opened a beer for me. "Beats living in a tent out in the field at Fort Lewis." He opened one for himself. "The old lady's out playing *bua tu* with their friends. Probably be out all night and come back in the morning down about two hundred bucks." He lifted his can and smiled. "So we can drink all day and night."

We all took big long swigs on the ice-cold beers. I felt the color coming back to my cheeks.

"Can't stay long," I said. "We're in the middle of an investigation."

"The CID never sleeps," Ernie said. He grabbed a huge handful of mixed nuts and stuffed them into his mouth.

"What do you know about General Bohler?" I asked.

"Bohler?" Milt said. "Why would you guys want anything to do with that old fart? He's dangerous."

"It's a long story," I said, carefully picking out a Brazil nut. "And I don't have much time for it right now."

"Okay." Milt held out his hand as if to stop me. "Say no more."

Milt finished his beer and the old woman padded into the room with three more. She served Milt first and then us and I hurried and finished mine and handed her the empty. Ernie crushed his can before he gave it to her. Can't take him anywhere.

"How much clout does Bohler actually have downtown?" I asked.

"Clout isn't the word," Milt said. "Anybody who holds the position of Chief of Staff owns the town. Everybody here—the mayor, the chief of police, even me, we're all dependent on the money that comes from Eighth Army."

"Not just the payrolls," I said.

"Of course not. There's a lot of Korean workers on the compound, but in addition to their paychecks, they manage to squeeze a lot of materiel out of the base: leftovers from the mess halls, used supplies that can be written off the property book. And occasionally there's even out-and-out theft," Milt said. "As long as it remains a tolerable percentage, the Army just writes it off. It's cheaper than the expense of trying to chase it down."

"And the Koreans know what the percentage is," Ernie said. He was getting drunk.

"Yeah . . . building contracts, the cleaning contracts, the maintenance contracts. It's endless." Milt made a helpless gesture. "And the big shots here have their chopsticks in every pot and they got to pay off the bigger guys down in Seoul. Hell, a lot of the money probably filters all the way to the top."

"Probably most of it," Ernie said.

"And if a commander tried to clamp down on it all," I said, "what would happen to him?"

"Not too much." Milt shrugged. "Depending on how hard he pushed. They might make life miserable for him, but mainly they'd just wait for him to finish his tour and be replaced by another guy."

"One who might be corrupt."

"Naw," Milt said. "Most of the COs aren't corrupt. Not in any big way anyway. It's just that they've got a choice. If they fight it, they won't win and they might be risking their military careers. If one pushed too hard, they'll find a way to cope with him."

"Like?" I said.

"Whatever," Milt said.

"But the smart ones just ignore it," I said. "Pretend it's not happening."

"Exactly," Milt nodded. "If he plays along, they treat him like a king. They give him awards and plaques and have ceremonies for him. And if any one of his Korean workers gets too greedy or doesn't live up to his responsibilities and embarrasses the commander, the Koreans in power will have his ass."

"Self-policing," Ernie said.

"Yeah. Exactly."

The old lady brought in three more beers and picked up the empties. Ernie forgot to crush his can this time.

"I suppose," I said, "it wouldn't be anything for them to set him up down in the ville with a little dolly."

"Whichever one he chooses," Milt said. He leaned back in his chair and took another sip of his beer.

"Would he have to pay her?" Ernie asked.

"The commander don't have to pay for nothing in Itaewon," Milt said. "Oh, she might hustle a little money from him and some stuff from the PX, shit like that. But she'd better not gouge him and piss him off. The Koreans'd have her little butt."

Milt sighed, staring off into space at the beauty of it all. He suddenly seemed to realize something. "Hey, you guys don't have something on General Bohler, do you?"

I shrugged my shoulders.

He sipped his beer for a moment and then looked at me. "What'd you find out, George?"

"Nothing much, really. Except that Bohler is a pervert."

"We all knew that."

"No, a real pervert," I said. "Chains, whips, all the basic equipment."

"Everybody's got to have a little fun," Milt said. "Gets boring fucking with the troops all day."

"There's more to it than that," I said. "He'd been seeing a Miss Pak, recently deceased. He's the last person that I know of to see her alive."

"George, you'd better forget about it." He sat forward in his chair. "The Army'd back him up all the way to the presidential palace. They'd find something to charge you with and burn you both. Don't mess with this. It's officer stuff. And if you really piss them off, they'll let the Koreans have you for lunch."

13

Ernie was particularly morose. Maybe it was the early hour. Maybe it was the fact that we were sitting in a canvas-covered jeep, it was cold, there was no heater, snow was on the ground, and we were freezing our balls off. Or maybe it was something else. I asked.

"Why so glum, chum?"

Ernie tightened his arms across his chest and grunted.

"The Nurse?"

He shifted in his seat and turned slightly away from me.

Bingo.

We were parked in what looked like a residential area but was actually nothing but small houses that were divided into individual rooms for field-grade officers—majors and above. We were at the bottom of a hill at the top of which sat Major General Bohler's official residence, a rambling ranch-style home surrounded by an electrified chain-link fence and security guards. The narrow street was lined with sturdy green shrubbery and the naked bark of elm trees gutting out the winter.

The purpose of this exercise was to spot General Bohler on his morning jog. I wasn't sure why. Maybe it's just that when I put somebody under surveillance I like to start from the beginning, at his first rising in the morning, like the first page of a book.

We'd kept our drinking to a minimum the night before, and when we parted in Itaewon Ernie had promised to meet me at the motor pool so we could pick up his jeep at 0530. Miss Lim, the one with the husband in Cincinnati, had been a little surprised that I had stayed so sober and that we'd gone to the *yoguan* so early.

I'd asked the old woman who owned the place to wake me at five in the morning. It had been hard to leave Miss Lim. I promised I'd meet her at the American Club tonight, which maybe was a mistake, because I had no idea where this surveillance would lead.

Ernie exhaled vapor in the chill air. He said, "Why would a major general be involved with a floozy like Miss Pak Ok-suk?"

"For the same reason most old farts get involved with beautiful young women."

"Altruism?"

"Right. And also they want to get a little nooky."

"Why would he kill her?"

"Maybe that's the way he gets his kicks, or maybe it was an accident, or maybe she had something on him and he wanted to keep it quiet, or maybe somebody else killed her and he wanted to cover it up to avoid scandal, or maybe . . ."

"All right, all right. I get the point. We don't know."

"Not yet."

"How do we find out?"

"Follow him. See what he does. Then ask questions when it seems appropriate."

"How do you put a tail on a major general?"

"The same way we normally do. Only it will probably be easier."

"I guess you're right. Everybody'll just figure we're extra security."

"Yeah. Even he'll probably figure that."

"Big ego."

"The biggest."

Ernie had been in a good mood after that. We had a chance to nail a big shot. But the Nurse must have put him through the wringer last night. Sitting in our cramped little jeep, his mood was foul and evil.

I heard heavy breathing and rhythmic crunching on the snow before I could see him. An Airedale, a big prancing puppy, bounded out of the morning mist, Major General Clarence T. Bohler plodding after him. Determined. Grim.

The general ran past us down the hill and then turned left, heading for the South Post gymnasium, which had been forced to begin opening at 0600 ever since he took over as Eighth Army's chief of staff.

"The son of a bitch didn't even pay any attention to us."

"Probably figures we're waiting to escort one of these officers somewhere."

Focusing his anger on the general seemed to make Ernie feel a little better. He sat up and started the jeep. We rolled down the hill a few feet and then he turned around and headed toward General Bohler's residence. Ernie sped up the long driveway, past the half-asleep gate guard, and pulled up in front of the house.

The gate guard was up now, and walking toward us. Another khaki-clad Korean paced the far fence, staring at us curiously, an M-1 rifle slung over his shoulder.

A rock planter fronted the house, and the windows were large and very clean. It was a big place and the old guy must have had plenty of room in there to knock around by himself.

I grabbed my clipboard, hopped out of the jeep, and strode toward the approaching gate guard.

"Security inspection," I said. I flashed my badge at him. "Why didn't you stop and check us at the gate?"

"I tried to but . . ."

I scribbled something on the clipboard. "Never mind. Show us the rest of the grounds."

A GI with a clipboard can do no wrong.

The guard walked us across the frozen lawn and explained how many guards were on duty at any one time and told us how the shift changes worked.

"Anyone in the house?"

"The housemaid. She always comes in early to help General Bohler with his jogging shoes."

"Help him with his jogging shoes?"

"Yes. Tie them for him."

Ernie's eyebrows just about ripped themselves off the top of his head.

"Who else is on the staff?"

"The cook. He'll be in first and later his assistant. And of course the housemaid's assistant."

We were behind the house now and had a good view of the Frontier Club, the skeet range, and far off in the misty distance the Chamsu Bridge stretching across the rolling Han River.

In the back were two oversized dollhouses. Plastic bowls sat in front of them.

"The dog?" I asked.

"Yes."

"Why are there two of them?"

"General Bohler, he had another dog, the brother of the one that he has now."

"She's a bitch?"

"What?"

"A girl. A girl dog?"

"Yes. But her brother, he disappeared, ran away. Almost two weeks ago."

"Was this dog a cherry boy?"

The guard looked up at me and his eyebrows arched.

"A cherry boy," I said. "He never caught a girl dog. Young dogs are very strong and if a man eats a young dog, then he will be very strong, too."

The gate guard smiled.

"And whoever finds this strong young dog, this cherry boy, he will be able to sell him to one of the special places in Seoul and make a lot of money."

The gate guard's frown returned.

"Maybe a hundred thousand won. Maybe more."

"I don't know. I never do that. I never eat dog meat."

"You ought to try it sometime," Ernie said. "It makes your *jamji* hard." He clenched his fist and held his forearm rigidly in front of his chest.

I stopped writing on my clipboard and I think the gate guard was starting to wonder if this was a real inspection.

"Who's working tonight?"

"Mr. Jung. He will be the chief. Starting at eight o'clock."

"Tell him we will be back to talk to him tonight."

The gate guards huddled in the center of the lawn and mumbled among themselves as Ernie careened the jeep down the slippery incline.

"Yo, Sarge. How goes it?"

The crewcut NCO looked up at Ernie from his chipped beef on toast, a little startled at friendliness so early in the morning. He was a stocky man, with a little gray at the temples and the weathered skin that comes when your face has been scraped by a razor about a jillion times. A tiny American flag pinned his black tie to his neatly pressed poplin shirt.

"Okay, Bascom, okay. How are you?"

"Hanging in there."

Ernie plopped his plate atop the plastic-coated tablecloth and sat down at the small table. So did I. One of the Korean waitresses, carrying a heavily loaded tray, shuffled over and offered us coffee, juice, or milk.

I took one of each.

The Eighth Army mess hall is huge and noisy but the food is cheap. Forty-five cents for breakfast. All you can eat.

"The old man treating you okay?"

The sarge snorted.

"Late hours?"

"Not so much that. He likes to be by himself at night. It's the seven days a week. He always has something going."

"From what I can see, the headquarters pretty much closes down on Saturdays and Sundays."

"For everybody else. But that's when he meets all these Korean businessmen. Plays golf with them. Goes to their houses."

"Why doesn't he just get their drivers to pick him up?"

"He likes his own sedan, I guess."

"None of those Koreans has a Lincoln."

"Only two in the country. Mine and the commanding general's."

There was pride and affection in the NCO's voice. For the car. I didn't detect any for Major General Bohler.

"What kind of guy is he?"

"General Bohler? He's like most generals."

"An asshole?"

"Got to be to get that much rank."

"I heard he lost one of his dogs."

"Is that why you're talking to me?"

Ernie shrugged. "Somebody's got to find it."

"So the CID's on the dogcatcher patrol." The sarge took a sip of his coffee. "Yeah. The old man took it pretty hard. The gate guards told him the dog had run away. They'd tried to catch him but he'd been too fast for them. I think he believed them. I guess it never crossed his mind that anybody'd do anything to hurt one of his babies."

"His babies?"

"Yeah. The old guy never has been married. What woman would have him? All he ever wants to do is work and chew people out and talk about how many Vietcong he killed riding around in his chopper. Sort of easy at two thousand feet. So he raises Airedales. He had to leave most of them back in the States, at his home in Virginia, when they sent him out here to be chief of staff but he brought these two puppies with him. You would have thought they were family the way he treated them. I've always liked a dog myself. A good working dog. One that will earn its keep and stand by you. But I've never been much for raising them for shows and stuff like that. What's the point? And it was sort of weird seeing the way he always tells GIs to tough it out. When that dog disappeared, he blubbered like a baby. For two days. It was a vacation for me. I just stayed in my room and waited for him to call me. Finally he did. To take him over to the chapel for the wake."

"The wake?"

"Yeah. He had that chaplain over there, what's his name?"

"Sturdivant."

"Yeah, Chaplain Sturdivant. He had him and his assistant perform a little ceremony for the dog. Since he figured he was dead and all."

"Who attended this ceremony?"

"I waited in the car. So it was just the chaplain and his assistant and General Bohler and Bonnie."

"Bonnie?"

"Yeah. The other dog."

"Did she cry?"

"Not hardly."

"Who do you think took the dog?"

"The gate guards. Who else? That sucker's worth some money downtown."

"Any proof?"

"Naw. You know they're slick. You'll never get anything on them."

"When did you have this wake?"

"In the afternoon. Over a week ago. It had to be a Sunday. I remember because it was the first Saturday I got off since I've been in country. He was so tore up and all."

"Did he go anywhere after the wake?"

"Yeah, he did. I let him off by himself. He said he just wanted to get out and walk a while. He told me to take the other dog back to his quarters, which I did. And then I went back to 21 T Car and parked the sedan."

"He just wanted to be by himself and walk a little?"

"Yeah."

"Was he in civilian clothes?"

"Sure. He'd attract too much attention with all those stars on his shoulder."

"Did he often go out by himself?"

"Not that I know of. Never."

"What'd he usually do at night?"

"Of course there are the official functions at the Officers' Club or the American Embassy or something like that. But other than that, I haven't got the slightest idea what he does at night. Stays home with his dogs, I guess."

"Sunday night, after the wake, where did you let him off?"

"Where else would a person go when they're feeling down?"

"Itaewon?"

"You got it."

Investigator Burrows craned his long thin body over Miss Kim's desk, trying to make her laugh with a glass rabbit filled with bubble bath he had bought in the PX. She ignored him. He stiffened and rose to his full height when he saw Ernie and me walk in.

"Where's your partner?" I said.

"He had to go on sick call."

"Got the clap again?"

"No. A skin condition."

Burrows swiveled his crane-like body and ambled down the hallway toward the first sergeant's office. I think he wanted to get there before us.

Riley said, "Yeah, okay," and slammed the phone down. "The truth is that those wires Slabem was hooked up to got overheated and he was engaged in an intimate conversation with some suspect at the time and was unable to turn them off or get the hell out of there, and as a result he was burned and his entire porky body looks like it was toasted in a wrap-around waffle iron."

"Sueño! Bascom!"

The first sergeant was bellowing from down the hall.

Burrows passed us on our way in, smirking.

"What's this I hear about you two guys not being out at the commissary or PX doing your job on the black-market detail like I told you to do?"

"It ain't true, Top," Ernie said. "We been staking out the commissary steady since you told us we were off Lindbaugh."

"Don't be bullshitting me, Bascom."

"No way, Top."

"What about it, Sueño?"

"The commissary, Top. I don't care what Burrows says."

"How many arrests did you get?"

"Things have been a little slow out there. They should pick up on payday."

"Don't *give* me that shit! I don't know what you two guys have been up to, but you better not be poking your noses into what don't concern you, and you'd better get on the stick and get out there and get me some black-market arrests . . . or I'll have your ass! You got that?"

Ernie and I nodded.

"Now get out of my office and get to work on the job that the Army's paying you to do. And don't let me hear about any more screwing off."

Miss Kim had her head down as we left; Riley winked. Burrows had disappeared.

Ernie made the jeep's engine roar. We were in just the right mood to see Strange.

"What's he doing during his off-duty hours?" I asked.

"Bohler? That old tight ass? Gets some strange, I guess."

"With who?"

Strange popped his bubble gum. "With whoever he can pick up. He's got two stars. It shouldn't be too difficult."

"Does he ever hang out in the ville?"

"I haven't seen him out there. But I've heard of a couple of guys who have."

"They've *seen* him running the clubs?"

"No. Not running the clubs. He wouldn't stoop so low. He sort of sneaks around, you know, with his escorts."

"His escorts?"

"Yeah. Those Korean guys who want to take good care of him."

"Like who?"

"Like that guy out there who runs one or two of the clubs."

"What's his name?"

"I don't know. He's a smooth character, expensive."

"How often does he go out there?"

"Very rarely."

"Does he have any regular hangouts? Places where we might be able to spot him?"

"No way."

"Well anyway, thanks, Strange. Thanks for the information."

"The name's Harvey."

"Yeah. Sorry, Harvey. See ya."

"Have you gotten any lately?"

"Not lately. I've been busy."

"Pity."

"Yeah."

Tinkling glassware and the smell of freshly sliced lemon. If we hadn't been in the Eighth Army Officers Club I would have been enjoying myself. It was your typical luncheon: honeyed ham with a pineapple ring and cherry on top, a baked potato wrapped in tinfoil, and succotash. We didn't eat. Of course, we hadn't been invited anyway. We stood off to the side, trying to stay out of the way of the waiters and the red-faced officers sliding over to the bar to belt down quick ones.

Someone clanged a spoon against a water glass. The room got quiet.

"We are here today to honor . . ." The speaker droned on. Finally, to a round of halfhearted applause, Major General Bohler was introduced. He was lean, like a gnawed sparerib, and the graying hair on the side of his head had been all but shaved away. The top of his pate glistened in the light, as if it had been oiled. He grinned. A wide toothy grin under square-lensed glasses.

His voice was raspy and thin. As if he were trying to soothe you before he cut your heart out.

The luncheon was in honor of the great improvements that had been made at the Korean Procurement Agency. Money had been saved. The taxpayers' interests protected. And great new edifices had been built to the glory of the Eighth Imperial Army. A series of Korean gentlemen, employees of KPA, received plaques and certificates of appreciation, bowing and shaking General Bohler's hand as they received their rewards. Bulbs flashed. And then Lindbaugh was on the stage, his chubby neck bulging out over his too-tight collar and tie. His moist-lipped grin revealed little gray teeth. Like a ferret. And then Mr. Kwok was on the stage. He was muscular and swarthy and seemed to take command of the room with his physical power. He didn't bow to General Bohler but kept his face impassive and shook his hand and accepted the big burnished copper plaque, emblazoned with little metal flags of the United States and Korea. Engraved words recorded forever the great contributions he had made to mankind and the cause of peace in Northeast Asia.

I looked at the barrel-chested officers along the bar. Some of them chuckled quietly to one another. I longed for a belt. Instead I went into the latrine and spit.

We were in the jeep at the base of the hill below General Bohler's quarters.

It was cold but there was no snow. There hadn't been any precipitation for over a week, since the night Miss Pak died.

The snow that was left on the ground looked like lumps of stale icing on mass-produced pastry. A thin sprinkling of soot lay atop it.

The frozen snow and the evergreen trees and the naked elms began to disappear as the sun went down. Soon all we could see were a few pale yellow bulbs serving as porch lights.

We waited an hour. Nothing. So we decided to shake things up. We got out of the jeep and walked up the steep winding drive-way. I carried my clipboard again. The two gate guards were smoking and joking but got quiet when they spotted us.

"Where's Mr. Jung?"

"Just a moment." The radio squawked.

Within about thirty seconds a stout, middle-aged Korean man in neatly pressed khakis appeared. We flashed our IDs.

"The report of inspection on the day shift is not going to look very good. So far, your men are doing somewhat better."

"We are particularly alert at night."

"The day shift is important, too."

"Yes."

"Would you please show us around the perimeter?"

"Yes."

We followed him along the chain-link fence but I kept my eyes on the house. The big Lincoln sedan was gone. The old sarge must have the night off. Inside, no one seemed to be moving.

The perimeter guards snapped to attention as we approached.

"What time do you expect the general to go out tonight?"

"He's already left."

"What?"

"Yes. He got off early from work today. Very unusual for him. He changed clothes and was gone before the sun went down."

"Where was he going? Do you know?"

"No."

"Was he alone?"

"Yes. And on foot."

The security chief didn't seem to be too worried about it. There is no terrorism in Korea. No kidnappings. No Red Brigades. The society is too well controlled. What they are worried about is a direct attack on specific targets by North Korean commandos. Thus, the heavy security at the general's quarters and the Eighth Army Headquarters itself.

"What time did he leave?"

"Just a few minutes before the sun went down."

We walked back down the hill to the jeep. I cursed myself for not getting here earlier. But who would have thought that a workaholic would cut out early from work?

Unless he had some more work to do.

We went to Itaewon but it was no dice. Kimiko was gone, she wasn't in her hooch or at any of the clubs. We just checked the main ones but it would have taken forever to check every little hole in the wall. Mr. Kwok's office was dark and he wasn't downstairs in the Sloe-eyed Lady Club.

Major General Bohler had disappeared.

"Why don't you go back to the compound?" Ernie said. "Get some rest. I'll hang around here until curfew to see if any of them show up and in the morning you can pick up on Bohler again. It's better to work in shifts."

Ernie was right. Trying to get something on Bohler could take a long time. Besides, there was something I wanted to do.

"Okay. You gonna see the Nurse tonight?"

"No. No way."

"Why not? You guys just had a big fight and then you made up. What is it this time?"

"She doesn't want to see me. She told me not to come to the hooch tonight."

There were lines on Ernie's face that I had never noticed before. I wondered if the Nurse had found a new boyfriend. He was wondering the same thing. I decided to drop it.

I said, "Don't worry about getting up early. I'll check out those security guards in the morning and find out what time Bohler got back tonight. Then we'll compare notes at the office."

"Okay."

I left Ernie standing in front of a dark alley with both his hands stuffed into the pockets of his nylon jacket. A girl approached him. He shrugged her off.

I caught a cab and was back at the main gate of the compound in about three minutes.

"You tell anybody I'm doing this and they'll have my ass."

"Don't worry, Jones," I said. "Nobody'd want it anyway. Been had too often."

"No, I'm serious. You know I'm not supposed to let anybody in here."

I said, "You're not supposed to black-market either."

He said, "You're an asshole, George." But he got out his keys.

"An asshole? I didn't turn you in, did I?"

"Well . . . hell, George. Everybody does it."

"But not everybody lets themselves get caught."

"Who would've thought you and Ernie'd be at Mama Lee's in the middle of the afternoon?"

"Anybody who knows us. Now get out of here."

The door to the chapel was unlocked. So was the door to Hurchek's office. I closed it behind me, pulled down the shade to the single window, and sat down at his desk. I pulled out my little flashlight and went through the logbook of the marriage packets that had passed through the Eighth Army chapel for the last few months. Taking my time. Getting it right.

I double-checked to make sure there were no entries signed out to "KMH" that I had missed. There were only the two: Li Jin-ai and Pak Ok-suk.

I found the marriage paperwork for Johnny Watkins and Miss Pak Ok-suk on Hurchek's desk in a box marked *hold*.

Talk about an understatement.

I thumbed through the folder carefully. The marriage application was on top, giving all the basic data on Johnny and Miss Pak: names, Johnny's Social Security number, Miss Pak's National Identification number, dates of birth, places of birth.

I made quick notes on a pad of paper I found on the desk.

An extract of Johnny Watkins's personnel record was also inside.

Basic training at Fort Leonard Wood, Missouri; advanced individual training at Fort Lee, Virginia; transferred to Korea eight months ago. Routine.

Somebody had typed out the security questionnaire on Miss Pak. It was signed and stamped with the chop of one of the offices down in Itaewon that did a good business helping GIs and Korean girls wade through the paperwork required by the Korean government and the Eighth Army.

Beneath that was a photostat copy of Miss Pak's family register. It told who her mother had been and nothing else. Not brothers and sisters and the usual information about everybody's place and date of birth. A family register in Korea was like their birth certificate. If you were born outside of a family, you were nothing. Miss Pak hadn't had much going for her.

Stapled to the back of the document was her picture. Her eyes seemed faded, protected, as if she didn't quite trust the man behind the camera. Permed hair covered her ears, more hair on one side than on the other.

Her cheekbones were high and prominent, the nose flat but not too wide, and her mouth small but full, making it almost seem as if she were pouting.

If the blow-by-blow description of her didn't sound too hot it was because the individual parts of her probably wouldn't measure up to Madison Avenue's idea of true beauty. And the quality of the black and white photo was lousy, too. But still, the spirit of Miss Pak Ok-suk shone through.

All the strange little parts of her face, thrown together, behind those sultry and challenging eyes, added up to a beautiful and desirable woman.

She was a knockout.

I pried the photo loose from the staple and slipped it into my wallet.

There was more paperwork. Her health certificate seemed to be clean. No TB. No abortions. No recorded cases of VD. That was unusual. The odds were that any girl who worked in Itaewon for just a few weeks would come down with some sort of venereal disease. But she hadn't. Maybe that said something about her clientele: older maybe, more cautious.

I shuffled the paperwork back into the same order I had found it in and placed it back into the hold box.

There was a stack of new marriage packets in Hurcheck's in box. They hadn't been logged in yet. I went though them. One of them was missing, replaced by a yellow eight-and-a-half-by-eleven Department of the Army sign-out/in sheet. The names of the soldier and the prospective bride were printed in Hurchek's neat hand. The Korean woman's name was Yoon Un-suh, which didn't mean anything to me at first, but the initials of the person who had signed for the packet did. KMH.

So did the name of the GI. He was my partner, Ernie Bascom. Yoon Un-suh . . . the Nurse.

14

Palinki was the armorer at the MP Station. A big Samoan, his smile seemed to fill the sky. So did his shoulders.

"No problem, brother. Keep it for as long as you want."

"Just for training," I said. "But I'd feel better if the First Sergeant didn't know about it. He gets antsy when we check these things out."

"Hey, you did me a favor before, George, and I haven't forgotten." He pointed to his big square head. "Nobody will know about this but you and me."

"Been staying out of the ville?"

"Yeah. And I haven't been drunk since it happened."

Palinki had nearly killed three GIs he caught harassing a couple of high school girls who were on their way home through the Itaewon market. Ernie and I managed to get him out of the way before the MP patrol arrived. The girls were frightened but unhurt and the GIs recovered after some hospital time. They just slunk around the compound nowadays, staying out of Palinki's way, and not going to the ville much anymore.

I looked around to make sure no one was watching. "I need one more thing, Palinki. You got any, you know, extra ammo?"

During peacetime the U.S. Army accounts for every weapon and every piece of ammunition with fanatical precision. But with so much of it floating around, a smart armorer can always squirrel some away for that rainy day when some ammunition is lost and he has to cover himself by replenishing inventory.

Palinki looked at the .45 in my hand. It was gray and had a big white number 3 stenciled on the grip.

"I can spare a little. How much you need?"

"Six rounds."

Palinki rummaged among the green metal ammo boxes, stood up, and held out six cartridges. They looked like bits of candy in his gigantic paw.

"Bring 'em back if you don't use them."

"Will do." I put them in my pocket. "Thanks."

"You got it."

He sat back down and hunched over the comic book that he had been reading. It looked like a brightly colored doily between his two thumbs.

Ernie had gassed up the jeep, and I told Riley that we'd be out all day trying to pump up our black-market statistics. We just drove.

"So what's the big mystery, pal?" Ernie said.

"I found out about your marriage paperwork."

Ernie looked at me, took a quick swig of coffee.

"I broke into the chaplain's office."

"Oh."

"Anyway," I said, "I found your paperwork and the paperwork of Miss Yoon Un-suh."

Ernie looked straight ahead.

"It wasn't any of my business, you got a right to your privacy, and I shouldn't have been poking around in there. Somebody signed out your paperwork."

"For what?"

"Shopping for companions."

"I don't like it, George. We ought to just go grab Bohler's ass and slap him with an assault charge."

"If he had a little less rank I'd agree with you."

"What do you mean?"

"This is a two-star general, the chief of staff to boot. They're not going to take the word of some low-level enlisted scum CID agents against his and they're definitely not going to even consider the testimony of some slut Itaewon bar girl."

"She's not a slut."

"Yeah. I know. Just trying to make my point." I shook my head in resignation. "The commanding general would probably put out the word and have the Korean National Police arrest us for pandering—for trying to corrupt the morals of some poor innocent two-star general."

"Sounds about right."

"Yeah. And we'd not only lose our jobs for bringing those kinds of accusations without proof, but we'd also stand a chance of getting court-martialed ourselves."

"For what?"

"The Uniform Code of Military Justice has a clause concerning the willful defamation of an officer's reputation. You can't call him a scumbag and you can't spread rumors about him that could hurt the morale of the troops by exposing the man in charge, who might lead us into combat someday, as the scrotum that he really is."

"They wouldn't charge us with anything," Ernie said.

I looked at him. He looked back at the road.

"All right. Maybe they would."

"You're damn right they would."

"So how do we nail this dick?"

"Get the goods."

It was nearly dark by the time I got to her place. I didn't knock but just slid the door back. The Nurse tilted her face slowly upward and looked at me as if she'd been expecting me.

She wore a tight black sweater and dark corduroy pants. The room was empty except for her purse and a coat and a broken mirror on the wall. I slipped off my shoes, stepped in, and slid the paneled door shut behind me. I sat cross-legged on the floor and faced her.

"Tell me about the General."

She looked down at her lap.

"That night," I said, "the last time you saw Bohler, did you bring him back here?"

She looked up, suddenly angry. "I never bring man back here! Only one man. Ernie."

"What was the marriage application for?"

"Ernie wanted to marry me." She threw her long hair back off her shoulder. "I thought about it. Maybe he was the first one who made me think about it. But I can't." She looked away. "I can't leave Korea."

"Why not?" I said. "What has Korea ever done for you?"

"I have to stay," she said.

"What about Ernie?"

"You don't understand. Me and my little brother, we need money. Nobody help. We have to get money. But we didn't want to hurt Ernie. Just for money. Ernie young. He's GI. He doesn't need money."

She took a slow breath and looked down at her lap. "I had done . . . it before. Some GIs . . . I don't know why." She waved her hand as if to dismiss something. "They like me. They all the time want to steady me, they all the time want to marry me. But they want do strange things. So I tell them I need money, bring money, and maybe then we can do."

"What about Bohler?" I said.

She looked down again. "I have to do."

"Have to do? Who says you have to do?"

"Everybody," she answered. "Policeman say, Korean man say. Everybody say General number-one honcho. I have to do."

"How did you meet him?"

"With Korean men."

"Who?"

She shrugged. "I don't know. They all same."

"What happened?"

"Korean man say I have to eat with him at party house. I pour him drinks, I laugh at what he say." She shrugged again. "He like me."

"And then he started coming to your place every night?"

"Not every night," she said matter-of-factly. "Maybe two, three times one week."

"And then you realized that he's not a normal man."

"Yes." She said it very softly. "He's not normal."

She became very tense, and very red, and very quiet.

She had been coerced by the local powers into assuaging the needs of the chief of staff of the Eighth Army. Despite the shame, it had given her a strange sort of power. No one would hassle her. In fact, she could probably count on a certain amount of protection by the local police. As long as she was taking care of the General, the police and the mayor and the local businessmen were all happy. Everyone was happy. Except her.

"What are you going to do now?" she asked. "You tell Ernie?"

"No," I said. "No."

"I don't know, Geogi." She looked sad.

"What about Bohler?"

"I don't ever want to see him again."

"Bohler will look for you," I said. "He might even send the Korean National Police after you. There are two of them outside now."

"Yes." She nodded.

"Aren't you worried about them?" I said.

"No. They are not looking for me. They are looking for you, Geogi," she said.

And then it hit me. The KNPs had been following me. Somehow they'd discovered that I had the film.

15

One of the things they teach you in the training course for the Criminal Investigation Division is that when you're getting chased by the bad guys never run into a dead end. Funny how that dictum stuck in my mind as I careened through the crowded streets of downtown Itaewon. But every time I turned a corner I prayed it wasn't a dead end.

The policeman kept blowing his whistle, which was sort of convenient because I could tell that he was falling a little behind. It stood to reason. The streets were crowded with pedestrians, carts, and vendors of all sorts. I knew which way I was going at each turn. He had to stop at every intersection and check which way I had gone.

I was heading in the general direction of the compound, away from the downtown. I turned down one road and it turned out to be a small outdoor market. Stalls on either side of the road were covered with canvas awnings supported by wooden poles. There were clothes and fish and produce but I didn't have to admire any of the goods. I was very rude pushing my way through the crowd. I'm afraid a few people were probably knocked to the ground but, like Satchel Paige, I didn't look back or listen for footsteps. I was afraid something might be gaining on me.

I estimated when the policeman behind me would hit the intersection and start looking. At that moment I crouched down low but kept moving, trying to make myself less of a conspicuous target.

As I plowed through the crowd, wave after wave of startled Korean faces came at me, like trodden grass rising to retake its shape. What they saw was a huge, crouching, wild-eyed Caucasian charging at them from out of the night. The Koreans fell back and opened a small path for me in the sea of humanity.

At the end of the long block, two more policemen trotted into the intersection, apparently having been attracted by their comrade's frantic whistle. I stopped for a moment and for the first time looked back. The policeman who had been following me was hopping up and down, straining to see past the jumbled stalls and milling crowds on the market roadway.

The police on both ends of the roadway started to close in. There was a small alleyway between a produce stall and a fish market. I ran down it and, as if to illustrate a point out of the CID training manual, it was a dead-end.

There was an eight-foot-high brick wall at the end and no doors on the tall buildings on either side. I ran for the wall and spotted a wooden crate at its base. I hit the crate running and bounded up, pulling myself up with my hands and kicking my right foot over the wall. It's amazing how much more acrobatic a person can become with a little incentive.

I stayed up on top of the wall for a couple of seconds, looking at the shards of glass under my hands and my legs. With a sick feeling, I rolled over, onto the far side of the wall, and fell—crashing—into a bush below.

It was somebody's back yard. A little fluffy white dog was barking his head off. I got up, moved away from the wall, and saw a gate. The dog bared his teeth and growled. I was in no mood to play with him and I think he could tell. He backed off.

Someone slid their door open and light spilled out into the small courtyard. A man in pajama bottoms and a sleeveless T-shirt gazed out the door. I waved and smiled and stepped through the gate out into a quiet residential street.

I decided not to wave anymore. Blood was running down my wrist.

I started running again but when I got back out to the large streets, there were too many pedestrians to go fast, so I slowed to a walk. I didn't want to attract too much attention to myself. The whistles were growing fainter behind me. I kept moving.

I checked my hands. The right was okay but the left had a pretty nasty cut. The flow of blood had slowed, no artery had been hit, but it was still pretty messy. I figured I'd need seven or eight stitches and I'd have a scar to jog my memory about this evening for the rest of my life—although I doubted I'd need the prompting.

I take long strides when I'm in a hurry, and I can walk as fast as some people can run, at least for sustained distances. I would stay off the main roads, if I could. If I ran into any police, they would most likely be walking patrols and I'd have a better chance. Then again, there would be fewer civilians to run interference for me.

I came to the MSR and the pedestrian traffic increased. The Koreans are an industrious people. Many of them were just coming home from work although it must have been past seven in the evening. Carts and trucks and vendors and people on urgent missions were everywhere. The Korean workday had not yet wound down.

I tried to hide my bloody hand by keeping it stiffly at my side. That probably just made it more conspicuous. I trotted across the street at a corner. That wasn't unusual. Everyone had to run to avoid getting hit by the speeding traffic. I disappeared down another alley. At empty lots or any break in the crowded skyline, I could see the lights of the helicopter compound that sat just about a half mile from the post. Then a chopper dropping lazily to land.

I picked up a handful of snow and wiped off the blood. A walking patrol approached at a stoplight and I held my breath. There were two MPs in the patrol, one American and the other ROK Army, and a Korean National Policeman. But they weren't looking for me, they were just on routine patrol.

"Just part of the scenery," I said to myself when they had passed.

The sweat was beginning to dry on my body and I shuddered from the cold. I was still in Korea.

My hand had stopped bleeding as long as I didn't move it. It was beginning to ache, a steady throb of pain running up my arm. No blood dripped down my pants legs. My shins must have been only scratched but I didn't have time to stop and take a look.

When I reached the walls of a factory compound I had no choice but to come out onto the main road. I put my hands in my jacket pockets and walked casually but with long strides down the road. There were Korean shops and restaurants blaring out their advertisements with music and light on either side of the traffic-clogged street. It was a long straightaway.

At first everything was written in Korean but gradually more and more signs appeared in English. CHICKEN HOUSE, DRAFT BEER, THE MANHATTAN TAILOR SHOP—all the things to entice a young GI into their places of business. I just wanted to make it to the bar district and blend into the crowd of off-duty soldiers.

Up ahead four streets ran off at odd angles. I took the road to the right. A half mile along, I hit downtown Itaewon.

The first thing I did was stop for a beer.

No one noticed me as I walked in despite my disheveled appearance. Huge, unkempt GIs were the norm around here. I walked past the pool players and the girls displaying their legs and bosoms at the cocktail tables to the one open seat at the bar. The attractive young barmaid poured the beer into a frosted mug. I made some inane but pleasant remark and tilted the mug to my lips, pushing past the white froth to the life-restoring fluid beneath. It was cold and wonderful.

The barmaid thought she knew me but she wasn't sure. She decided to play it safe and confided in me that she was on the rag, "men-suh," she called it, and that was why she had to work behind the bar tonight. I patted her hand gently with my one good one and assured her that I understood. She took another long look at me, I think realizing that I wasn't the guy she thought I was, and then shrugged and walked away.

The place was bright and bubbled with music and colored lights that flashed and bounced off the walls at crazy, repetitive angles. I felt like I was in a pinball machine.

It was only a one-room club, bar along the back wall, the latrine to the right, and a door to a flight of stairs, apparently to the girls' rooms upstairs.

Besides the adolescent ambiance, the club's other attraction was the girls. Taking their cue from the decor, they were dressed like a bunch of wild women: miniskirts, hot pants, halter tops, see-through blouses all surrounded by nyloned legs below and flamboyant, explosive hairdos above.

The music punched at my eardrums and the beer was served in frosted mugs. What more could anyone ask? I was starting to feel good again. Ernie would probably put this place off-limits. Not cave-like enough for him.

One of the girls approached me and I let her and before long she was massaging the knotted muscles of my neck and cooing to me about going upstairs. I had another beer and reveled in the attention. Her short blouse hung loosely over her pert breasts and stopped short of her midriff. She swiveled me around on the bar stool, turned herself around, and pushed her butt as close as she could get it. She looked triumphantly around the club, with a little half smile on her face, all the while wiggling her can up against her trophy. Then she took my good hand and placed it underneath her blouse. She wasn't wearing a brassiere.

The MP patrol walked in just then.

The patrol was composed of law officers from three jurisdictions. Their job was to police the bars and the red-light districts near the U.S. Army bases, to make sure Korean-American relations didn't get out of hand.

The young ROK Army MP struggled valiantly to keep the disgust he felt from crawling onto his face. It wasn't working. The American MP adjusted his shiny helmet and shifted his hands from his pistol belt to his holster, then back to his pistol belt again.

One of the girls scurried up to him and thrust out her hips. "Hi, Freddy," she said. "What time you gonna catch me tonight?"

Birdlike hoots rose from the gaggle of girls. The MP's face flushed and the lower half of his face grinned while his eyes darted around. He walked around the girl, leaving his Korean partner to stand guard, while he checked inside the bathroom. Standard procedure.

The one I was worried about was the KNP, a man older than the two MPs. He was a seasoned veteran of the Korean National Police. He ignored the antics of the girls and seemed to be searching for something. I stifled the urge to run and turned against the bar to hide the blood on the side of my jacket. As I did, I pulled my newfound paramour along, my hand pushing even further up into her blouse. I grabbed both her breasts with one hand. She giggled and bounced compliantly until she had resituated herself in my lap. I started kissing her neck. She laughed, grabbed hold of my forearm and pressed my groping palm even more firmly against her.

I kept my blood-soaked left hand deep inside my jacket. The KNP made a slow circle around the club, looking closely at all the GIs. I whispered in my girl's ear, "We most tick go short time, can do?"

She leaned back a little and turned her head slightly. "No sweat," she said. "Can do easy."

The KNP was watching us now.

I whispered again, "How much money *mama-san* need?"

"Ten dollar, can do." She reached back and grabbed my joint.

"Ten dollar too much," I said. The KNP loomed over us. We ignored him.

"Ten dollar *skoshi* money." She let go of my privates and held up her hand, thumb and forefinger held parallel about a quarter-inch apart, to indicate how little money ten dollars really was. And then she said, "Number *hana* short time. Everything can do."

I said, "Five dollars."

The KNP walked away.

"*Aigu!*" She slapped me on the thigh. "Whatsamatta you? You Cheap Charlie?"

"*Tone oopso,*" I said. No money.

She looked at me like I was out of my mind, yanked my hand from under her blouse, and threw it down so hard it banged against the side of the bar. Her little buns quivered as she clatterd across the club on her three-inch-high heels.

The MP patrol was on its way out, but before the swinging door could shut completely, I saw the KNP look back at me. I swiveled around on the bar stool and watched him in the large mirror behind the bar.

They were gone. My former girlfriend was sitting on a chair, her arms crossed over her small bosom, nylon-sheathed legs balanced one over the other. She was talking indignantly to her friends, occasionally shooting a withering look my way. I finished my beer and crossed to the latrine.

There was only a commode and a small sink clinging to the wall. The mirror had been torn off ages ago. I took off my jacket, placed it atop the commode, and tried to turn on the water faucet. All I got was a dry hiss. I turned back to the commode. The water looked clean. What the hell.

I flushed the commode and, when it refilled, I leaned down and washed my bloody hand. The blood was caked over the torn areas but there didn't seem to be any glass inside. As I washed, the wound started to bleed a little. I let it drain and continued to ladle water until the contents of the little toilet turned the color of beets.

A blast of music hit me, followed by cold air, as a GI walked in.

He stood at the door with his mouth open.

I looked up and smiled. "I'll be finished in just a minute," I said.

He backed out of the room and shut the door.

I flushed the toilet again and rinsed off the hand one last time. When I had finished, I stood there letting it drip dry. There were no towels.

I managed to get my comb out of my left hip pocket with my right hand and ran it a few times through my short hair. Then I flushed the toilet once more and rubbed a splash of the fresh water on my face. What with the beer and a little freshening up, I was starting to feel okay again.

My hand was dry and no longer bled. It looked a little bit better. I still needed an aid station and some stitches, but I wasn't anxious to go on an Army compound at the moment.

Carefully, I put my jacket back on and tucked in my shirt. When I turned to check myself in the mirror all I saw was a blank wall.

Back in the club, my girl was still sitting in the same chair, same position, and still pouting. I winked at her and gave her a big smile on the way out. She turned her head and gave a little snort.

There were business girls and GIs and neon lights and little old ladies in front of wooden pushcarts full of snacks and gum and sundry items, but no patrol visible anywhere on the street. I turned away from the large street and headed toward the darkened alleys.

In a few blocks I was in a residential area again. There were older children, some with packs, heading purposefully toward home.

The number of clubs and GIs faded. I was getting a little lost but finally came out onto a larger road and saw a neon sign: the Rose Club. I trotted out into the traffic and dodged the careening kimchi cabs. Just as I got past the glare of the Rose Club's neon, two white Korean National Police jeeps pulled up to a screeching halt out front. Policemen jumped out of the first and the other jeep pulled up alongside. I heard shouted instructions but couldn't make them out, and then the second jeep peeled off down the road.

A small neon sign up ahead had an arrow pointing down a narrow alley. The sign said "THE KEY CLUB." Some of the KNPs looked over the GIs walking into and out of the Rose Club but they didn't go into the club itself. It was an unwritten law—KNPs didn't go into GI clubs without MPs along with them.

Two of the policemen had left the group and were coming in my direction, trotting. As soon as I got into the shadows of the narrow alley, I ran. The surface of the alleyway was uneven and I had to be careful not to twist my ankle. The alley wound around at weird angles and then took a sharp left. I was in front of the brightly lit back door of the Key Club and slowed to a walk to get my breath back before entering.

Something leapt out of the shadows and grabbed me.

"Jesus!"

"*Yoboseiyo*," it said. A young girl. She couldn't have been over eighteen, heavily made-up with mascara and powder, and rouge rubbed all over her cherubic face.

"You wanna catch me?" she said. She wrapped her arms around my elbow and bicep. Bleary-eyed, eyelids half closed, she waited for her answer.

"No," I said and pulled away. "I go Key Club." She stumbled after me but kept her grip on my arm.

"*Yoboseiyo*," she said again. "*Yoboseiyo*." She wouldn't let go.

Footsteps of police were coming down the alley. I stopped. Her head lolled down on my injured arm, but her grip was still tight. There was no time to fight her off and, if I did, the KNPs would have me. I grabbed her hair and tilted her face up to mine.

"*Agashi*," I said. "We go Key Club, I buy you drink, then we go short time most tick."

Her face brightened. "Short time?" she asked.

"Yeah," I said, as I pulled her toward the door. She nodded happily and followed, leaning into my side as we walked up into the club, never releasing my arm from her vice-like grip. I could hear the KNP coming as the swinging doors slammed shut.

We staggered toward the bar and I realized that her death grip was making the pain in my arm a whole lot worse. There were a few GIs playing pool and about fifty girls scattered around the place. They all stared at us as we hobbled across like two survivors of the Bataan Death March.

The women looked younger than any group I had seen before. The legal age for prostitution in Korea is eighteen. I didn't believe that most of these girls were that old.

I sat down at the bar. She just stood at my side, still clinging to my arm. She seemed to be struggling to stay awake. I ordered a beer for myself and a drink for her. Hers came in a cocktail glass, was colored bright red, and had no alcohol in it. The cost was three times what I paid for my beer.

The barmaid pushed the brown OB bottle in front of me. "You want a glass?" she asked. I said yes. She seemed surprised.

The glass had dust on it and I had to pour the beer myself. Not as much class as the Lucky Seven Club.

I managed to get her to sit down on the stool next to me and held up my beer glass for a toast. Her eyelids opened a little bit. She was trying to figure out what I was doing. The barmaid was standing there, watching us, and said something to her in rapid Korean. The girl just leaned down and slurped some of the liquid out of the glass.

I said, "Cheers," smiled at the barmaid, and took a long drink.

"I go banjo," I said. The girl just sat there, staring at the bright red liquid in her glass. I looked at the barmaid. She nodded and I crossed the floor to the small door marked WC.

I didn't have to take a leak but I was checking for windows. There was a small one with bars across it, but it only led to a cement wall.

This latrine had toilet paper, the Key Club did have some things going for it. I ripped off a little and dabbed at the fresh blood seeping from my left hand. I threw that in the commode and then wadded up a bunch of toilet paper and stuffed it into my jacket pocket. Now the Key Club was out of ass wipe, too.

I walked out and, instead of returning to the bar, headed directly for the front door. I didn't open it, but the swinging doors were a little off center and there was a slight opening with a cold draft coming through.

I could see a KNP standing outside. He reached toward someone, probably a partner, and traded cigarettes and matches, performing the ritual of lighting up and preparing for a long wait.

The back door was already covered by the other policemen. I was trapped.

I returned to my seat at the bar and woke up my girlfriend. She opened her eyes as wide as she could get them and asked reflexively, "We go short time?"

I took another pull of my beer and looked at her for the first time. She was wearing exceedingly tight hot pants that seemed to be molded like plastic wrap to her. Her legs were bare, no nylons, and a few bruises spotted the otherwise creamy brown skin. Inscribed on her T-shirt above the nipples was an advertisement for American Express travelers' checks. Her cheeks were a little pudgy and her straight black hair was cut short, accenting the roundness of her face.

She was actually very cute and would have been an attractive young lady had it not been for all this.

I didn't answer but reached out, took her arm, and pulled it toward me to look at her wrist. She came awake immediately.

"Whatsamatta you?" She yanked her arm back and became shrill. "You no touchey Judy, okay?" She wagged her finger at me and stood up. I half expected her to punch me. The she looked over at her cherry red drink, reached for it, and downed it in one gulp. She turned back to me, fully coherent now.

"You wanna catchey Judy, get short time now, or you wanna catchey 'nother girl?" She waved her arm around the room.

"Where's your room?"

"Upstairs," she said.

I finished my beer. "Let's go."

On the way up I watched her pretty backside sway back and forth—soft, youthful. And I thought of the raised scars on her wrist, like high mud rows between rice paddies, and the neat circular burn marks from flaming cigarette butts put out on her skin.

When we got to her room, we took off our shoes and entered. There was nothing but a rolled-up mat on the floor and a small table covered with cosmetics and a little mirror. Some of her clothes were hanging from nails in the wall and the rest were wadded up and piled in the corner.

She started to unroll the mat but I walked to the window. We were on the second floor and there was a drop of twenty feet to the alley below. I turned to her. "How can I get out of here?"

She just looked at me.

I said, "I no can go. Korean policemen front door and back door. How I get out?"

"No can do," she said.

I reached in my pocket, pulled out a ten-dollar bill, and handed it to her. She folded it and stuck it inside her hot pants. "Let's go," she said.

I followed her down the hallway and up another flight of stairs until we came out on the roof. "Which way?" I asked.

She just waved to the buildings on either side. Both were almost the same height as our building but there was about a ten-foot space between each.

"How?" I said. She shrugged. I looked around. There were no fire escapes or footholds to use to get down.

I weighed going back to her room and waiting them out. But that wouldn't work. After curfew, when most of the GIs had left, the police would make short work of finding me.

There was an iron grating that had been left up on the roof to rust. I paced it off but it wasn't nearly long enough to cover the gap to the next rooftop. There was nothing I could use to span the space. Actually, it was about twelve feet and, looking across, it looked very close. A twelve-foot jump. I could make it. It's just that if I missed, it would be a three-story drop. Just a matter of confidence, I told myself. If it were twelve feet paced off on the ground, it would be no big problem. It was just the fear of the abyss below.

Judy seemed to sense what I was planning to do. I thought of the KNPs below. This might not work. They might spot me or be waiting for me even if I made it to the building next door. I handed her the film.

"You hold this for me?" I asked. "I don't want to break it."

"When you come back?"

"Tomorrow."

"Ten dollar," she said.

"Five."

She shrugged her narrow shoulders and slipped the roll of film into the snug front pocket of her hot pants.

I got back against the far side of the building, ran across the roof as fast as I could sprint, pushed off from the top of the cement parapet, and leapt into space.

The parapet had been higher than I thought, and rising up the three feet or so to breach it had taken away most of my forward momentum. I was hurtling through the air, halfway between the two buildings and the edge still seemed a long way away. I hit the ledge of the opposite building flush on my stomach.

I thought it had killed me and I almost blacked out, even as my body began to slide down the side of the building. I grabbed on to the ledge with my elbows and stopped myself. It bit into my chest, and I kicked and found a toehold, pushed up with my foot, and managed a better grip so I could pull up. Struggling for every inch, I shimmied up onto the roof.

I lay there for nearly a minute but still couldn't breathe. After a while I was getting some air. My hand was bleeding again.

I found the stairwell in the center of the roof and walked carefully down the steps. It was a small apartment house, and the pungent aroma of kimchi and fish became stronger as I descended toward street level. I encountered no one. When I got to the front door, I lay prostrate and peered around the corner. The policemen were still standing in front of the door but Judy had just walked out of the club into the cold night, still in hot pants and T-shirt. She started talking rapidly to the police. I prepared to make a run for it, but by then the policemen were laughing. One of them came forward and offered her a cigarette. The other one good-naturedly lit it and, while they were enjoying themselves, I walked out of the building, down the alley, and onto the large road.

I was glad I had taken that toilet paper. I had the entire wad gripped tightly in my left hand inside my jacket pocket. I felt some blood seep slowly out and I gripped the soggy paper harder, trying to stanch the flow.

Along the road, past rows and rows of clubs and bright lights, GIs swarmed everywhere. I became less worried about the KNPs. As long as the blood didn't seep through my jacket—

I wanted to go on the compound, to the dispensary, and get some stitches in my hand. I didn't think the MPs were looking for me. I was pretty sure it was just the KNPs. As far as the Army was concerned, my only offense was being AWOL, and that probably hadn't even been reported yet. Even if it had, nobody wastes any time looking for U.S. Army deserters in Korea. There's nowhere for them to go. Eventually they'll either turn themselves in or come to no good end. But the KNPs were looking for me pretty hard. I had to figure it was to protect General Bohler. The mayor and the chief of police must have put out the word that I had to be apprehended, prevented from snooping around anymore.

If I told my story, no one would believe me. Just another jealous enlisted man trying to make an officer look bad. But the powers in Itaewon definitely didn't want me out here unattended. Somehow they knew about the film and figured I had it.

There was a steady stream of ROK military vehicles traveling down the Main Supply Route, heading toward Yongsan Compound and the ROK Army headquarters beyond. Riding in one of them would be safer than hoofing it. I stepped out into the street and waved one of them down. The cab was made of sheet metal rather than canvas and painted a dark green. The soldier on the passenger side slid one pane of the divided window forward.

I spoke to them in Korean. "I'm sorry to bother you," I said, "but I have to get back to my post right away. Can you help me?"

"We are on our way to the Ministry of National Defense," the young man said. He was a ROK Army lieutenant.

"There is an emergency in my unit. They need a translator right away."

"Have they caught an intruder?" The lieutenant sat up, suddenly interested.

"I'm sorry," I said. "But I can't talk about it."

"Get in," he said, and opened the door for me.

The ROK lieutenant shifted into the back to make room for me in the passenger seat. I ducked into the front seat, hiding my hand in my pocket.

Then I felt it. A dull thud behind my left ear. Dazed, I just sat there, wondering what it was. Then I felt it again, this time to the back of my head.

Just before I passed out I glimpsed something in the rearview mirror. A Korean National Policeman, grinning.

16

"These guys aren't too happy with you." It was the first sergeant.

"That's funny," I said. "I thought we hit it off quite nicely."

We were talking through an iron grating.

I was in the holding cell in back of the Itaewon Police Department. It was a charming place really. The room was about thirty feet square with a cement floor and two huge wooden platforms, the living quarters for the inmates, elevated about three feet high on either side of the central aisle. Broadcasting its presence from the rear was the *byonso*.

They say learning is best accomplished when the tactile senses are employed. The fetid waves of aroma pulsating out of the *byonso* left the meaning of the word indelibly impressed on my cerebral cortex.

Earlier that morning an old man had sloshed a bucketful of water onto the cement floor. I had been sitting on the edge of the platform and he had unceremoniously doused my shoes and my socks. My cold feet reeked of the stale water and disinfectant. I was hungry, I was dirty, and a series of fresh bruises arrayed about my torso added their drumbeat to the huge aching knot on my head.

Other than that I was fine.

One of the blue-suited policemen came up beside the first sergeant, pulled out a large ring of keys, and opened the iron door. I stepped out quickly and took a deep breath. At the front desk they gave me an envelope with my identification, my keys, and my wallet. I checked to make sure it was all there.

I slipped my Army ID card and my Criminal Investigation Division badge into my hip pocket. "What about an apology?" I said.

Top looked at me. "An apology?"

"Yeah," I said, "from Captain Kim. His boys got a little rough. While I was conducting an investigation."

"That's not the way they see it."

"Well how the fuck do they see it?" My neck stiffened and made the pain from my head pulse louder. The sullen eyes of the half-dozen Korean policemen around the room were on us.

Top faced me directly. "Let's go, George."

I straightened my jacket, looking around the room at each policeman in turn.

"They charged you with resisting arrest," Top said.

Standard police procedure. The first thing you do is cover your ass.

"And then they charged you with breaking and entering."

"But I didn't break anything," I said.

"Well," he said, "something's probably broke now."

I couldn't argue with logic.

"I was on a goddamn investigation."

"I claimed you were on an investigation," Top said. "I told them that. And I told them that you're in the CID, at the moment."

"So they dropped the charges?"

"No. They told me to get you out of town."

"They don't have any jurisdiction to tell me to get out of town." I said it but I didn't believe it. It was their town and their country. "What happened to cooperation between Korean and U.S. Investigative agencies? What about the KNP Liaison Office?"

"It's your own fault," he said. "You know what we were supposed to do here. It's obvious to everybody that no one else was going to get murdered and the whole thing could be forgotten."

"That's not the way I saw it," I said.

"No," he said, "You have to go and start investigating all this shit again, get people all in an uproar, and end up with the whole fucking world down on your ass."

"I was just trying to earn my pay," I said.

"Yeah," he said. "I guess."

A Korean doctor approached. He wore a black suit and a black tie and black horn-rimmed glasses. So as not to clash with his jet black hair, I thought. The man nodded to Top and then to me. He took off his coat, handed it to a cop, opened his bag, and went right to work. He made me open my hand on a countertop and used water and a washcloth to rinse off the dried blood in a plastic basin. After the wound was cleaned to his satisfaction, he pulled out a bottle of peroxide and with a cotton swab drenched the open gash in the fiery solution.

I tried not to let the pain show on my face. Top sat quietly off to the side and looked at me without expression. Every time I twitched, the cop grinned a little wider. I was impressed that so much pain could come from such a small part of my body.

The doctor pulled out a syringe and a small vial and deftly filled the syringe with a clear fluid. The cop's feverish interest seemed to be growing. By the time the doc reopened my reluctant hand and stuck the needle flush into the middle of the open wound, the policeman was in rapture. My arm convulsed with the pain. We all stood there silently while the doctor waited for the Novocain to take effect. Then he pulled out a needle that looked like an oversized fishhook and laced some black nylon string through it. He took my hand again and pushed the needle through my flesh, across the wound, and under the flesh edging the other side. The string followed the needle through and he quickly laced up the largest parts of the gash. His hand movements were quick and sure but he kept having to tell the officer to get out of his light. His nose was almost in my palm.

When the doctor finished, he knotted off the string neatly and pulled a small pair of scissors out of his bag and cut off the loose ends. It looked as if the black fossilized remains of a primordial sardine were resting in my palm.

He stood up, Top helped him put on his coat, and I nodded my thanks to him.

When we got outside, Top laid into me.

"Sergeant Sueño," he said, "these are not people you want to be in bad with. I won't be able to help you if you keep pushin' on this." He paused. "I'm not hearing you say what I need to hear you say."

I didn't say anything.

The first sergeant shook his head, sighing, and went on ahead to the jeep.

The security guards at the gate remembered us as the guys who had been doing the inspecting lately and waved us right through.

"Is the general in?"

"Yes. He just got back from work."

It had already been dark a couple of hours.

We parked the jeep, walked up to the front door, and rang the bell. An elderly Korean woman in traditional dress opened the door. We told her we wanted to see General Bohler. She looked confused for a moment and then a voice rang out from the back room.

"Let them in."

She led us to a large room, a study, I guess you would call it. A fire crackled. Plaques and photographs hung on all the walls. In the center of the room was a carved statue of a nude African woman. General Bohler sat in a large leather lounging chair, wearing only sandals and a bathrobe. He set a book down when we walked in. Something thick and nonfiction: *The Enemies of Security.*

"Evening, boys."

Slowly, he put his glasses back on. He seemed completely relaxed. Too relaxed.

"Sit down. What can I help you with?"

"You're under arrest, General."

He began to laugh. "Aren't you going to read me my rights or something?"

"We can do that. But it always seemed a little corny to me. You already know them, don't you?"

"Sure I do. Now what am I being charged with?" He was a man playing along with a joke.

"The murder of Pak Ok-suk."

"Who?"

"Miss Pak. The young girl you tied up, sodomized, and then strangled to death before setting fire to her apartment."

"Hold on just a minute, son. I didn't start any fire."

"I'm not your son."

I locked my eyes on his and fought the urge to punch his face in.

"No," he said. "No, you're not. You're Hispanic, aren't you? You could pass for Eastern European or Greek but you've actually crossed the border and come north, haven't you? I'm a good judge of these things."

"I didn't cross the border. You crossed it in 1846."

Bohler laughed. "Good answer. The Mexican War. When we took all that real estate away from your ancestors. Looks like we might have to take some more here pretty soon if you don't clean up all those Commies you got running around down there."

"I don't have any Commies running around anywhere. Why'd you kill her?"

"Now, now. You're sort of jumping to conclusions, aren't you?"

"We got the photos, Bohler."

Bohler's facial muscles didn't move but slowly the blood ran from his face. When his voice came out, his throat seemed to be clotted with cotton.

"I can make your careers. What are you now? Buck sergeants? In two years you'll be E7s. In three, first sergeants. I've got friends at the personnel center. It'll be a snap."

"Get your clothes on, General."

"You don't know what you're doing. You don't know what kind of buzz saw you're going to run into. I've got money to hire lawyers and I've got friends who will rip you to shreds."

Ernie blew a bubble and let it pop.

Bohler's face purpled.

"You're nothing but shits. Shit ass maggot enlisted men! I'll have you chopped up for C rations."

He jumped up and reached for something behind the end table. Ernie sprang forward and grabbed him and I yanked the whip out of his hand. We put him facedown on the sofa and handcuffed him. Ernie wandered around the big residence until he found his bedroom and his wallet.

"Fifty-six dollars, his ID card, and a bunch of plastic. I had to rummage through an assortment of leather straps and dildos before I found it."

The hands of the housemaid quivered as she put on his slippers. We threw him in the backseat of the jeep and yelled at the security guards to call the MPs because we wanted an escort.

While we waited, Bohler curled up in a little ball.

"They took Buster, I know they did. They all had their eyes on him, watching him every day, and finally they got him. I couldn't just let it go or else they would have gotten his sister, too. They're all a bunch of cannibals."

When the MPs got there I didn't give them a chance to figure out what was going on. Three of their jeeps, red lights swirling, followed us in a mad little convoy over to the Yongsan provost marshal's office.

Ernie leaned toward me. "Who in the hell is Buster?"

"His dog. Apparently some of the security guards had a little barbecue."

Ernie sat back up and kept his arms stiff as he made a big right turn.

"Only sensible use for the mutts."

"There's no doubt in my military mind that you are completely out of your gourd!"

It was the staff duty officer. The nervous desk sergeant had called him when he heard who we were bringing in. He didn't want to take the responsibility, by himself, for booking a two-star general.

The staff duty officer was thin, small, and pugnacious; an infantry officer from the honor guard and absolutely flabbergasted that anyone would even think of arresting a general.

The room had filled with MPs waiting to see what would happen. I kept telling the desk sergeant that I wanted the guy booked and I wanted a key to the holding cell so I could put him in it but he kept stalling.

The staff duty officer strutted around like he owned the joint, which caused a few grumbles from the MPs who didn't particularly like an outsider coming in and throwing his weight around. After all, a staff duty officer is supposed to stay up at the headquarters building and notify the Eighth Army staff in case of alert, not come messing around in military police business. I figured the desk sergeant would never be forgiven for calling him but that didn't help me much now.

The staff duty officer, whose name was Captain Manning, had figured out who the real culprit was. Me. He got up close, the brim of his cap just a few inches below my chin.

"You've got the *temerity* to drag a flag officer of the United States Army out of his quarters in the middle of the night—"

"It's not the middle of the night, sir."

". . . and stand him here in *front* of all his men, half *naked*—"

"He refused to put his clothes on."

"You could have dressed him!" His face was flushed but I think even he realized how silly his statement was. A couple of the MPs snickered. He cleared his throat and continued. "And then you try to coerce a conscientious desk sergeant—who after years of military training is well aware of the proper way to treat his superiors—into booking Major General Bohler and locking him up as if he were some sort of common criminal!"

"I'm booking him for first-degree murder."

Ernie held Bohler by the elbow. His arms were still handcuffed behind his back and his knobby knees stuck out of his silk lounging robe. His face had been hanging down but he looked up when he realized that he had gotten some support from a fellow member of the officers' corps. He got his regular voice back. It was a growl.

"I'm going to have somebody's ass for this, Captain. You'd better square it away."

Captain Manning flinched and turned to the general, thrusting his shoulders even further back. "Yes, sir."

Ernie jerked Bohler towards the desk. "Enough of this bullshit. Give me that goddamn form. I'll fill it out and book him myself."

The MPs glowered at the desk sergeant. One of them

shouted, "Book the son of a bitch!" Another obscenity faded away. A murmur filled the room.

"At ease!" Captain Manning walked up to the desk sergeant. "Don't you give him any form. This officer will not be booked, do you understand me?"

I got between him and the desk sergeant. "Interfering with an official investigation, sir? Obstructing justice?"

A moment's confusion entered Captain Manning's eyes. Ernie grabbed the paperwork out of the desk sergeant's hands and started filling it out while I held on to Bohler. When Ernie asked the general for his service number and full name, Bohler wouldn't answer, so we took it off his ID card.

Ernie slapped the completed form down in front of the desk sergeant and Captain Manning started yelling at him that it wasn't valid. The MPs closed around us in a tight circle. A couple of them were fed up.

"We ought to book the captain for interfering with an arrest."

"Yeah. Get back to the headquarters building where you belong."

One of them reached out and put his hand on Captain Manning's elbow. He swung his arm around like someone who had just been seared with a blowtorch. He actually hit the MP and then two MPs grabbed him. He tried to push them away and then the whole crowd started jostling. Ernie and I were trying to pull General Bohler out of the melee when someone slammed the door and hollered, "Attention!"

Everyone froze. Colonel Stoneheart, provost marshal of the Eighth United States Army, strode into the room, silver eagles glistening off his fatigue uniform like attack planes making their dive through the sun.

"What the hell is going on here?"

Everybody talked at once and General Bohler got his courage back and pretty soon Colonel Stoneheart was bowing and scraping to him and Captain Manning kept jumping in on their conversation like a puppy trying to get in with the big dogs. More MP jeeps rolled up, sirens blaring, Colonel Stoneheart gave some crisp orders, and the next thing I knew, Ernie and I were looking at each other in the relaxing quiet of an eight-by-ten holding cell.

We were alone, there were no hooks or sharp edges on the walls, and we couldn't hear any of the commotion going on outside.

Ernie turned toward me slowly.

"Nothing like a career in military law enforcement, eh, pal?"

I let my head wag.

"Fun, travel, and adventure."

17

When they released us, the first sergeant was waiting at the front desk looking as if he'd outlived his normal life span by about five hundred years.

"Don't say it, Top," Ernie said.

"I'm beyond words now."

The desk sergeant had us sign some paperwork and we walked out to a green Army sedan with a Korean Army driver waiting behind the wheel. The morning was cold but bright and fresh, like a new chance on life. The first sergeant didn't say anything until we got back to the CID Detachment.

The walk down the hallway resembled a funeral procession. Riley stared at us and when the phone rang he just lifted it off the receiver and set it back down. Miss Kim's eyes were red and she fumbled with a well-worked handkerchief.

"Sit down, you guys."

We took the same chairs we had sat in so many times while we received ass-chewings and braced ourselves for what was certainly going to be the El Primo of all time.

The first sergeant cleared his throat.

"The charges against Major General Bohler have been dropped."

Ernie hissed through his teeth.

My stomach tried to swallow itself and maybe it was the lack of sleep but the world got green again for a moment.

Ernie was the first to be able to speak.

"How can they do that, Top? They haven't had a chance to look at the evidence we got."

"The commanding general saw the prints first thing this morning. He and Colonel Stoneheart were up at dawn going over them. The people from the judge advocate general's office told him that it doesn't prove anything as far as murder but only proves that he once had an affair with a young woman who looks somewhat like Miss Pak Ok-suk."

The first sergeant held up his hands so Ernie would be quiet and he could finish.

"Even if we could prove that the woman was Pak Ok-suk, it still doesn't prove that he killed her because apparently a number of men had formed sexual liaisons with her, and having been one of them doesn't make you the killer."

"But we have corroborating witnesses," Ernie said. "Kimiko can put him there, at the scene, on the night of the murder."

"A bar girl convicting a general? It won't fly, Bascom. Her word won't hold up in court. The CG reviewed all the evidence, along with Colonel Stoneheart and the Eighth Army judge advocate, and they came to the conclusion that the only thing to do was to get General Bohler out of the country right away so this thing doesn't get blown out of proportion. The ROKs have agreed. They saw no reason to jeopardize our bilateral relations by going forward with such a flimsy case."

The first sergeant walked over to the coffee urn, poured himself a cup of coffee, and came back to his desk. Neither Ernie nor I made a move.

"There is some good news to come out of all this, though. The ROKs have agreed to drop the charges against Spec-4 Johnny Watkins. He was freed this morning and is on his way back to Yongsan. They're putting out the word to the Korean papers that subsequent investigation has shown the fire and resulting death to have been accidental. We've already booked Watkins on a flight back to the States this afternoon."

"Getting rid of everybody involved," Ernie said.

"That's no way to look at it, Bascom. This is an ugly situation and now it's over." The first sergeant fidgeted in his chair. "The CG talked to Colonel Stoneheart about you two. He says to let you know what a good job you did and he's proud of your tenacity in going after the case. And he's sorry that you were held while we tried to unravel everything. I've been authorized to give you some time off, too, to sort of unwind." The first sergeant stood up. "Take off the rest of today. That will give you a long weekend and then be back here Monday ready to go to work."

He shook both our hands and we stumbled down the hall.

"Can you believe these assholes?" Ernie said.

"Yeah. I can believe 'em. But they forgot one thing."

"What's that?"

"I still have the negatives. Stashed in a safe place." For five bucks, Judy would protect that roll of film as if it were gold bullion. "We make a few more prints, a cover letter, and I bet there's a few congressmen around who'd love to ask some questions up at the Pentagon."

"It means they'd shaft us," Ernie said.

I shrugged. "I never wanted to be a first sergeant anyway."

Ernie looked at me. "Me neither."

Ernie dropped me off at the barracks and I got on the horn and after a few tries I got through to Ginger at the American Club. Her voice was flat as she told me that Miss Lim was in the hospital.

"Which one?"

"The Peik Sim Byongwon. Near East Gate." She paused and I thought I could hear her swallowing. "Take care Georgie."

I held the receiver away from me and then I dropped it and then I was out the door.

The receptionist in her crisp white uniform looked down the list of patients for people with the last name Lim.

"She's young," I said, "and beautiful."

"Lim Hong-su, Lim Chong-kyu . . ." Finally she looked up at me. "Miss Lim Mi-hua, age twenty-nine, room 334." The unblemished oval of her face was impassive. "That is in the trauma center," she said.

An old woman in a heavy overcoat sat in a chair at the side of the bed. When she looked up at me, I could see through the dried tears and the wrinkles that she was Miss Lim's mother.

"I am Georgie," I said.

She stared at me for a long time, as if by looking she could somehow figure out how I had brought so much grief to her daughter.

Miss Lim was in traction. One arm broken, two legs. Bandages surrounded her face, a tube ran into her nostrils, and there were stitches along her forehead, her cheek, and her chin. Her eyes were puffed and closed.

I heard some murmuring down the hallway. The nurses had noticed the big American walking the ward. A dapper Korean man in rimless glasses and a white coat walked in.

"Good morning," he said. "I am Doctor Ahn."

We shook hands.

"Are you a friend of hers?" He nodded toward Miss Lim.

"Yes."

"I am afraid the news is not good. Most of her hip has been shattered. She will not walk again."

I looked at the doctor.

I looked at Miss Lim. She didn't seem to be breathing. The big cold cement walls of the hospital closed in on me but I fought the blackness and somehow remained standing.

I thanked the doctor and walked out of the room.

Miss Lim's mother had never taken her eyes off me.

After I retrieved the film from Judy and paid her five bucks, Riley used his lunch hour to help us print more photos. He had a lot of experience in photography. Ernie and I fidgeted outside the darkroom. Finally Riley poked his head out.

"Did you guys do something unusual to the chemical bath when you were developing these prints?"

We shrugged.

"Well, the negatives have gone funny. Come in and take a look."

We went into the darkroom and, after our eyes adjusted, he held up one of the wet photographs. A big halo emanated from Miss Pak's head and from General Bohler's and they were bright enough to leave barely a trace of facial features. That was the best print. All the others were totally ruined.

"You guys need a little work on your lab techniques."

"Yeah," Ernie said. "We need a little work on a lot of things."

"Where is the first set of prints you made? You can just make more from those."

"We turned them over to the provost marshal's office."

"History, huh?" Riley said.

"I'm sure they'll have an honored spot in the Eighth Army archives."

"Where's that?"

"The incinerator."

"Hey!" Riley said. "One piece of good news—the initials of the party who signed out the marriage packets?"

"Yeah?" I said. "Who?"

"Bohler's secretary."

The first thing I did was go back to my room and get a whole lot of sleep. Or at least I tried to. The houseboys kept bustling around the barracks, making a lot of noise, and my head kept popping off the pillow with a new thought of how I should have handled the case. A couple of times I shuffled down the hallway in my shorts and shower shoes and bought myself a can of Falstaff out of the big PX vending machine. Finally I gave it up and took a shower, shaved, and got dressed.

I went to the ville.

The reason for all the changes at the Korean Procurement Agency was that General Bohler had been using his influence to get new companies, under the auspices of Mr. Kwok, the lucrative Eighth Army contracts that had routinely been going to another group of entrepreneurs. Lindbaugh had been the facilitator for this at KPA, and since he was in the right place at the right time—and willing to go along with the program—he made a lot of money. Bohler, meanwhile, got what he wanted—an organization headed by Mr. Kwok that would do his bidding. If he spotted a woman he wanted, he got her, and I could only guess what other sorts of services were provided.

For some reason he got a perverse pleasure out of coercing young women who were about to marry servicemen from his own command into doing his sexual bidding. Maybe he made his choices from the photos and something interesting he saw in the marriage packets. Maybe it was just the safety of medically screened brides-to-be. However he made his choices, the women I knew about were exceptionally beautiful.

Li Jin-ai looked good even in the poor-quality black-and-white photograph in her marriage paperwork. The Nurse was a knockout and, of course, there was Miss Pak. Probably there had been others.

The ville on this late Friday afternoon was subdued. No hustle. No bustle. Just the smell of fish and fresh vegetables from the Itaewon market and the feeling that bars and whores and GIs were as inevitable and eternal as the slow changing of the seasons.

The early-morning sun had melted some of the ice but now the sky was overcast again and a slight wind had picked up and the ice on the roadway had refrozen into a smoother, slicker consistency. I slipped two times trudging up the hill to Itaewon.

The doors of the American Club were barred and locked. The King Club was open. Instead of my usual beer, I had a straight shot of Korean-made bourbon. It was rough but I held it and then I had another. The stuff can grow on you.

The jukebox spun out some good sounds and a couple of girls at one of the tables were giggling and looking at me and trying to get up the courage to talk to me or hoping that, better yet, I would talk to them. The place was warm and cozy and, as the bourbon started to seep into my body, I wondered what I was worried about. I told myself that I had no reason to feel anxious.

I wished that Miss Pak Ok-suk were here, to dance for me, in her tight blouse and miniskirt. But the Jade Lady was relegated to my dreams.

Freezing air burst into the room, trailing a bustling little woman, hair in disarray, eyes wide. She spotted the two girls at the table in front of me, sat down, and immediately launched into breathless exposition.

Something had happened. Something big.

I tried to pick out the words but she was running them all

together and waving her hands for emphasis. The girls ignored their Cokes and sat with their mouths open, all their attention focused on the ranting woman. The young man behind the bar and the adolescent girl who was the daytime cashier also stopped what they were doing and listened.

I managed to pick out a couple of words. Something about her apartment. Her landlady. And then I realized what it was. Her rent had been raised. That's all. Nothing serious. It didn't affect me in any way. But I also realized what I had been so anxious about all day and if I hadn't been so tired and so nervous and now so drunk, I might have realized it a long time ago.

Kimiko.

I finished my bourbon and headed toward the door.

Snow had begun to fall. Very lightly. It was a rough climb heading up the hill toward Kimiko's hooch because the road was slick and the fresh snowflakes were not making it any easier. The long gray stone walls loomed ahead of me. For some reason the gate to Kimiko's hooch seemed farther up the road than it had been before, farther from the main road and farther from the pulsating life of Itaewon. But that was impossible. Gates in stone walls don't move. It had to be my imagination, or the cheap bourbon.

When I reached the gate, the rusted metal swung back easily at my touch. I clanged it shut behind me, making sure the latch caught.

It seemed that no one was home. All the hooches were closed and shuttered. The burned-out hooch, Miss Pak's hooch, was still blackened and charred. Fresh petals of snow landed on the scorched wood, as if to mock the ruins, and then melted—disappeared.

I almost turned around and walked out, but something made me decide to check Kimiko's room. An obsessive sense of detail that the Army had drilled into me. Someday I would get rid of it. I hoped. As I crossed the courtyard, I made the only footsteps in an untouched field of white. The door to Kimiko's hooch seemed to be stuck but I pulled and it rattled and then the door slid back.

She lay there in a long white dress. A dress I had never seen before. She was flat on her back on the cold vinyl floor, a pillow under her head. Her hands were crossed serenely across her stomach and her long black hair had been combed and neatly arranged beneath her. She wore no makeup, the first time I had ever seen her this way. Her mouth and eyes were closed and it seemed that calmness had finally overcome her. She was almost beautiful. Except for the huge gash across her neck.

But there was no blood. Only caked flecks along the jagged opening. And there was no blood on the floor or on her clothes. It had all been wiped up, cleaned, and someone had washed her and put on the fresh clothes and combed her hair and set her here, on display—like some great leader millions of people would file by to pay their last respects. But there were no other people. Just me.

Just me and what was left of the woman Kimiko.

Curiously, I didn't feel bad. Maybe this was what was best for her. But I guess that sort of instant reaction is always there with people like Kimiko. Others just wish they would go away, that they wouldn't be seen anymore, that they wouldn't flaunt their needs in public anymore. I didn't exactly miss her myself. It was a relief that she was no longer around, no longer able to cadge drinks and embarrass me when I was trying to impress other women. And I tried to harden my heart with the thought of her blackmailing and the way she had used Miss Pak-Ok-suk for her own designs. Still, she looked small lying there.

18

When we strolled into the American Club, Ginger didn't come running down the planks, and when we sat down at the bar and ordered a couple of beers, she continued her halfhearted conversation with one of the retirees down at the end of the bar and sent the young girl who was her assistant to fill our order.

Ernie hit the beer pretty hard. The girl had hardly finished pouring for us when it was gone. Ernie ordered another, fished some money out of his wallet and, without asking me, told the girl to bring us two shots of brandy on the rocks. Korean brandy is pretty jagged stuff, but this brandy was not too bad. Probably California brandy poured into the Korean-made bottle, so Ginger wouldn't have to pay import tax.

When we finished that shot, Ernie ordered two more, and

another beer for me and another beer for himself, then set about busily pouring and slurping, hunched over the bar like a craftsman at his workbench.

"Building a drunk, eh?" I said.

"It's time."

I waited. I knew he'd tell me about it when he was ready. He was ready.

"The Nurse is much better now. But old Bohler did scare the shit out of her. She's quiet most of the time, and she doesn't even want me to get close to her.

"She doesn't look any different. But I guess it's on the inside. Like maybe she can't trust anybody anymore and maybe she can't relax with a man anymore. To me, that's always been the greatest thing about the Nurse, that she was so relaxed. She took everything in stride, nothing fazed her."

"She didn't seem so relaxed the night she came in here with a stick."

"That was different. We were supposed to have gone to see the chaplain that day, for the marriage processing interview, but I skipped out. We were busy and, besides, I didn't feel like going."

I took a sip of the brandy and had to widen my lips and pull in some air with it. Ernie was rough on her, very rough, but I wasn't one to be casting stones.

"I can understand why you didn't feel like going. After you hard-assed Chaplain Sturdivant like you did."

"He's a jerk."

"No argument on that one."

Ernie waited and then he spoke again. "I don't know about this marriage paperwork stuff. It's too much of a hassle."

"So's marriage," I said.

"Yeah."

I guess I wasn't helping much.

Ernie squinted at me, mulling over what passed for a thought.

Was something eating me, he wanted to know. I shook my head no and tried to look innocent.

A scraggly-looking little country band came in and started tuning up. Another night in Itaewon. But this would be the first one in a very long time without Kimiko.

I didn't tell Ernie about what I had seen at her hooch today. Better to keep him out of it.

Finally, after a number of dead soldiers had fallen off the bar's ramparts in front of us, Ginger came over and stood in front of me.

"Miss Lim, she was never sure when she was going to see you and she was afraid she might have to get on the plane to Hawaii without saying goodbye."

She thrust something at me.

"Here."

It was a little package made of brightly colored wrapping paper, intricately folded. I thanked her and slipped it in my pocket. Korean custom is not to open gifts in front of others. Good custom. Helps you stay hidden.

We had a couple of more brandies and a few more beers and then launched ourselves unsteadily out the door to hit as many bars in Itaewon as we could until we passed out.

In the morning I unraveled the package. It was a jade medallion. A little circle with one Chinese character in the middle.

The character was *ai*, which means love.

Riley met us at the snack bar and after getting himself a big cup of coffee, and loading it with about half a cup of cream and four spoonfuls of sugar, he took a sip and started filling us in.

"Bohler's on his way back to the States, in disgrace. They've lined him up with a training job down in Georgia and it's understood that he's supposed to set himself up for retirement in Florida and be out of the Army within six months."

"What about the Koreans?"

"That was a little more tricky. They wanted to cooperate but they had a complicated public-relations problem on their hands. The Itaewon fire marshall reopened the investigation and came to the conclusion that although Miss Pak Ok-suk might have been having sex with someone earlier that evening, they believe that the man, whoever he was, left and that then Miss Pak, under the influence of alcohol and drugs, attempted to change the *yontan* charcoal by herself and dropped one of the flaming briquettes in the center of the floor. Possibly she thought that there was a metal pan there to hold it. And then she lay down on her bed and went to sleep."

"What about the abuse to her body?" Ernie said.

"Never mentioned in too much graphic detail in the Korean papers. They ignored it."

"And Spec-4 Watkins?"

"Charges against him were dropped. He's down at Osan Air Force Base right now, under MP escort, being sent back to the States."

"Are they kicking him out of the Army?"

"Not right away. They assigned him to The Presidio of San Francisco. Better to keep him on active duty, so they'll have him under jurisdiction of the Uniform Code of Military Justice, until this thing blows over."

"So it's all just going to blow away, huh?"

"Except for you guys. They discussed sending you up to the DMZ—discussed it very seriously—but decided against it right now because if they do, you're liable to start mouthing off to the wrong people."

"Like our congressman."

"Or a reporter," Ernie said, looking encouraged.

"Right." Riley sipped his coffee. "So they're going to keep you here, keep an eye on you, and give you an attitude check. Your prospects around here, though, are not too bright after being foolish enough to lower the hammer on the chief of staff of the Eighth United States Army. But the one ray of hope is that they've definitely taken you off the shit list."

"What? You're kidding."

"No. Seriously. They've taken you off it. And put you on a whole new list that they've created just for this situation. They're calling it the disembowel-as-soon-as-possible list. You're both tied for first place."

"Anybody else on it?"

"No. Just you two."

"You've been a great help to us, Riley."

"Glad to be of service."

19

The monks kept their vigil for two days and finally they took Kimiko's body away, back to the mountains.

The landlady seemed relieved and had a couple of young men helping her clear the remains of Miss Pak's apartment while she got Kimiko's little closetlike room in shape for a new tenant. When she saw me she stopped what she was doing, tensed, and just waited. I nodded, turned around, and went away.

She didn't nod back.

Palinki wasn't the type to hound me about the .45, so I held on to it for a while, keeping it in my wall locker, checking the cold steel and counting the cartridges every day, just to make sure they were still there.

I wasn't sure why but it was important to me.

Ernie and I went on a huge drunk, reeling from bar to bar, starting early in the morning, sometimes taking a nap in the afternoon, and then getting drunk again at night. When we went back to work Monday, we were just going through the motions on the black-market detail and found plenty of time to slip away to little isolated draft-beer halls out in Itaewon and have a few cold ones for lunch. We went on like this for quite a while. I can't say how long now. The time faded into a dismal blur.

Ernie never once mentioned the Nurse.

Finally one morning I woke up and was sick about how I'd been acting. I made a special effort to get over to the gym and see Mr. Chong for the noon tae kwon do workout.

"Where have you been, Georgie?"

"Busy."

"You should not get so busy. It is dangerous."

I sobered up, worked out steadily, and my midsection started to firm up again. It was as if my body had taken hold of my fate and slowly its resolve started to become apparent to me.

Mr. Kwok, meanwhile, had made more and more inroads into the economic life of the village. A couple of his competitors had closed down and a couple more had sold out to him. He closed their clubs down for a while, remodeled them, and reopened the doors with big, flashy grand openings. I started hanging out in the ville, supposedly for the black-market detail, but mostly watching his comings and goings. I kept particular track of his thugs, sipped on Coke, and somehow stayed sober.

The winter should have been over but a last flurry of cold, ice-laden air whistled through Seoul. The snow wasn't heavy but just enough to make the roads slick and life a little uncomfortable. I loved the long overcast days and the freezing crispness that seemed to tighten and enflame my body.

I started carrying the .45.

My Spartan regimen had kept me a long time without a

woman, and one late afternoon, while slogging through my black-market rounds, I turned—without thinking about it much—down the alley that led to the hooch where the girl lived, along with her sisters, in the brothel behind the Sloe-eyed Lady Club.

She was wary. I had cut out on her before, without giving her any money, and made her lose face. This time I gave her the money up front and went into her hooch to relax while she got a pan of hot water ready.

She was very young, very small, and I was very excited. When I finished, I got dressed and went back to the latrine. Most of her sisters were out, or sitting quietly in their rooms, gossiping, playing cards. I found a toehold in the fence and climbed over.

Kwok was usually in his office this time of day. He got up late so the afternoons were like mornings for him. Time for the mundane things in life. Paperwork. Bills. The flamboyance came after the sun went down.

His thugs were rarely around during the daytime. They slept even later than he did. Sometimes he had late-night things for them to do.

I climbed the rickety metal staircase on the outside of the building, unable to keep completely quiet but trying to keep my advance as rhythmic and as calm as I could.

One of the things that had bothered me from the first was the pair of straight metal tongs in the middle of Miss Pak's room. Someone had found the half-submerged heater outside and then used the tongs to pull out one of the flaming briquettes and bring it inside and put it on the vinyl floor. Maybe Miss Pak had done it herself, if she was very drunk or very loaded on drugs. But that seemed unlikely because if she was that far gone she would have just passed out and not paid any attention to the underground heating system. If, however, she had actually tried to change the charcoal briquettes in the heater, it would have been second nature to her to replace one of the flaming briquettes with a new one and leave its red-hot embers in a metal pan outside near the stove. She was a farm girl, she knew how to do these things, and for her to have started the fire herself seemed unlikely. Major General Bohler, however, had little knowledge of the workings of Korean households. This was his first tour in Korea—they didn't need underground heating systems in Vietnam—and since he'd been here, his servants had done everything for him, including tying his jogging shoes.

If he had choked Miss Pak until she was either dead or she had passed out, it didn't seem possible to me that he would have put on his clothes, gone outside in the freezing cold, searched around until he found the heater, opened it, used the tongs to pull out one of the charcoal briquettes, and then brought it back into the house to start a fire and destroy the evidence. He would have exposed himself to too many prying eyes.

It was more likely that he would have panicked and put his clothes on and run to the one person in Itaewon who could help him: Kwok.

I could imagine the frantic Bohler, telling Kwok that he thought he'd just killed a girl. The solicitous Kwok telling him to go home, that he would take care of everything, and then going to the hooch and . . . But that's where it broke down. Why not just remove the body? Business girls disappeared from Itaewon all the time.

So the blackened tongs festered in my mind.

But then we saw the photos. I felt sorry for Miss Pak, who was being so ravaged, but still it was exciting and I searched every part of her body. The clarity of the photos was bad, and Bohler was all over her, but I did manage to make out, in a couple of the shots, the medallion that she was wearing around her neck. The one that said *ok*. Jade.

It seemed sort of strange to me that a young girl like her, having money for the first time in her life, would buy herself such an old-fashioned piece of jewelry. Jade, from antiquity, and Chinese characters yet.

Not exactly trendy.

And if she did like that sort of thing, why wasn't she wearing it when she had her photograph taken for the marriage paperwork? Maybe she hadn't bought it yet, sure, but there was another possibility. Maybe a man had bought it for her. As a gift. And it wouldn't have seemed appropriate to her to wear it in the photograph intended to accompany her request for betrothal to Johnny Watkins.

And I doubted that it was a GI who had bought it for her. When GIs buy gifts for Korean business girls they usually come straight out of the PX. After all, what value does a thing have if you haven't seen it advertised on television?

But a Korean man could have bought it for her. He would have had to be rather infatuated with her, though. Kwok didn't seem to be the type, but who knows?

If he were, that would explain his desire to destroy Miss Pak Ok-suk along with the evidence of Bohler's debauchery. A man can fight jealousy, put himself above it, but not forever.

Another factor was the silence of the neighbors. If the person lurking around Miss Pak's hooch just prior to the fire had been a GI, even Major General Bohler, the Koreans would have had no hesitation in reporting everything to the police.

Had it been a known thug, they might have hesitated, but the police would have gotten the truth out of them and taken care of the thug.

If it had been Kwok, however, the neighbors would have been frightened to death to talk about anything, and the police wouldn't have pursued the case either. They probably received more money from Kwok's operations than they did from their regular paychecks. In some ways he was their employer. And even if they had decided to throw him in the can, they would have to put up with a lot of heat from up top.

All that trouble for a GI whore? Not likely.

But all this was really just a mind game I was playing with myself. Even if Kwok hadn't killed Miss Pak, I knew he had killed Kimiko, or had one of his boys do it. And he'd crippled Miss Lim.

That was enough for me.

I opened the door to Kwok's office and walked in.

His head was in a big safe. He sat up abruptly and swiveled around in his chair when he heard me enter.

The office was spare. A small wooden desk, a couch, a coffee table, a green-shaded lamp on his desk fighting the gloom of the overcast afternoon.

"What do you want?" he said in Korean.

I closed the door behind me, reached in my coat, and pulled out the .45.

His body sagged, just slightly, as breath escaped from his body. Slowly, he gestured toward the safe. "I have money," he said in English.

The bullet slammed into his body and he spun back off his chair. I stepped forward but he was down, a puddle of blood growing on the floor. The gun had been sighted on his chest when it went off. The .45 had a heavy slug. He would die soon. If not, maybe he deserved to live.

I looked at the money. Some of it was greenbacks and some of it bank notes, but most of it was Korean money. Stacks of it, in various denominations. I took a bundle of worn-looking ten-thousand-won notes, folded it, and stuffed it into my pocket. Expenses.

The puddle of blood was getting bigger now, almost reaching my shoes. I stepped towards the door but halfway there I stopped. Something was holding me. I went back to the desk and quickly looked through the drawers. In the top middle drawer I found it. The jade medallion. Ok. I left it there, closed the door to the office behind me, and walked hurriedly, but not frantically, down the steps.

I climbed the fence back into the brothel. As the cold night approached, all of the girls were indoors, fixing their hair and putting on makeup. No one noticed me as I slipped through the hooches and left quietly through the front gate.

One loud noise. Maybe a backfire. That's all anyone would think. The next day I cleaned the .45 carefully, threw the two remaining cartridges into a septic tank, and returned the weapon to Palinki.

"Everything go okay, brother?"

"Yeah. I got in a little target practice."

"If you need to use it again, you let me know, you hear?"

"Yeah, Palinki. Thanks."

There was no mention of Kwok's death in the Korean newspapers. He wasn't the type anybody makes a fuss over after they're dead.

Out on black-market detail I watched the comings and goings of his underlings. They seemed agitated and never stopped ranting at each other. We heard from the KNP blotter report that a couple of them were killed. Knifework. And three or four of Kwok's nightclubs closed. Pretty soon somebody must have taken his place because things got quiet again. The closed nightclubs were reopened, one of them under a new name and another as a Japanese nightclub, catering to tourists from Tokyo.

Itaewon is going to hell.

Ernie and I didn't get to work together anymore. The first sergeant kept us separated and kept finding more and more menial tasks for me to perform.

Finally Riley broke the news to me.

"You're being transferred, George. Up north."

"At least they waited a decent interval."

"They're claiming that it doesn't have anything to do with your arrest of General Bohler, just manning requirements."

"Bull."
"Yeah."

The DMZ is beautiful. I mean that. I'm at a little firebase over-looking a valley with hills marching off as far as you can see in either direction until you run into the snow-capped mountains. There are no trees, just shrubs, because no one wants their field of fire obstructed.

The hills are capped by sandbagged positions and in the valleys below, rows of barbed wire parallel chain-link fences, and between their fences and ours about a jillion land mines lurk underground, like lethal subterranean mushrooms.

The North Korean across the valley, looking at me through field glasses, sports a brown uniform and a floppy cap with a red star on it and there is no doubt that he is my enemy.

He sits on one side of the line and I sit on the other.

Neat.

I often think about Kimiko and Miss Lim and Miss Pak Ok-suk. And when I get a night off I take the Army bus across the half-frozen Imjin River, but I never go to Seoul. I stay in a village of thatched-roof hovels and drink rice wine and cuddle with country girls who haven't yet learned how to speak English.

It's only when the rice wine flows, and won't stop, that I think of Kwok and Miss Pak, and the Jade Lady dances, burning in my soul.

Turn the page for a sneak preview of

SLICKY BOYS

MARTIN LIMÓN

1

"**Y**ou buy me drink?"

Eun-hi coiled her body around my arm and leaned over the bar, her shimmering black hair cascading to the dented vinyl counter. I inhaled lilacs.

"*Tone oopso*," I said. No money. "Payday's not until Friday."

She pouted. Red lips pursed like crushed cushions.

"You number ten GI."

Ernie leaned back on his bar stool. "You got that right, Eun-hi. George is definitely number *ten* Cheap Charley GI." He tilted his head back and swigged from a frosty brown bottle of Oriental Beer.

We were in the U.N. Club, in Itaewon, the greatest GI village in the world. Shattering vibrations careened off the walls, erupting from an out-of-tune rock-and-roll band clanging away in the corner. On the dance floor Korean business girls, clad in just enough clothing to make themselves legal, and American GIs in blue jeans and sports shirts gyrated youthful bodies in mindless abandon.

It felt good to be here. Our natural environment. My belly was full of beer and my petty worries had been flushed away by the gentle hops coursing through my veins. Still, I was surprised Eun-hi had talked to me and I wondered why. Usually she remained aloof from all GIs except those who were willing to spend big bucks, which—on a corporal's pay—didn't include me.

Eun-hi stood up and pushed a small fist against her hip. She was a big girl, full-breasted, tall for a Korean woman. Long leather boots reached almost to her knees and white hot pants bunched into the inviting mystery between her smooth brown thighs. Dark nipples strained to peek out at the world from behind a knotted halter top bundling her feminine goodness. Eun-hi was a business girl. One of the finest in Itaewon. Finer than frog hair, to be exact. A GI's dream, a sailor's fevered vision, a faithful wife's nightmare.

My name is George Sueño. My partner Ernie Bascom and I are agents for the Criminal Investigation Division of the 8th United States Army in Seoul. We work hard—sometimes—but what we're really good at is running the ville. Parading. Crashing through every bar in the red-light district, tracking down excitement and drunkenness and girls. In fact, we're experts at it.

Gradually, over the last few months, more girls like Eun-hi had drifted into the GI villages. More girls who'd grown up in the twenty-some years since the end of the Korean War, when there was food to be had and inoculations from childhood diseases and shelter from the howling winter wind. Eun-hi was healthy. Not deformed by bowlegs or a pocked face or the hacking, coughing lungs of poverty.

She must've felt the heat of my admiration. At least I hoped she did. She took a step forward.

"Geogie," she said. "Somebody want to talk to you."

Ernie shifted in his stool, straightening his back. I stared at her. Waiting.

"A girl," she said.

My eyes widened.

She waved her small, soft palm from side to side.

"Not a business girl. *Suknyo*." A virtuous woman.

Ernie leaned forward. Interested now.

"Why in the hell would a good girl want to talk to George?"

I elbowed him. He shut up. We both looked at Eun-hi. She shrugged her elegant shoulders.

"I don't know. She say she want to talk to GI named Geogie. In Itaewon everybody know Geogie. So I tell you."

"Where is she?" I asked.

"At the Kayagum Teahouse. She wait for you there."

"Is she a friend of yours?"

"No. I never see before. She come in here this afternoon when all GIs on compound. Ask me to help her find Geogie."

"How'd she know I'd be here?"

Eun-hi laughed. A high, lilting warble, like the song of a dove.

"She know. Everybody know. You always here."

It wasn't true. Not always. Sometimes Ernie and I hit other clubs. But it was true that we were in Itaewon almost every night.

Ernie set his beer down. "What does she want?"

"I don't know. She no say. You want to know, go to Kayagum Teahouse. Find out."

She placed one shiny boot in front of the other and thrust out her hip.

"You no buy Eun-hi drink, then Eun-hi go."

With that, she performed a graceful pirouette, held the pose for a moment, and sashayed her gorgeous posterior across the room toward a group of hell-raising helicopter pilots.

Ernie looked at me, lifting his eyebrows.

"A *suknyo*," he said. "Looking for you?"

"Yeah. What's so surprising about that?"

"Oh, nothing. Except you're a low-rent, depraved GI and no decent Korean woman would get within ten feet of you."

It bothered me. Where did he get the idea that I was depraved? Sure, I preferred girls who were young. Eighteen or nineteen. But I was only a few years older than that myself. What was wrong with that?

"Not so depraved," I said.

Ernie stood up. "Shall we go?"

"Aren't we going to think about this first?"

"What's to think about?" he said. "A virtuous woman wants to talk to you. You think of yourself as a knight in shining armor. Maybe a horny one but still a knight. Besides, I'm curious."

He was right. It was enough to get anybody curious. Itaewon was, by edict of the government, for "tourists" only. Translated— American GIs. And any woman caught in the area of the GI clubs, without a VD card proving that she was a registered prostitute, was subject to arrest. Whoever this suknyo was, she had risked losing a hell of a lot of face by coming down here.

"Yeah," I said, standing. "I'm curious, too."

I slugged down the dregs of my beer. We grabbed our jackets off the backs of the bar stools and headed toward the big double doors. Outside, the smoke and noise and smell of booze faded behind us. The young doorman bowed. I figured him to be about thirteen years old, either a distant relative of the owner or some urchin they took in off the streets. He was wrapped in three layers of grease-stained sweaters. A gauze mask protected his mouth and nose from the cold.

I took a deep breath and felt the fresh bite of winter.

Itaewon was layered in crusts of snow. Neon lined the road running up the hill, flashing and sparkling through the latticework designs of frozen white lace. Shivering business girls, half naked, stood in alcoves, arms crossed, peering out over the rims of their dark-lined eyes, searching for the next customer.

A GI winter wonderland.

We twisted up our collars and shoved our hands into our pockets. Ernie blew a great billowing breath through tight lips.

"Cold out," he said. "Colder than a GI's heart."

At the Kayagum Teahouse it was easy enough to spot her. She wore a white cotton blouse buttoned all the way to the neck, and her face was a smooth oval, like an oblong polished pearl. Her mouth was moist and red, and shining eyes gazed steadily at the world in dark seriousness. Her name was Miss Ku.

She handed us a note, intricately wrapped into the shape of a flower, and asked us to deliver it to Cecil Whitcomb, a soldier of the British contingent of the United Nations Honor Guard.

As a civilian, she wasn't allowed on the compound to deliver it herself.

I was hesitant at first but Miss Ku pleaded with her eyes. They'd been lovers. They'd broken up. She wanted to see him one more time.

Each word was pronounced carefully. Precisely. As if the English had been memorized after long hours of study in a library. She told me that she was a graduate of Ewha, the most prestigious women's university in the country.

She apologized for becoming involved with Cecil. It was a mistake. She'd met him at a British-Korean Friendship Day at the British Embassy. He was in civilian clothes and she didn't know he was in the army. She bowed her head.

Soldiers are low on the Confucian hierarchy. Almost as low as prostitutes and actors.

Ernie and I waited. Something was screwy. I didn't know what, but something.

I noticed her hands. Long and slender with short cropped nails and small calloused knots on the fingertips. She slid an envelope across the table. It was stuffed with a short stack of five-thousand-won notes. About a hundred bucks' worth. This changed everything. Greed usually does.

Ernie snatched up the money and shoved it deep into the pocket of his nylon jacket.

I looked around. No Americans in the Kayagum Teahouse. Only young Koreans of college age, boys and girls, hunched over steaming cups of ginseng tea. No one to spy on us. And besides, we weren't taking a bribe. Just working a side job. Nobody could say we were doing anything wrong.

We'd do it. Why not? Easy money.

I picked up the paper flower and slid it into my breast pocket.

When Miss Ku smiled, the radiance of her gemlike face filled the room.

That alone would've been payment enough.

The next morning we gave the note to Lance Corporal Cecil Whitcomb.

Looking at Whitcomb, I wondered why a woman as gorgeous as Miss Ku would bother with a guy so unimpressive. His body was bony and pale. Dark brown hair fell over eyes that made him seem as if he hadn't quite woken up.

Ernie and I towered over him. Ernie is over six feet tall and I'm almost six foot four, and I was about two shades darker than the nearly translucent Cecil Whitcomb. On duty, CID agents have to wear coats and ties, which is what we had on. Cecil was on a work detail. He wore baggy fatigue pants and a grease-smeared woolen shirt.

He was nervous about two cops cornering him outside the unit arms room, but he unfolded the paper flower and read the message, showing no expression on his long, shadow-eyed face.

Somehow he had managed to bedazzle Miss Ku, and now he'd turned his back on her. It didn't make sense. But it wasn't any of our business. Our job was just to give him the note.

I glanced down at the printing. It was in English—in a careful hand—and said something about a meeting downtown and something about "I haven't told anyone yet."

When he finished reading, we waited for him to talk. He didn't. We decided to hell with him and walked away.

Ernie shook his head. "A couple of goofballs."

That summed it up. At least it seemed to at the time.

After work, the sun lowered red and angry beyond the hills overlooking the Yellow Sea. I noticed how cold it was. The temperature must've dropped ten degrees in the last couple of hours. A flake hit my head. White fluff whistled through the air. Snow would complicate things, but it wouldn't stop us from running the ville. Nothing would.

A half hour before the midnight curfew, we stood at the central intersection in Itaewon, gazing at the sparkling neon through a steady sprinkle of snowflakes. Kimchi cabs slid on the road and people had to grab handholds to climb up even the most gentle incline.

"Another world of shit," Ernie said.

"Looks like it," I said.

Ernie and I were discussing which bar to hit next, when an ice-laced gust of Manchurian winter roared up the main drag. An Eskimo trudged through the swirling wind. When he came near, I saw that he wasn't an Eskimo at all. Another long nose. And then my eyes focused. It was Riley, the Admin Sergeant from the CID Detachment.

He pulled a thick wool scarf off his neck, scanned the street, and spotted us.

"What does *he* want?" Ernie said.

The first glimmer of worry shot through my brain. "We're on call tonight, aren't we?"

"Sure," Ernie said. "But I left *ajjima's* phone number." He was talking about the landlady of the Nurse, his steady Korean girl-friend. "She would've come and found us if we had a call."

I wasn't so sure. Not in this blizzard.

Riley stormed up the road, stopped when he reached us, and motioned toward Ernie's right hand. Ernie handed him the liter of *soju*, a fierce Korean rice liquor. Riley rubbed the lip of the bottle with the flat of his palm, tilted his head, and glugged down a healthy shot. His Adam's apple undulated down his skinny neck as the searing liquid fell to his stomach. When he finished, he blew some breath out between his thin lips, thought for a moment, and slugged down another swallow. With red-rimmed eyes, he looked back and forth between us.

"Where have you guys *been?*"

"Right here," I said.

"But you're on call tonight."

"Ernie left *ajjima's* phone number."

"But she wasn't there when the First Sergeant called and her daughter answered and she can't speak English."

Ernie spoke up. "So the First Sergeant ought to learn Korean."

Riley looked at Ernie as if he just realized that he should be committed to the looney bin.

"You know the First Sergeant hates Koreans."

"That isn't our problem," Ernie said. "We left a good number."

Riley let his head loll on his long neck, as if his skull was suddenly too heavy for his shoulder muscles.

"Okay, okay. So you guys have an excuse. What else is new? But when the First Sergeant can't get through, he calls me in the barracks and orders me out of the rack and sends me down here to find you. At the Nurse's hooch the daughter draws me a map and says '*soju*' and pretends like she's jolting down shots and I wander around the ville until I find you." Riley spread his hands. "So it's over now. So forget it. But we got bigger problems. Problems downtown."

Suddenly I was worried. Not about the First Sergeant or about not being available when we were supposed to be on call—I'd been through that sort of trouble before—but about what had happened downtown.

"What problems?" I asked.

"Dead GI," Riley said.

Ernie and I waited.

"Well, not a GI exactly."

One of the business girls standing in the shadows plucked up her courage and sashayed toward us. Riley saw her coming and waved her off. She pouted, a gentle snort erupted from her nose, then she turned and marched back to her comrades waiting in the darkness.

"They found him downtown, near Namdaemun," Riley said. "Gutted with some sort of big blade. Body in a snowdrift. Blood everywhere."

He was warming to the subject, but I didn't need the details. I'd examine those when I arrived at the site. I interrupted him.

"What do you mean, not a GI exactly?"

"I mean he's not a GI. Not technically."

Ernie leaned forward. "Then what the fuck is he?"

"He's British. Member of the United Nations Honor Guard. A Lance Corporal. Name's Whitcomb." Mustard gas slammed into my nostrils. An old man pushed a cart past us loaded with the still-burning cinders of perforated charcoal briquettes. Things that had burned brightly, heating the flues beneath the floors of Korean homes, but that now were dead. And useless.

It took about five seconds for our brains to start working again. We left Riley standing in the snow and stumbled and slid down the hill, running toward the line of kimchi cabs waiting patiently in the somber night.

2

After stomping through the snow to the 21 T-Car motor pool, Ernie flashed his badge and managed to get the keys to the jeep from the half-asleep dispatcher. Twenty-one T-Car is a military acronym that actually means 21st Transportation Company (Car), which maybe makes a little more sense.

Despite the frigid air, the motor started right away. Ernie grinned.

"Amazing what a bottle of Johnnie Walker Black will do for an engine."

The bottle went every month to the head dispatcher who made sure the jeep was properly maintained and always available when Ernie needed it.

We drove through the gate and out into the city.

All vehicles were off the street now because it was past curfew, the midnight-to-four lockup the government slapped on a battered populace over twenty years ago at the end of the Korean War. The theory is that it helps the authorities spot North Korean spies who might be prowling through the cover of night. The truth is that it reminds everybody who's boss. The government and the army. Not necessarily in that order.

We rolled through the shadows.

Seoul was dark and eerily quiet and looked like a town that had been frozen to death.

The jeep had four-wheel drive and snow tires, but still Ernie slid on the packed ice every now and then. He turned out of the skids expertly and I felt perfectly safe with him at the wheel. Safer than I would've felt if I were driving. He's from Detroit. He's used to this kind of thing. But I hadn't learned how to drive until after I joined the army and, in East L.A., where I come from, it doesn't snow very often. Only during Ice Ages.

I thought of the long summer days when I was a kid, running with packs of half-wild Mexican children through alleys littered with gutted mattresses and stray dogs and broken wine bottles. There were no swimming pools in the barrio. We poured buckets of chlorine-laced water over our heads in a futile effort to keep cool. And during the hottest days of the season, when I was fortunate enough to land a job, I breathed in the tang of warm oranges and overripe limes fermenting in a metal pail as I knocked on door after door in Anglo neighborhoods, hustling for a sale.

Every kilometer or so we were stopped by a ROK Army roadblock. The soldiers looked grim and tired. Their breath billowed from fur-lined hoods and they kept their M16 rifles pointed at the sky, which was okay with me. After we showed our identification and the twenty-four-hour emergency dispatch, they waved us through without comment.

Neither Ernie nor I talked. We were both thinking the same

thing. We were in deep kimchi, the fiery-hot fermented cabbage and turnips that Koreans love. Kimchi up to our nostrils.

We'd taken money to deliver a note to Cecil Whitcomb, and now he was dead. Military justice doesn't know much about mercy. If anybody found out, we'd be kicked out of the army with a bad discharge or end up doing time in the Federal Penitentiary in Fort Leavenworth, Kansas, or both.

This wasn't going to be a routine case.

I was also beginning to feel a little guilty about maybe getting Whitcomb killed. Maybe a lot guilty. But I decided to put that away for now. I needed to think. And concentrate on the job I had to do when we arrived at the murder site.

Despite all the boozing we'd done in Itaewon, Ernie and I were both sober. But it wasn't from the cold air. It was from the tarantula legs of fear slowly creeping up our spines.

The upturned shingle roof of the Great South Gate was supported by stones weighing more than half a ton each. The gate had been built during the Yi Dynasty about four centuries ago, and was once part of a wall that surrounded the city. Now, in the deepness of the Seoul night, it sat somber and unmoving, as if it were watching us.

We circled the great edifice twice, creating lonely tracks in the snow, until I spotted a glimmer of light in one of the roadways running up a hill.

"Up there," I said. "Vehicle moving."

"Right."

Ernie swerved up the incline and rushed through a narrow road until the walls widened. We turned and almost ran into a gaggle of official-looking vehicles clustered around the mouth of another, even more narrow alley. Ernie found a spot up the road, parked the jeep, and padlocked the steering wheel.

As we walked back toward the lights, a grim-faced soldier stepped out of the night. He leveled an M16 rifle at us, blowing chilled breath through brown lips.

"*Chong ji!*" he said. Halt. "*Nugusho?*" Who is it?

I put my hands up slowly. "We're from Criminal Investigation," I said, "Eighth Army. Here about the body."

When he didn't respond I said the same thing—or almost the same thing—in Korean. The creased brow above the chiseled planes of his face crinkled a little tighter.

Ernie grew impatient. He pulled out his identification and thrust it forward. The soldier flashed a penlight on it, then studied our faces.

He waved his black gloved hand.

"*Chulip kumji yogi ei.*" No admittance here.

Ernie took a step toward the guard, staring at him, talking to me.

"Who does this asshole think he is, telling us we can't go in there? We're on an investigation."

I reached my hand out toward Ernie's elbow. The guard's face hardened.

"Relax, Ernie." I couldn't blame the guard much. We didn't look like investigators right now, dressed in our blue jeans and nylon jackets with dragons embroidered on the back. It was oh-dark-thirty, just a few hours until dawn. We were tired and it occurred to me that we must smell like a rice wine distillery.

"We don't have jurisdiction out here," I told Ernie. "He's just doing his job."

"Fuck his job."

Ernie turned and walked down the alley.

"*Chong ji!*" the guard yelled. When he aimed his rifle at Ernie's back, I stepped in next to him and spoke in soothing Korean.

"We're here for the investigation," I said. "A foreigner has been killed." I raised my open wallet in front of his eyes. "We're from Eighth Army. If you try to stop us, you will have many problems."

The guard looked at me warily. I saw the indecision in his eyes. "Don't worry," I said. "You won't get in trouble."

I wasn't sure if that was true, but I knew he'd be in a lot more trouble if he shot Ernie—or me.

I backed down the alley, hands raised, identification held over my head. When I was convinced that the guard wasn't going to shoot, I turned and hurried into the darkness.

Korea is a divided country—north and south—and a country under the gun. Over 700,000 armed Communist North Korean soldiers breathe fire across the Demilitarized Zone only thirty miles north of Seoul, the capital of South Korea. It's not surprising that paranoia seeps into everything.

The alley near Namdaemun was like most alleys I've wandered through in Korea. Narrow. High walls of brick or stone or cement on either side. Spikes and shards of broken glass atop the walls to keep out intruders. Flat, uneven stone paving. Water seeping out of open pipes, running freely down the indented center of the walkway, reeking of decay.

Around the bend Ernie waited for me.

"Did you get him straightened out?"

"Yeah, Ernie. Jesus. Why didn't you wait until he checked it out with his Sergeant of the Guard? They would've let us through."

"Fuck that shit. They see a *Miguk* face and they just don't want to let us in."

"They would've had to. Patience pays in Korea."

Ernie snorted.

"You're going to get us shot one of these days," I told him.

He grinned at that. I don't know why the idea seemed appealing to him.

At first glance Ernie appears quite normal. He has short sandy brown hair, combed straight to the side, and a pointed nose and big green eyes that shoot out at people from behind round-lensed glasses. In uniform he looks as if he belongs on a recruiting poster. It's after you get to know him that you realize he's cracked.

A white sign pointed up a flight of stone steps. "Peikchae Yoguan" the sign said. The Peikchae Inn.

Peikchae was the southernmost country on the Korean Peninsula during the Three Kingdoms Period, about 1,300 years ago. Koreans don't forget much.

We walked up the steps. The stone walls followed the stairway and then turned. I felt as if we were in some ancient place. The alley was stuffed with the smell of rusty water and cold stones and frozen hay.

During the Korean War, much of Seoul had been leveled. But many of these old walkways and flights of stairs had survived. Not worth wasting a shell on. New buildings had been constructed on the old foundations. The Peikchae Yoguan was one of those, although the inn was made of cheap wood that was already splintering and starting to rot.

An open spot in the flights of stone stairways spread out enough to make room for a stone bench. Flashlights swirled. Men mumbled. Some squatted and took photographs of footprints or collected minuscule items from the snow with tweezers and dropped them into plastic bags.

The Korean National Police. The all-pervasive law enforcement arm of the government of the Republic of Korea. A federal police force with representatives in every city, town, and village in the country. None of them looked back when we walked up.

The spot was isolated. The high walls around us were the backs of two- and three-story buildings. Tiny windows gazed out on us like half-shut eyes. The entrance to the Peikchae Yoguan was around another flight of crooked stairs with no direct line of sight from the front door. Whoever had chosen this place had chosen it well.

No lighting. At the bottom of a pit of stone and brick in the middle of an indifferent city. The perfect spot for a killing.

We scanned the soot-flaked ice looking for a stiff.

Ernie stepped closer to take a look at a drift of snow up against a short stone wall. He walked back.

"Tried to deep-freeze the son of a bitch."

"What?"

"Yeah. Hid him under the snow."

I sidled my way in closer, watching where I stepped.

In the center of the clustered policemen lay a body, already turning blue. When a beam of light slid over the corpse I saw what resembled the guy we had talked to this morning: Cecil Whitcomb. But it was a lifeless thing. As drained of color as death itself. Eyes wide. Blood spattered like spreading satin on the frozen sheet beneath him.

Whoever killed Cecil had dug out a hole for him in the drift and tried to cover him up. It hadn't worked well because the body made a lump in the smooth blanket of white lace that covered the city. But to the unobservant it would pass unnoticed. And probably all the killer wanted was a few minutes to make his getaway. This frail camouflage had given him that time.

Somebody finally decided to notice us. A tall Korean man. Almost six feet. A long gray overcoat, slicked-back hair, and a hawk nose under almond eyes. I wondered if he didn't have an ancestor who had ridden as one of the Middle Eastern auxiliaries with the hordes of Genghis Khan. He approached slowly. I nodded and we greeted one another. His English was precise. Careful. As were his movements.

"Are you Inspector Bascom?"

Mexican or Anglo, we were all just Americans in the eyes of a Korean policeman. When I was growing up in Southern California that attitude would've come in handy if more people had shared it. Saved me a few lumps.

"No," I said. "I'm George Sueño. This is my partner, Ernie Bascom."

Ernie ignored the tall cop and continued to gaze at the body and chomp on a fresh stick of gum.

"I'm Lieutenant Pak. Namdaemun Police Precinct."

He stuck his hands farther into his pockets and turned his head toward the corpse. "I understand that this person is not an American."

"No. British. Cecil Whitcomb."

"You knew him?"

"I've seen him." Lieutenant Pak waited, as if expecting a fuller explanation. I gave it to him. "He was in the United Nations Honor Guard. Since they're such a small contingent they've turned over police power to us at Eighth Army. They fall under our jurisdiction."

Pak shook his head. "Murders in Seoul fall under my jurisdiction."

He was right. According to the treaty between the U.S. and Korea, any crimes involving United Nations personnel that happen off a military compound can be handled by the Korean National Police if they choose to exercise jurisdiction.

Our role would be as observers, unless Pak asked for our help. I expected he would.

Two men in blue jumpsuits trotted past us, carrying a folded canvas stretcher. They knelt near the body and hoisted it out of its capsule of ice.

Whitcomb's necktie and white collar had been twisted askew. Dressed for an appointment downtown. No American GI would wear a white shirt and tie unless he had to. Who could understand these Brits?

I motioned for the men to wait and knelt near the stretcher. I grabbed one of their flashlights and played it over the body. The sleeves of Whitcomb's jacket had been shredded, as if someone had slashed them repeatedly with a sharp, razorlike blade. His hands and wrists had also been cut, along with portions of his ear and cheek. None of the cuts were deep, except for the big one in the center of his chest.

I pulled open a fold in the white shirt. He wore green woolen underwear. The caked blood made me think of the colors of Christmas. Apparently the knife had entered just below the sternum. One deft gash into the heart.

I lifted his lifeless hand and checked under the fingernails. Nothing. Maybe a lab could find a trace of flesh, but I couldn't see any. I dropped the limp hand and turned back to Lieutenant Pak.

"What have the neighbors said?"

"So far, nothing. My men are out now." He waved at the high canyon walls surrounding us. "Asking questions."

In the flickering beam of the flashlight, I studied the footprints in the crusted snow, "There was a fight. Someone must've heard something."

"Maybe." Pak looked at me steadily. "But sometimes men fight and don't make noise."

He was right about that. Sometimes you're too preoccupied with saving your life. Screaming can wait.

Ernie checked the body as the men with the stretcher lifted it up. He sniffed the air above it, as if examining a side of beef, and chomped more furiously on his wad of gum. He didn't say anything.

I glanced up the stairway leading to the *yoguan*. A light blazed yellow and the front door of the inn was open. At least someone in the neighborhood had taken note of all the commotion. I started up the steps. Ernie followed. So did Lieutenant Pak.

The big wooden double doors of the rickety wooden building were unbarred, and an elderly man and woman peeped out around the entrance. They stood at the end of a long wood-slat hallway that had been varnished and revarnished maybe a million times. The floor squeaked beneath our feet.

The woman wore a long cotton housedress and folded her arms over a thick sweater. A black bandana tied around her forehead hid almost all of her liver spots. The man was thinner, with wispy white hair. He wore the loose pantaloons and shiny silk vest of the ancient Korean patriarchs.

Even though Ernie and I walked in first, they ignored us and bowed to Lieutenant Pak.

"Oso-oseiyo." Come in, please.

Lieutenant Pak nodded back. Before he could speak I shot a question at the couple in Korean.

"Yogiei junim ieyo?" Are you the owners here?

Both nodded. Lieutenant Pak leaned back, mildly surprised that I could speak the language. Not many GIs bother to learn.

"Did you see any foreigners tonight?" I asked.

They both shook their heads. The husband smiled, as if he had suddenly encountered a talking horse, but the wife found her voice.

"No. No foreigners."

I twisted my head toward the murder site. "Did you hear anything—shouting, fighting—earlier this evening?"

The woman shook her head again. "Once curfew comes, we lock up and go to bed. We never stay open past curfew."

Not unless they have customers, I thought. The old woman was parroting the lines because of the presence of a Korean National Police officer. Not that Lieutenant Pak would give a damn if the inn stayed open past midnight, but Koreans are a cautious people. Especially when dealing with government officials.

"Did you see a young woman in here tonight? A very attractive young woman. A university student?"

Lieutenant Pak looked at me. Ernie fidgeted. Suddenly, I realized that I'd made a mistake by bringing it up.

"College student?" The old woman shook her head. "No."

"Maybe not a college student, but a young woman. Waiting for someone."

She shook her head again. "There have been no young women here tonight."

Right, I thought. There were probably three or four bar girls upstairs right now. With paying customers.

I asked a couple more questions but the old couple stuck to their story, which boiled down to they hadn't seen anything and they hadn't heard anything. With those big bolted doors it was possible. Maybe.

On our way down the steps, Lieutenant Pak walked next to me. Snow started to fall again, in moist clumps.

"Who is the young woman you asked about?"

I shrugged. "All soldiers—British, American, or Korean— always look for young women."

"Yes. But you . . ." He stopped and searched for the word. "You *expect* something."

"I expect GIs to look for women," I said. "That's all."

The blue-smocked technicians at the crime scene were wrapping up their work. The Korean police—and the U.S. Army overseas—don't rely much on high-tech methods of crime detection. They rely on shoe leather. And on interrogation techniques, the most reliable of which is a fist to the gut.

I turned to Lieutenant Pak and waved my arm toward the jumbled buildings and shacks that ran up the hill away from the murder site.

"Will you let me know if you learn anything from your interviews in the neighborhood?"

"Yes." He handed me his card. One side was printed in English, the other in Korean. It gave his phone number and his address at the Namdaemun Police Station. I didn't have a card, but he knew where he could find me. "Will you be talking to his unit today?"

"First thing," I said.

"And will you tell me what you find out?"

"Yes. I will."

He nodded. Not quite a bow but good enough for cop to cop. I nodded back.

As Ernie and I stepped down the treacherous stairway, Lieutenant Pak stood at the top, hands thrust deeply into his overcoat, watching us.

So far, this case fell fully under Korean jurisdiction. But Lieutenant Pak knew he'd need my help to ferret out information on the military compounds. And I'd need his if the assailant turned out to be a Korean. So far, we were cooperating.

We'd see how long that lasted.

When we got back to the jeep, Ernie unlocked the chain around the steering wheel and started up the engine. "You almost stepped on your dick back there, pal," he said.

"Yeah. You think he was suspicious?"

"Of course he was suspicious. He's a cop, isn't he?"

"But we're the investigators assigned to this case for the U.S. side. He's not going to think we had anything to do with it."

"Not as long as you keep your trap shut."

Ernie backed away from the wall, turned the jeep around, and swooshed through the growing blanket of snow. On the way back to the compound, slush and shattered ice ran after our spinning wheels. Frozen ghosts vanishing in the night.

I thought of Cecil Whitcomb and how pale and shriveled his body looked. Just yesterday I'd talked to him, gazed into his eyes, watched as he dispassionately read a note from a beautiful woman pleading for a rendezvous. And I thought of the two women who'd maneuvered us into this mess.

All the shit started with Eun-hi, the sexiest bar girl in Itaewon. For quite some time I'd wanted to get my hands on her flesh. Before it was for lust. Now I had a different motive.

OTHER TITLES IN THE SOHO CRIME SERIES

Quentin Bates
(Iceland)
Frozen Assets
Cold Comfort

Cheryl Benard
(Pakistan)
Moghul Buffet

James R. Benn
(World War II Europe)
Billy Boyle
The First Wave
Blood Alone
Evil for Evil
Rag & Bone
A Mortal Terror

Cara Black
(Paris, France)
Murder in the Marais
Murder in Belleville
Murder in the Sentier
Murder in the Bastille
Murder in Clichy
Murder in Montmarte
Murder on the Ile Saint-Louis
Murder in the Rue de Paradis
Murder in the Latin Quarter
Murder in the Palais Royale
Murder in Passy
Murder at the Lanterne Rouge

Grace Brophy
(Italy)
The Last Enemy
A Deadly Paradise

Henry Chang
(Chinatown)
Chinatown Beat
Year of the Dog
Red Jade

Colin Cotterill
(Laos)
The Coroner's Lunch
Thirty-Three Teeth
Disco for the Departed
Anarchy and Old Dogs
Curse of the Pogo Stick
The Merry Misogynist
Love Songs from a Shallow Grave
Slash and Burn

Garry Disher
(Australia)
The Dragon Man
Kittyhawk Down
Snapshot
Chain of Evidence
Blood Moon
Wyatt

David Downing
(World War II Germany)
Zoo Station
Silesian Station
Stettin Station
Potsdam Station
Lehrter Station

Leighton Gage
(Brazil)
Blood of the Wicked
Buried Strangers
Dying Gasp
Every Bitter Thing
A Vine in the Blood

Michael Genelin
(Slovakia)
Siren of the Waters
Dark Dreams
The Magician's Accomplice
Requiem for a Gypsy

Adrian Hyland
(Australia)
Moonlight Downs
Gunshot Road

Stan Jones
(Alaska)
White Sky, Black Ice
Shaman Pass
Village of the Ghost Bears

Lene Kaaberbøl & Agnete Friis
(Denmark)
The Boy in the Suitcase

Graeme Kent
(Solomon Islands)
Devil-Devil
One Blood

Martin Limón
(South Korea)
Jade Lady Burning
Slicky Boys
Buddha's Money
The Door to Bitterness
The Wandering Ghost
G.I. Bones
Mr. Kill

Peter Lovesey
(Bath, England)
The Last Detective
The Vault
On the Edge
The Reaper
Rough Cider
The False Inspector Dew
Diamond Dust
Diamond Solitaire